McA
M

FRAMINGHAM PUBLIC LIBRARY

3 13 00328 9297

W9-DFZ-562

DISCARD

DATE DUE

DATE DUE

JUL 0 5 2000		
AUG 7 2000		
DEC 2 6 2000		
GAYLORD		PRINTED IN U.S.A.

Printed in USA

MAY 2 0 1993

FINAL APPOINTMENT

By the same author

A POSITION OF TRUST
SEASCAPE WITH DEAD FIGURES
A PRETTY PLACE FOR A MURDER
A FOX IN THE NIGHT
REMAINS TO BE SEEN
ROBBED BLIND
BREACH OF PROMISE
BLOOD KIN

FINAL APPOINTMENT

ROY HART

St. Martin's Press
New York

*All characters in this publication are fictitious
and any resemblance to real persons, living or dead,
is purely coincidental.*

FINAL APPOINTMENT. Copyright © 1993 by Roy Hart. All rights reserved. Printed in
the United States of America. No part of this book may be used or reproduced in any
manner whatsoever without written permission except in the case of brief quotations
embodied in critical articles or reviews. For information, address St. Martin's Press,
175 Fifth Avenue, New York, N.Y. 10010.

Library of Congress Cataloging-in-Publication Data

Hart, Roy.
Final appointment / Roy Hart.
p.   cm.
ISBN 0-312-08777-2
I. Title.
PR6058.A694857F56   1993
823'.914—dc20   92-43179   CIP

First published in Great Britain by Little, Brown and Company.

First U.S. Edition: April 1993
10 9 8 7 6 5 4 3 2 1

FINAL APPOINTMENT

ONE

HE GLIMPSED THE FLASH OF light in the distance. He accelerated, and responded by flicking his dip-switch. It was the last conscious movement he ever made. In the same instant he was dead, and at midnight, when his headless body was wheeled into the mortuary on a squeaky trolley, his death was assumed to be the result of a particularly bizarre traffic accident.

Martin Craven twitched in his sleep. He was having the nightmare again, clambering shakily out of his car and walking back on buckling legs to where the battered and bleeding body lay at the edge of the road, thinking it was dead, then, as he stood over it with the bile of terror rising in his gorge, his heart pumping like a steam engine, watching it struggle to its hands and knees and reach out for him, slobbering blood all over his shoes as it toothlessly mumbled 'help me, help me'. At which point, as always happened, his feet were glued to the road so that he couldn't move; and then he was sitting in his car, the door swinging open while he struggled to remember where the ignition key was and where the handbrake was, and all the time the creature was crawling after him on its hands and knees in the dark, and when he did find the ignition key it wouldn't turn and when he struggled with it and finally made it turn the engine wouldn't start, and even in his sleep the cold muck sweat drenched him all over again, and he was moaning, praying, swearing, because the foul

1

thing had crawled up beside the car, was looking in, one wet red hand on the door sill. Then suddenly the car was moving, rocketing off with a squeal of rubber, the door still swinging open, its headlights piercing the dark—

He shot upright in the claustrophobic blackness, the fear still sawing in his throat and the sweat still bathing him, struggling to remember if all that had happened just now, yesterday, last week, last year, if it had ever happened at all. Not yesterday, because he remembered leaving the office early, remembered calling in on Giles Weston, then slumming around a few pubs in the City, vaguely remembered Giles helping him on to the train at Waterloo, and his staggering off it alone at Bournemouth. He vaguely remembered eating curry, could still taste it sour in his mouth. Somewhere near the station he'd eaten that, must have been because he'd still been bloody nearly legless and couldn't have walked far. Then what?

Gerry Pope springing out of the dark in the car park of the Hanging Man. There had been a row. Pope had counted the money and said it wasn't all there. He wanted the rest on Friday. Or else.

He remembered it all then. The accident had happened. He'd had the new radiator grill and fender fitted in Birmingham a week later.

There had been no witnesses to the accident, but Pope had dug deep. In the end he had found out everything. Absolutely everything.

Martin Craven fell back to his pillow. Sleep did not come to him for a long, long time.

Dawn came with a miserable grey drizzle, the first rain in this part of Dorset for a week or more. One of the first early risers to feel it on his face was Tasker Hobday. Up since just after seven o'clock, old Tasker, as he was locally known, was carrying his yellow plastic bucket down to the stream that bordered the edge of his woodland domain. His elderly collie bitch trudged along beside him, lurching

2

away occasionally to investigate an unfamiliar scent, but never straying far because she was deaf and partly blind and relied upon old Tasker for everything.

They reached the stream. Tasker eased himself cautiously down the slippery bank, and clinging to the bough of an alder he crouched and leaned out and drew his bucket through the water. Tasker Hobday was old enough to remember when the stream was a full-blown river, twenty feet wide and deep enough to drown in, and could only be crossed by swimming it or by the footbridge along at the village. In those far-off days the water had been like crystal; a lad on a hot summer's day could dunk his face in it and lap it up to his heart's content. It used to taste of iron and folk said it was medicinal and would put right anything from gripe to carbuncles. Nowadays he had to boil it before he could even wash his face in it, and had to get his drinking water from old Elsie. But then nothing was what it used to be; although Tasker was philosophical enough to wonder sometimes if it ever had been.

With his bucket filled, he straightened and clambered back up the treacherous bank. He looked around anxiously, a little short of breath. The last time he had seen old Trix she had been flopped down only a couple of feet away on the grass.

'Trixie,' he called, in his cracked dry voice. 'Where are you, girl?'

When she didn't reappear, he put down his bucket and called her name again, louder this time, making a megaphone of his cupped hands so that she would hear him better.

'Trixie,' he called. 'Trix!'

But all that he heard was the sound of his own voice, and the soft patter of the rain among the trees.

Elsie Wicks had also felt the cold rain on her face. She had risen at a quarter past seven. A big, dark, flamboyant woman of boundless energy she was soon at the business

3

of the day. By seven-thirty she was washed, dressed, had put the kettle to boil on the Aga and was out in her henhouse collecting eggs. There were three today, so there would be a spare one for old Tasker when he called to collect his bucket of water at a quarter to eight.

She was soon sipping her first mug of tea of the day and doing the small crossword puzzle in the *Daily Telegraph*. The larger crossword she always saved until bedtime. At seven forty-five, two boiled eggs and three slices of well-buttered toast inside her, the small crossword completed and the headlines briefly scanned, she rose from the table and unhooked her work-list from the side of the wooden dresser.

Three jobs to do today. That brooch to be finished, Mrs Craven's engagement ring to be fitted with a new claw and she really had to make a start on those ear-rings for Ashley's up in the King's Road; in a few more days they'd be chasing her for those. And there was shopping to do today too. The housework would have to wait. She abominated housework, life was too short.

She glanced at her watch. Ten minutes to eight. Tasker was late. By the time he got here the tea would be stewed. They usually had a chat for a few minutes, but today that was definitely out; she simply had too much to do.

Martin Craven did not so much wake as tentatively stir, the aftermaths of his heavy evening a midget quarrying away in his skull with a pneumatic hammer and a fur-upholstered tongue that still tasted of sour whisky and even sourer curry.

He swung his feet to the carpet. The inert figure in cerise pyjamas in the next bed, sprawled on its back and with its mouth open, snored on. He wondered if she knew how much he detested her. He had been crazy for her, but that was a long time ago. What had initially caught his eye had been a pair of long tanned legs and a glittering cascade of long blonde hair. And when she had jutted her stomach invitingly and sparkled her eyes at him over her wine glass, and asked him, 'Und how long for heff you been in Oslo, Meester Craven?' he had suffered a rush of brain from his head and a surge of blood to his loins, from both of which it had taken him a full six months to recover. But by then he was married to her and it was far too late to rectify the matter, although he was now thinking seriously about doing so. Because he knew now that she had a lover, he had proof. He had had a few mistresses too but that was different, and he had never been found out. She had been, and he had the evidence. All that had inhibited him hitherto were the provisions of the Married Woman's Property Act, but Giles had told him yesterday that if he could prove that Dagmar had been knocking it off with someone else, the Divorce Court judge might consider her counter-petition with great disfavour.

He had, oft-times, fantasised about wringing her neck. Killing was not so difficult, after all, and it would certainly have been cheaper than divorcing her. But not now. The police would check up on him, work back, and he had too many things to hide.

She grunted and shifted irritably as he stood up and knocked over his bedside lamp. He set it upright again. A few exploratory movements told him that everything was still functioning more or less as it ought to be, and a cold shower in the en suite bathroom shocked him most of the way back into the human race. He had to shave with more than usual care. He used a cut-throat razor, and his hand was shaking abominably.

Hughie Lee had also been up and about in the rain that had stopped now and was giving way to a thin, watery sunshine with no warmth in it.

'See you've 'ad a bit o' luck, then,' his sister said, sitting in the doorway of the battered and rusty old single-decked bus they used for getting about the country. She dropped the potato she had been peeling into the bucket of water between her feet.

'Yeah,' he said. 'Just a bit.' He climbed the two wooden steps and skirted the bucket. He laid the two snared rabbits on the table beside the door and opened the drawer beneath to take out his skinning-knife.

'I seed an owl on your shoulder when you come in last night,' she said, over her shoulder.

'Don't talk daft,' he said, not looking at her.

'But I did,' she insisted. 'A big brown 'un. An' you were late. Later 'an you ever bin.'

'Yeah, well,' he said, trying to fob her off. 'I 'ad a bit of business to see to, didn't I.'

'But you 'ad an owl, 'Ughie. A big brown 'un. Sittin' on your shoulder it were.' Her tone had dropped to a whine of acute anxiety as she persisted. She had risen from her corner by the door and come to stand beside him. 'It 'ad horns.'

'It were probably just these two bunnies,' he said, laughing, deftly skinning. 'You could make yourself a nice pair of gloves out o' these.'

But she would not be turned. 'It's people you get owls for, 'Ughie. Not rabbits.' Her anxiety deepened. 'You're not in no trouble, are you, 'Ughie?'

'No,' he scoffed, loosing a harsh dry sound that was supposed to be another laugh. 'Course I'm not. Anyway, you were asleep when I got back, your curtain drawn an' everything. You couldn't 'ave seen nothin'.'

'I don't 'ave to see, do I, 'Ughie? I just know, don't I?' She plucked anxiously at the sleeve of his jacket. 'I always know, don't I?'

It was true, she did. Up in Birmingham, the local kids had called her Mad Annie. In Hereford, she'd got accused of being a witch, and the police had come visiting because of a missing kid, a little girl it had been, just because Annie had been seen talking to her once. Annie had told the police the little girl was in the river. And she had been.

And she was right about the owl on his shoulder last

6

night too.

'Per'aps we ought to be movin' on agin,' he said, starting work on the other rabbit.

'I like it 'ere,' she grumbled. 'It's the best place we've ever bin. I get sick of travellin'.'

'We're travellin' people, girl,' he asserted. 'It's bred in.'

'Know what I think, don't you,' she said, staring up at him. 'I think you're just tryin' to take me mind off that owl.'

'All right,' he said wearily, laying down his knife and turning to face her. 'There *were* an owl.' He gripped her arms as her eyes widened in fear. 'But you're not to fret, see, 'cause it weren't nothing to do wi' us. And if the police come, you don't say nothin' about no owl. You remember how it was wi' that little girl in the river, an' all the trouble it give us, don't you?' He put a finger under her chin and lifted her face to make her big worried eyes look at him. 'You do remember that, don't you, Annie? So this time you don't say nothin'. All right?'

She nodded dutifully. 'I'll get back to peelin' those tatties,' she said, reluctantly drawing away. 'Make us a stew.'

'Aye,' he said. 'That'd be the best thing. An' no more talk of owls. Just you mark that.'

Nicholas Chance had been out of bed since soon after five o'clock. By six-thirty he had overseen the milking, by seven he had made himself coffee and toast, and at seven forty-five he was in the office at the back of his extensive farmhouse and separating those bills he was able to pay from the ones he could stave off for a little longer.

He heard his wife clomping down the stairs just before a quarter to eight and her iron-shod heels ringing on the quarry-tiles of the kitchen floor, the clatter of a cup and saucer as she poured herself a coffee. Some days she came in to see him before she went out, sometimes she didn't. It depended how the fancy took her. Today was one of the days when she did. She was dressed in her riding-gear, as she was most mornings.

'I'll be about an hour,' she said, from the doorway, crop in one hand and hard-hat in the other. 'Want anything up in the village?'

'No, thanks,' he grunted sourly. 'I wonder how the hell you find the time.'

'Meaning what?' she retorted, her beautiful mouth tightening into a thin bitter line.

'Meaning I'm trying to run a bloody farm,' he said. 'It would be gratifying to get a little help from time to time.'

'I told you when we started out, old darling, all that mud and animal crap just isn't in my line. I did say, didn't I?'

'Repetitively,' he said.

'Then stop bloody whingeing,' she threw back at him. 'See you about half-eight,' she added, but the last words were mostly lost behind the closing door.

When she was well and truly gone he delved into the pocket of his old jacket slung over the back of his swivel-chair and took out a blue envelope, the one that had arrived in the first post this morning. Then, hooking his wastepaper tub closer with the toe of his boot, he painstakingly tore the envelope and its contents, a receipted invoice, into tiny shreds.

That was one bill he had had to pay.

Elsie Wicks drew a strip of thick platinum wire out of the antiquated wall-safe in her bedroom, snipped off a quarter-inch with a pair of pliers, then put the strip back in the safe and swung closed the heavy door behind it. Having turned the key in the lock, and spun the combination a couple of times to confuse any would-be housebreaker, she rose to her feet and pushed the end of the bed back to cover the safe.

At which juncture she heard old Tasker shouting his head off from out in the kitchen. She noted that the time was five to eight.

'Elsie!' he called again wheezily. 'Where the 'ell are you?'

'Here,' she sang cheerily. 'Coming.' She hurried back down the passage.

He was standing on the coconut mat just inside the kitchen door, shaking all over, and his usually ruddy cheeks were as white as his beard. He'd got his dog on the end of a piece of string and was holding out his yellow plastic bucket at the end of a trembling arm.

'The old girl just found this,' he croaked. 'What d'you think I ought to do?'

She closed on him, and peered into the bucket. She saw only the wet grubby top of a motor-cyclist's red crash helmet with a black visor, and wondered what all the fuss was about.

'Wear it,' she joked. 'It'll keep your ears warm in the winter.'

'Not likely,' he retorted, holding the bucket higher. 'It's got a bloody 'ead wedged inside it. Look!'

And, for the first time in her life, Elsie Wicks almost fainted.

TWO

ROPER TAPPED HIS FOOT BRAKE as he recognised the yellow-jacketed figure prowling about the edge of the heath on the opposite side of the road. He drew his Sierra into the verge a few yards behind the line of traffic cones and climbed out. A pale sun shone but a cold wind blustering across the heath made the morning feel more like the scrag-end of winter than the middle of spring. A lean man of middle years, he buttoned his flapping raincoat as the wind cut him to the very bone as he crossed the carriageway. Parked on the grass on the heath side of the road was Chief Inspector Brake's white Land Rover with its hazard lights winking, and behind that a Panda car was drawn up, probably the local beat-officer's. Further back along the road another yellow-jacketed figure was quartering the gutter, and amongst the cones two more were stretching a measuring tape between them over a length of nasty-looking bloodstains. Two more blue-capped heads were bobbing about above the shrubbery on the edge of the heath.

'Morning, Charlie,' said Roper, coming up behind Brake as he crouched to pick up something from the grass, a small green plastic ferrule like a bootlace tag, decided it was of no interest and tossed it out into the road. Chief Inspector Brake was from County Traffic Division and it was rare to see him out and doing his own leg-work. 'Big one, was it?'

'Morning, sir,' said Brake, straightening up and jotting a

note on his clipboard. 'We're still trying to work it out. Not even sure which way he was travelling. We think he was on a motor-cycle, poor sod.'

'You only think?' Roper proffered his cheroot packet. Brake plucked one out. Roper lit it for him, shielding the flame from the breeze across the heath, then one for himself.

'Still haven't found his bike,' said Brake, exhaling smoke. 'Nor his head.'

'You serious?'

'Dead serious,' said Brake. 'All we've got's a body and some blood on the carriageway over there.' He pointed with his cheroot to where the two constables were still measuring the stains behind the line of cones. 'No head, no identification, no anything. He was wearing protective gear, so odds on he was on a motor-bike. His head was taken clean off.' One of Brake's black-gloved thumbs drew a line across his throat from ear to ear. 'Clean as a bloody whistle. Never seen anything like it.'

Roper grimaced. It was only twenty minutes since he'd been eating his breakfast. His own job was messy enough, but he wouldn't have swapped it for Brake's at any price.

'Perhaps he came up too fast behind a lorry with an open tailgate,' suggested Roper. 'And forgot to put his brakes on.'

'Something sharper than the edge of a tailgate,' said Brake. 'The mortuary attendant reckoned it had been sliced off with something like a blunt carving knife. But whatever he hit, he must have been going at a fair old lick.' He broke off to shout for Sergeant Mallory, whose radio could be heard squawking metallically from the open window of his Panda car. Further along the road, two women on horseback, riding along the verge at a walk, were waved out into the carriageway by one of Brake's constables. They dropped into a single file as they approached the traffic cones. It was coming up for five past eight and the road was getting busier as the morning

11

rush hour got under way.

'Well, I'd best be getting along,' said Roper. 'Wish you luck.'

'Thanks,' said Brake. 'And if you happen to find a head lying about,' he added with grim humour, 'you won't forget it's mine, will you?'

Roper walked back to his car. The local beat-sergeant was still sitting half in and half out of his car and talking over his radio.

A dozen paces from the Sierra, the two women passed him on a couple of well-kept brown hacks, close enough for him to feel the heat coming off the horses. The women, tightly breeched and trimly jacketed, looked like a matching pair, the sort you saw in the perfume advertisements in the Sunday supplements, too smart and too good-looking to be quite real. One was dark, the other fair; the fair one said something – she had a foreign accent of some kind – and the other one laughed, the deep throaty laugh of a woman who was very sure of herself. Beyond the cones and Roper's car they swung back on to the grass and broke into a canter, then a brisk gallop as they turned on to the heath.

As he climbed back into the Sierra and turned the ignition key he glimpsed, in his door-mirror, Sergeant Mallory slam his door and hurry back along the verge to Brake. Roper buckled his seat-belt and thought no more of it as he drove on to County to start his day's work. Not that he had all that much to do. Things had been very quiet just lately.

He stepped out on the third floor and the lift doors gasped shut behind him. He made straight for the coffee-machine further along the green-carpeted passage – he could barely function without that first plastic cup of coffee of the day – popped in his tenpence piece and dialled his selection of coffee, milk and sugar. The machine buzzed, clicked, had a moment of indecision, then performed.

'Ah, Douglas. Morning. Got a job for you,' a crisply

12

martial voice said at his shoulder. It was the Assistant Chief Constable (Crime), aka, at least in the canteen where he never set foot, the Speeding Spectre, mostly because of the machine-gun delivery of his instructions and, so it was alleged, because he was the only living human who could move at the velocity of light. A pinched-faced and narrow man who smiled rarely, he was however, in Roper's opinion, a proper hands-on copper and the two of them rubbed along pretty well together.

'About half a mile due west of Appleford. On the heath. Brake and the local beat-officer waiting for you. Gipsy feller came across a body lying in the road last night. Didn't have a head.'

'I heard about it,' said Roper. 'I passed the place on my way in this morning. Had a word with Brake.'

'Good,' said the ACC. 'So you know all about it then. Keep in touch.' He paused, but only for dramatic effect. 'Thing is, seems they've just found his head. In entirely the wrong place. Odd, eh?' And with that he was gone, striding on down the corridor, turning right, and then smoothly creating the illusion that he had managed to pass cleanly through his office wall.

At nine o'clock the same morning, in company with Detective Sergeant George Makins, Roper was back on the edge of Appleford Heath and talking to Brake and Sergeant Mallory.

It was Mallory, the neighbourhood beat-officer, who had come across the body at eleven thirty-five last night, although his was not the first sighting.

'Bloke called Hughie Lee,' said Mallory, who was young, thickly-set and chunkily filling his uniform, a touch on the cocky side and so recently promoted that the chevrons on his sleeve still glittered. He spoke disparagingly, with traces of a Dorset burr in his voice. 'Gipsy. Him and his sister turned up here about three weeks ago. They live in a clapped-out old bus between Downlands Farm and Elsie

13

Wicks' place; she's the woman who made the phone call after old Tasker's dog found the head.' He turned and pointed. 'I caught Lee in my headlights when I was going home for a bit of supper. He was crouched there, about halfway along that line of cones, close to the verge. I thought he was grubbing about in a rubbish sack that somebody had dumped.'

Only it had not been a rubbish sack, but a body clad in motor-cyclist's black leathers and protective boots. As Mallory's headlights had picked him out, Lee had leapt to his feet and darted away; but in the few seconds that had taken, Mallory had recognised Lee and was able to call him by name and thereby flush him out from the shrubbery in which he had obviously intended hiding himself.

They had returned to the body together, Lee with some reluctance. It was only then that Mallory saw that the body was missing its head. It also did not escape his notice that the two breast pockets of the man's one-piece leather suit were unzipped. A brief probe inside them also showed that they were empty, although there were several keys on a ring in the body's shirt pocket. Breaking off only to radio for an ambulance and some assistance from the Traffic Division, Mallory had at once searched Lee, not only frisking him but making him turn out his every pocket and even demanding he took off his boots. Which sounded to Roper a bit heavy-handed, but then Sergeant Mallory looked that sort.

Lee was clean, as the jargon has it, apart from a coil of lightweight brass picture-wire and a pair of pliers, but Mallory had still not been satisfied. When the ambulance had taken the body away, and the site investigation placed in the hands of a sergeant and constable from Traffic, Mallory had taken Lee back into the shrubbery into which he had tried to make his hasty exit. For a whole half-hour Mallory had searched the paths and bushes with a hand-lantern, his gut telling him that it could only have been Lee who had emptied the victim's pockets, despite

14

Lee's vehement denials.

'Dodgy, is he, Sergeant?' asked Roper. 'This Lee?'

'They all are, aren't they, sir,' said Mallory, with a sneering assuredness that made Roper like him even less. 'They're not in a place five minutes before they turn it into a tip. It's a fair bet he does a bit of poaching; and all his sister's got between her ears is a chunk of bloody wood.'

Roper was becoming less enamoured of Sergeant Mallory by the minute. He was too self-assured, too hasty at drawing conclusions. 'Caught him poaching, have you?'

'No, sir,' Mallory confessed. 'He's too bloody sharp. But I will. It's only a matter of time.'

Mallory had finally let Lee go on his way at half-past midnight. At which juncture he had joined the two baffled officers from Traffic who had coned off part of the road and set up hazard flashers. At one o'clock this morning they had still failed to find either the victim's head or his motor-cycle anywhere within a reasonable distance of the body. At two o'clock they had shut up shop for the night with a view to making a more thorough search in the daylight.

Which was more or less when Roper had arrived on the scene on his way to work and stopped to chat with CI Brake. When he had glimpsed in his mirror Mallory doubling back to Brake from his car, Mallory had just received the message that one Tasker Hobday, or, rather, his dog, had found what was reasonable to assume was the motor-cyclist's head, still jammed in its crash helmet.

'Where is it now?'

'Still at Mrs Wicks' place, sir. I wasn't quite sure what to do with it. And I thought you might want to take a look at it.'

'You're kidding,' said Roper, with some considerable feeling. 'But I suppose we've got to.'

His first sighting of Elsie Wicks' ramshackle, isolated and slate-roofed bungalow was a bird's-eye view from the road. Set in a clearing amongst the trees, when they were in full

15

leaf it would be almost obscured. Access to it was given by a long steep driveway of grass, gravel and rutted earth, at the bottom of which was parked a plum-coloured Volvo estate car of uncertain vintage, plastered with dried mud around the wheel arches and door sills and sadly in need of a respray and a fair bit of panel bashing.

Closer to, the bungalow looked even more dilapidated. The stucco was falling away from around one of the windows and the front door was a particularly revolting shade of recently applied apple green, its bottom half repaired with a patch of hardboard from which most of the nail-heads were already beginning to exude rust. Rainwater was still dripping down from the leaking gutter above another window.

The woman who answered Mallory's summons on the rusty door-knocker had been cast in the heroic mould, smooth skinned and big-boned, well over six feet tall and with her wealth of black hair caught up at the nape of her neck in a tortoiseshell clip that looked like the real thing. Roper and Makins showed their warrant-cards as Mallory effected the introduction.

'Frankly,' she said, plainly relieved at their arrival, opening the green door wider and marching ahead of them down the narrow and dark little hallway with the hem of her scarlet kaftan flapping around her ankles, 'I wouldn't mind if you were the King and Crown Prince of bloody China, just so long as you get that awful bloody thing out of my greenhouse a bit sharpish. Cuppa tea all round, is it? Been quaffing the stuff since half-seven this morning.'

She led them into the kitchen, most of it taken up by a battered white deal table with a tablecloth draped over one end of it and surrounded by half a dozen handmade wheel-backed chairs that were definitely quality antiques. Sitting at one end, and looking up expectantly as they all marched in, was a stocky little man with a shock of white hair and a square-cut white beard, in the throes of lighting a pipeful of tobacco. Flopped on a rag-mat in front of an old iron range was an elderly collie basking in the warmth. It viewed their entry with sleepy disinterest then closed its eyes again and somnolently dropped its chin back on its paws.

Roper was introduced to Hobday, who was one of those men who was no taller standing up than he was sitting down. Bow-legged, he looked a sprightly seventy or so, his handshake an enthusiastic one.

While the jovial Mrs Wicks made the tea, Mallory showed Roper and Makins out to the overgrown garden and the grimy-windowed greenhouse. Tasker Hobday's yellow plastic bucket stood on the flagged stone floor just inside the door. Somewhere not too far away chickens were clucking.

'If you tilt the visor,' suggested Mallory, 'you can just see a nose and a bit of beard.'

Roper plucked up the knees of his trouser-legs an inch and dropped to a crouch beside the bucket. The crash helmet, its top uppermost, was an expensive one, dark red, quite plain and crusted here and there with damp earth. There were several deep scratches too, and a couple of dents that looked recently made on the crown. The visor was of translucent black plastic, the kind you can see out of but not into – and has bank cashiers reaching for their panic-buttons the moment it appears at their windows.

He took a long deep breath, and steeled himself. Then, easing a gloved finger down between the visor and the wall of the bucket, he felt for the bottom edge of the visor and gingerly lifted it. As Mallory had said, all he could see was the tip of a nose and a few bloodied straggles of black moustache and beard. He could have lifted the helmet out and taken a good look at the rest of the face, but he wasn't in the mood at this early hour of the morning, besides which the less the helmet and its gruesome contents were handled at this stage the better. He pushed the visor down again and levered himself upright, still doing battle with

17

his stomach. Blood was still seeping into the wet and muck in the bottom of the bucket, and in the damp warmth of the greenhouse as the sun climbed higher, the whole was beginning to smell.

Mrs Wicks passed the mugs of tea around the table in her kitchen. George Makins had gone back to his car to radio for a mortuary van to take away the yellow bucket.

'The old girl found it,' said Tasker Hobday, flourishing his pipe in the general direction of his collie who still lay prone on the rug in front of the range. 'I'd been down to the river for me washing-water, turned round, and there she was, gorn. I hollered for her. She didn't come. She don't see all that well and she don't hear all that good either, so I started roaming about a bit and shouting louder. I knew she couldn't be far 'cos she's got a bit of rheumatism in her back legs, and I'd only turned me back on her for a couple of seconds. Then I heard her whining, soft like, like she does when she comes across a fox hole. I tracks her down. And there she is, up to her belly in the stream and pawin' away at this red thing. Looked like a ball only it weren't floating about. I calls her. She comes. But then she goes back and starts whining again, sort of urgent, like. So I took me shoes and socks off and rolled up me trouser-legs and paddled in to see what it was. But old Trixie had stirred up a lot of mud from the bottom, so I couldn't see it proper, so I picked it up and saw it was one o' them skid-lids. Dead heavy it were, like it had a couple o' housebricks stuffed inside it, and it slipped clean out o' me hands and went splashing back into the water. Got soaked all up me front, I did. That was when I saw it had a bit o' meat and bone sticking out the bottom. Give me a bit of a turn for a minute, it did. But I knew I had to tell somebody, so I empties me bucket, stuffs this thing in and comes rushin' back here to get a bit of advice from Elsie.'

'And I rang for Sergeant Mallory pretty damn quick,' said Mrs Wicks.

Roper sipped at his mug of tea, strong enough to dissolve iron bars and drenched with sugar. 'Did you hear anything unusual last night, Mrs Wicks? Anything that might have sounded like a traffic accident, up there on the road?'

'Not a thing,' she said. 'But then I don't hear much of the traffic down here. It's one of the reasons I stopped on after my hubby turned his poor old toes up.'

'Mr Hobday?'

But Hobday too had heard nothing untoward; but then he had spent most of the previous evening playing dominoes along at the Hanging Man in the village and a good mile from here. He and his dog had walked back from there at a few minutes after eleven o'clock. He had got home to his hut around twenty-past eleven and had heard nothing thereafter except his radio.

'You didn't happen to see a body lying in the road? Might have looked like a rubbish sack. About two hundred yards up the road from here, going towards Dorchester.'

Hobday shook his head. When he came back from the pub he always turned off the road down Elsie Wicks' driveway, because she always had the light on over her front door and it helped him to find his way. He completed his journey along the bank of the stream.

'Did anything like a motor-bike happen to pass you between the pub and here?'

Hobday pursed his lips and went into deep meditation, champing on his pipe.

'No,' he said eventually, slowly shaking his head. 'Not as I remember. The only motor-bike I recall seein' last night was pushed up in the corner of the car park.'

'Which car park?' asked Roper, with rising interest.

'The Hanging Man,' said Hobday, as if Roper should have known that all along. 'Shoved up beside the gents' privy.'

'What time was that? D'you remember?'

'Couldn't say exactly,' said Hobday apologetically. 'Bit

19

before eleven, I s'pose. I don't take much account o' time, 'cept when the pubs open and shut. Don't have the need, y'see.'

Makins returned. 'All done,' he said. 'Van's on its way.'

'How long's it going to be?' asked Mrs Wicks, still not reassured, rising to fill another mug for him.

'About half an hour,' said Makins, unbuttoning his raincoat with one hand as he took the mug from her with the other. 'Thanks.'

'Can't be soon enough,' she said, with a shudder. 'Got a feeling I'm going to be haunted by that bucket for the rest of my life.'

Roper waited for Makins and Mrs Wicks to settle again.

'Did you see the rider of this motor-bike, Mr Hobday?'

'Can't say I did,' replied Hobday, scratching thoughtfully at his hairy cheek with the stem of his pipe. 'But then old Dick and me were in the snug-bar; they always keep a nice fire goin' in there. He might have gone into one of the other bars o' course. Old Maurice'll prob'ly know.'

'Maurice Hapgood,' explained Mrs Wicks. 'He's the landlord along at the Hanging Man. Been there for years. Knows everybody.'

Roper made a note of that. Out here in the country, a pub landlord was usually the eyes and ears of the world. But, on the other hand, the world was awash with motor-cycles and one, unless you were a connoisseur, was very much like another. And there were probably a dozen or more that had travelled this way last night, and the riders of several of those could easily have stopped off to wet their whistles in the Hanging Man public house.

Their tea finished, Hobday and his collie led Roper and Makins through the overgrown fastness of Mrs Wicks' back garden, and then through a broken wire fence and into the trees, busily chattering away all the while. He was an ex-Navy man, Leading-Seaman, minesweepers mostly, during the war. Lived now on his Navy and old-age pensions. Had a little hut along the way a bit. Nice and private, like. Woke up in the morning to the sound of birds. Nothing like it. A good stick, old Elsie Wicks was. Clever an' all, she was. Made joolry, rings and brooches and bracelets an' all that sort of stuff. Some of it went up to London. Designed it herself. Did a few repairs too, but only for the locals.

And that was the river, leastways it used to be a river, only a trickle now, though. And there, just there, was where he filled his bucket each morning, and way along there was where he first found old Trixie whining and splashin' around when he'd finally caught up with her.

It was a secluded, shady place, deep among the trees, last autumn's damp rotting leaves still carpeting the ground.

Roper glanced up the steep slope to his left, towards the road. There was a difference of about thirty feet between the two levels between which the helmet could have bounced and rolled and finished up in the water. Except that the accident had occurred a couple of hundred yards further along the road.

'Just here, it was,' said Hobday.

George Makins dropped to his heels on the bank and picked over a few damp leaves. Several were darkly blotched. Before Hobday and his dog had come on the scene earlier and disturbed everything, those leaves had probably lain close together. It would have been better if the old man had left everything alone, but then what he had initially observed had simply been a red helmet sticking out of the water, and there was no reason why he should have connected it with a road accident of which, so he had said, he had no knowledge. Interest had drawn him to it, interest had caused him to wade out and pick it up. The golden rule, even for Roper, was to observe everything and touch nothing, but that rule, on this occasion, had been broken and it was too late now to do anything about it.

'Blood, is it?' asked Roper.

'Looks like it,' said Makins. Still down on his hunkers, he

21

reached inside his raincoat and brought out a couple of plastic evidence bags. Into one he dropped two of the leaves and closed the envelope's patent seal between finger and thumbnail. A blood-match would at least confirm that Hobday hadn't made a mistake about the actual site of his find.

Roper's interest was drawn then to a rusting iron boundary fence, over on his right and almost obscured by more trees and shrubbery. Beyond it the trees ceased abruptly and gave way to grassland, ploughed fields, and in the far misty distance a solitary farmhouse with a clutter of outbuildings behind it.

'Whose land's that, Mr Hobday?' asked Roper.

'Downlands Farm,' said Hobday. 'Mr Chance's place. Biggest spread in miles, that is.'

Roper and Makins returned to the road. The sun was warmer now and up here on the higher ground it was drying off the last of the moisture left by the rain.

'What do we do now?' asked Makins.

'Not sure,' said Roper. 'Might be worth having a word with that gipsy, of course.' He glanced at his watch. It was almost half-past ten. 'I think I'd like another chat with Charlie Brake first, though.' Because he had come across some strange old businesses in his time, but this one was downright grotesque. What it surely had not been was a straightforward traffic accident.

'Looks like he wants a chat with us too,' said Makins.

And Brake obviously did, for his was the distant figure frantically signalling to them with his clipboard.

'Things are getting curiouser and curiouser,' said Brake, when Roper and Makins joined up with him again. 'We've been jogging along on the assumption that him and his bike couldn't have stopped all that far apart. But they did.'

'How d'you know?' asked Roper.

'Because we've just found it,' said Brake.

THREE

BRAKE LAID HIS CLIPBOARD ON the bonnet of his Land Rover. 'The body was found here,' he said dabbing at a cross on his sketch-map with the capped end of his ballpoint. The road at this point ran almost due west to due east. At its eastern end it linked up with the A351 to Poole and Bournemouth, whence Roper had been driving when he had chanced upon Brake and his team earlier that morning. A lightly trafficked stretch of road outside the rush-hours, he used it as a shortcut when the weather was good because there was less chance of a traffic hold-up on it. North of the road lay the heath, on the south side and behind them Elsie Wicks' bungalow, Downlands Farm and several others. Appleford village straddled the road roughly a mile to the east.

'And where's the bike?'

'Just here,' said Brake, sliding his ballpoint a couple of inches westward on the map, in the direction of Dorchester. The pen was lifted and used to point along the road. 'Where my two lads are. I was just on my way to give it the once-over, as a matter of fact.'

'We'll join you,' said Roper.

They walked the three hundred yards or so along the verge of the westbound carriageway, to where Brake's sergeant and constable were up to their waists in the dense shrubbery that separated the carriageway from the downward sweep of grazing land behind it. Between the two was a stout wooden fence.

23

The motor-cycle, a red Honda, its front wheel buckled and rammed hard up against one of the fence-posts, looked as if it had negotiated its own way through the bushes and had barely scathed them. It had plainly been travelling westward. From the road it had been completely concealed.

'It's got to be a freak accident,' proposed Brake's baffled sergeant. 'He hit something, got snatched off and the bike just travelled on under its own steam and landed up here.'

'And his head was inside his skid-lid and nearly a quarter-mile back down that way,' Roper reminded him, jerking his head in the direction of Elsie Wicks' bungalow. 'So it's even freakier than that.'

'You know what I think, don't you?' said Brake grimly.

'Probably,' said Roper. 'Somebody stretched a piece of cheese-wire across the road.'

It was the only plausible answer.

It was George Makins, examining the verge of the west-bound carriageway near where the body had been found, who stopped at the road sign bearing the legend 'Cattle Crossing', ran his fingers down the grey painted post and found the horizontal depression in the aluminium and the postage-stamp sized chip in the paintwork. And Brake's constable, on the other verge, who discovered what, at first sight, appeared to be a penknife slash around half the circumference of a silver birch tree which was within a foot or two of being exactly opposite the Cattle Crossing sign. Both marks were chest-high, and added substance to the wire theory. Like most long stretches of rural road, this one was without streetlights, and the length of wire would have been invisible in the dark until it was too late.

Brake's sergeant came back from the Land Rover, where he had spent the last ten minutes being patched through to the DVLA at Swansea on the radio in order to run a check on the motor-cycle.

'Any luck?' asked Brake as the sergeant joined them.

'Gerald Michael Pope,' said the sergeant. 'He bought it

second-hand just after Christmas.' He flipped open his pocket-book. 'Twenty-one A, Jubilee Walk, Dorchester.'

But if Roper and Brake heard the address they showed no sign of it. The name had been enough for both of them. Brake's jaw had stiffened belligerently.

'Something up?' enquired Makins in the ensuing silence.

'Bet your life there is,' said Roper. 'If he was who we think he was.'

'Hit and Run Pope,' said Brake. 'He used to be a copper.'

'Allegedly bent,' added Roper. 'But he quit the Force before we could catch him. Where are those keys you picked up at the mortuary last night, Sergeant?' he asked Mallory.

'In the safe at my cottage,' said Mallory.

'Go and get 'em,' said Roper. 'As quick as you like.'

'He was a sergeant,' said Roper, as Makins turned out on to the road to Dorchester and changed up another gear. 'One of Brake's lads on Traffic. Dead keen. Used to get through a pocket-book every week. Seemed to spend half his time in court giving evidence.'

'Over-zealous, was he?'

'Not so's you'd notice,' said Roper. 'He also did a lot of work after hours. Everybody used to reckon he hung about in pub car parks, waited for a likely victim to reel out and climb into his car, let him get out on to the road, then flash his warrant-card, breathalyse him and nick him. He did a lot of work in civilian clothes and his own car, did Sergeant Pope.'

'Dirty,' agreed Makins. 'But we're paid to be on duty twenty-four hours a day, aren't we?'

'So we are, old lad,' said Roper, as Makins slowed behind a juddering tractor, waited for a gap in the oncoming traffic then pulled out to overtake it. 'But we don't take bribes, do we?'

'He did that, did he?'

25

'One verbal complaint,' said Roper, 'and one very fulsome letter to the Chief Constable. And that was probably only the tip of a very large iceberg.'

It was Roper himself who had conducted the covert investigation into the affairs of Sergeant Pope, after Pope had vehemently denied the two alleged offences and had wriggled out, apparently scot-free, from both of them. Both complainants had positively identified Pope, and one had even been able to recite from memory the number Pope wore on the shoulders of his tunic. But the problem lay in the fact that both gentlemen had previously been charged by Pope for serious motoring offences, one of them twice, and on each occasion had been found guilty and heavily fined, so that both would have known Pope well enough for him to be etched deep in their memories, which is what Pope had suggested at the time. Grudge-bearers, he'd said. It happened all the time. They were just trying to get back at him.

On one occasion when a back-hander was allegedly suggested by Pope, he had been in his uniform and astride his police-issue motor-cycle. On the other he had been in civilian clothes in his own private car at two o'clock in the morning, so that both times he was without a witness. But then so had been the complainants; one of whom had subsequently withdrawn his allegation when Pope threatened to take a private libel action against him.

As far as Pope had been aware, both matters had been quietly shoved under the carpet. The investigation of him, however, had continued. Roper himself had looked into Pope's bank account, his mortgage repayments, his tax returns, even the extent of the monthly repayments he made on his several credit cards. By the end of a week he even knew to the penny what Pope's new car had cost him and which finance company had lent him the money for it. He had turned up nothing suspicious; but then a bribe to a police officer was hardly likely to be paid by cheque, nor passed over the counter of a bank.

Six months later, a year ago now, Pope had fallen out with his wife, resigned from the Force, and dropped from sight. Few were sorry to see him go, for Pope had been an unappealing colleague; a loner, said some, crafty, said others, neither trait an endearing one in a job that required at least a modicum of trust and cameraderie between fellow officers.

'But why was he called "Hit and Run"?' asked Makins.

'Because he attended more of those than anybody else,' said Roper. And that had been true. Pope had been the attending officer at more hit and run accidents than the rest of Brake's officers lumped together. Which might or might not have been a string of coincidences but, statistically, had been highly unusual. And, investigatively speaking, few of those accidents had ever been cleared up and the files on them were still open.

Now Pope was back, albeit dead. And that had been no traffic accident last night.

Jubilee Walk was a dark narrow alley off High West Street in the centre of Dorchester, its entrance and exit blocked off to vehicles by black iron bollards. Numbers 21A, B and C were engraved on three doorbells beside the new mahogany door that fronted directly on to the street and was squeezed between a second-hand clothes shop on one side and a kebab parlour on the other.

Roper experimented with the two Yale keys Mallory had given him. The second one fitted. There was mail on the doormat. Roper stooped and picked it up. Two of the envelopes were for Pope, one of them an electricity bill printed in red, the other from the Inland Revenue. He kept those and dropped the rest back on the mat.

The stairs were uncarpeted, the walls lined with embossed paper that someone had smartened up with a lick of pink emulsion paint.

There was another doormat on the landing in front of 21A. Roper reached for the light switch. Either the bulb had blown or the fuse had. From somewhere higher up came the steady clatter of a typewriter.

It was the other Yale key that opened the white painted door of 21A. Makins followed him in. The darkened room was plainly Pope's office. Diagonally across the corner near the window, and facing the door, was a smart new desk, a chrome and leather swivel-chair behind it and a less ostentatious visitor's chair in front. A grey steel filing cabinet stood against the wall opposite the door, and another door on the right gave access to another room at the rear of the building. The faint smell of kebabs was probably a fixture.

Makins opened the Venetian blinds on the window overlooking the street and let in some light. The green carpet was threadbare and shabby, the walls painted the same dusty pink as the walls of the stairs, as if somebody had bought the paint as a job lot and been determined to use every last drop.

Roper went behind the desk. The mechanical calendar was set for today. The few letters in a wire filing tray were all circulars and bills. All the bills were addressed to Pope. The wastepaper bin was empty. An electric kettle, plugged into a wall socket, sat on the floor beside it.

He depressed the replay button on the combined telephone and answering machine beside the filing tray, and started going through the desk. The top right-hand drawer contained only the usual office paraphernalia – stapler, paper-punch, scissors, Prittstick, Sellotape, a few cheap ballpoints bundled together in an elastic band and a packet of paper-clips. The answering machine whirred on. Several incoming callers had been recorded, three of whom had rung off without leaving a message. Another call had been from someone called Lennie who had Pope's television in for repair. It was going to cost eighty quid, and did Pope want him to do the job? Someone else, who called herself Kathleen and sounded Irish, asked Pope to phone her back in the morning at work.

'Looks like he's camping out here,' said Makins, who was checking the drawers of the filing cabinet. He was holding up a tin of tomato soup. 'This drawer's full of canned grub.'

'How about the others?'

'All empty,' said Makins.

A girl's adenoidal and whining voice came from the answering machine. She was Sharon from the Six Ways service station, pointing out that Mr Pope had still to settle up for the work carried out on his motor-cycle last month. In case he'd forgotten, it was a hundred and eighteen pounds including VAT and Mr Banks wanted it settled this week or he was going to take advice from his solicitor.

Roper opened another drawer. Inside was a cardboard box of freshly printed stationery, a sample of the paper Sellotaped to the lid. He opened the drawer wider to read the printed heading on the sample.

'Well, wouldn't you just know,' he muttered.

'What's up?' said Makins.

'He's a private investigator,' said Roper. 'Or so it says here.'

'Cheeky sod,' said Makins.

'Damn right,' said Roper.

Makins went into the back room. Metal rattled hollowly. Makins came back again.

'Can I borrow those keys a minute?'

Roper handed them to him. 'What's in there?'

'A couple of metal cabinets. Locked up.'

Makins went away again. The remainder of the desk drawers, apart from one containing envelopes that matched the new stationery and a box of business-cards, were empty. Whatever Pope had been investigating there had clearly not been much of it.

'Guv'nor,' called Makins. 'Come and look at this.'

Roper skirted the desk and joined him in the small back room. Uncarpeted and pink walled, a handbasin in one corner, its only items of furniture were two tall, green metal cupboards and a rickety little table beside the basin, one of its legs standing on a wad of folded paper. The cupboard that Makins had opened had started life as a five-shelved filing cabinet, but three of the shelves had been unbolted and were lying in the bottom. Standing on them was a folding camp-bed, a pile of untidily folded bedding beside. On the shelf above was a microwave oven, a Pyrex casserole dish, an assortment of cheap crockery and a few bits and pieces of cutlery standing in a jam jar. All of which lent more credence to Makins' suggestion that Pope, for some reason or other, was shacked up here.

On the top shelf was an array of photographic equipment, an old Pentax 35-millimetre camera fitted with a long-focus lens, a carton of black and white film with two rolls missing, a small developing tank, again for 35-millimetre films, two small print-developing trays, postcard sized, several bottles of developing and printing chemicals, again for black and white film, and printing paper.

'Who uses black and white films these days?' said Makins.

'Private detectives, probably,' said Roper. 'Means they can do it all themselves and not farm it out to somebody who might be partial to collecting dirty pictures.' He took down the camera and its heavy lens, experimented with the film rewind button, found it loose, then opened the back. The camera was empty.

Makins was at the other cupboard. It had been stripped of all its shelves and converted into a wardrobe for Pope's few clothes. Standing on the floor at the bottom was a photographic enlarger, a cheap, tinny-looking thing, but good enough for its purpose and further evidence that Pope did all his own photo-processing and printing. A sheet of hardboard tucked behind the cupboard was an exact fit into the window recess and plunged the room into darkness until Makins took it down again. So the room was plainly Pope's makeshift darkroom. The grimy window opened on to an iron fire escape, a tiny courtyard and the unlovely backs of the buildings in the next street.

'. . . I don't give a shit,' a man's gruff muffled voice exploded angrily from the front office. 'Just be there.'

'For God's sake,' came a plaintive male response. 'The banks are shut now, aren't they?'

'You should have remembered earlier then, shouldn't you? See you in the car park. Eight-thirty. Bring it!'

There came a sharp click, and apart from a whirr the answering machine fell silent again.

Roper and Makins went back quickly into the front office. Roper rewound the tape a few inches and played the last exchange again. Too much time had passed for him to remember the sound of Pope's voice, but the nearer-sounding of the two men was more than likely him. And his voice had sounded threatening. And that had not been simply a recorded incoming message. It had been a heated exchange and for some reason Pope had seen fit to monitor both ends of it. And money was concerned. So perhaps Pope had been up to his alleged old tricks again and was demanding money with menaces.

'Excuse me,' a woman's tart and businesslike voice demanded from behind them, 'but what the *hell* do you two think you're doing in here? And how did you get in?'

Roper turned. She was standing in the doorway out to the landing, a handbag under one arm, a weighty briefcase dangling from her other hand, plump and fortyish in a trendy grey suit.

'Well?' she said. 'Who *are* you exactly?'

'Police, madam,' he said, fishing out his warrant-card and holding it out at arm's length. 'Superintendent Roper, County CID; and this gentleman is Detective Sergeant Makins.'

She came warily closer and examined his card, then Makins'.

'And you are who, madam?' asked Roper, when her curiosity was satisfied and had given way to interest as he

31

tucked his card away again.

'Shirley Cracknell,' she said. 'Mrs. I run the secretarial agency upstairs. I was on my way out, heard voices and saw the door was open. Then I saw you two fiddling about. Been up to no good, has he?'

'Who's that, Mrs Cracknell?' asked Roper, with winning ingenuousness.

'Mr Pope,' she said. 'I wouldn't put it past him. I still haven't worked out yet what he does for a living. And *I'm* his landlord.'

'But surely you didn't rent him this place without his telling you what he was going to do in it?'

'Oh, sure,' she said. 'He told me he was starting up in shop and office cleaning, and all he needed was a desk and a telephone and somewhere to keep his paperwork. I thought it was a bit odd because he seemed extra keen to take this office, which has two rooms, when he could have taken one of the single-roomed offices on the top floor at half the rent.'

Mrs Cracknell had not at first been suspicious of Mr Pope but merely curious. She rarely saw or heard him arrive in the mornings and just as rarely had been aware of his leaving in the evenings. She herself turned up each morning at half-past eight and left, as a rule, at some time around half-past five, depending on her workload. She ran a one-woman typing and word-processing operation, and such was the pressure of work sometimes that she was forced to stay on until ten or eleven o'clock at night. On those occasions, she had often noticed that the lights were on down in 21A all evening and were still on when she passed the door on her own way home for the night. A couple of times she had heard Pope going out, quite late, ten o'clock or half-past, but on both occasions he had been back within half an hour or so; and sometimes, as she was going home, she had met Pope returning. He was dressed in motor-cycling gear, as he had been last night – although last night he had been going out as she had been coming in; he kept his motor-cycle in the courtyard downstairs.

'What time last night, Mrs Cracknell?'

She frowned. 'Oh,' she said shrugging. 'About half-ten, I suppose. I was feeling a bit peckish and went along to the café for a roll and a cup of soup. I got back here and he was just coming down the stairs. He'd got his helmet on and everything.'

'Did he speak to you?'

'Just the usual token grunt. He isn't a great talker.'

She had worked extra late last night, the end-product in the briefcase she was carrying now, and had not left until nearly midnight. She had not heard Pope return.

'How long's he been here?'

'Since the week before Christmas; four months or so.'

'Pay his rent on time, does he?'

'In advance. First day of every month.'

'Cash in hand, or cheque?'

She hesitated, so it was probably cash in hand and H.M. Inspector of Taxes didn't know about it.

Then she came clean and said, 'Cash. Two hundred a month,' and was obviously gratified when Makins omitted to record that detail in his pocket-book.

'Know anything about him?'

'No,' she said. 'Not much. Except that he's divorced.'

'And he was no trouble?'

'Not particularly. I hear his radio playing in the evenings sometimes, but then he must hear my printer hammering away; so there's no point complaining.'

Roper and Makins had turned the place over thoroughly enough to know that there was no radio here, so what Mrs Cracknell had heard must have been the television set presently undergoing repair by the as yet unseen Lennie.

Mrs Cracknell knew little else about her tenant. He paid the rent on time and behaved himself; it had obviously never occurred to her that he was living here as well, nor did Roper, for the time being, enlighten her.

'Look,' she said. 'I really do have to go now, but is it a deep dark secret why you're here or can you drop a hint? I mean, what's he been up to exactly?'

'Mr Pope's dead, Mrs Cracknell,' said Roper. 'Traffic accident, near Appleford village. Some time late last night.'

'Oh, Lord,' she said, paling. 'Poor man.'

Maurice Hapgood, the landlord of the Hanging Man in Appleford village, knew they were coppers the moment they walked into his saloon bar. The older, canny-looking one, who sounded like a Londoner, had ordered two cheese and pickle rolls and a half of bitter, the baby-faced fair one a lager shandy and two rounds of salmon and cucumber sandwiches. They were muttering away together by the fireplace and the fair one had his notebook beside his plate, and very deedy it all looked.

'Perhaps it's about that accident last night,' whispered Hapgood's wife, Jackie, standing beside him behind the counter and drying the glasses as he sluiced them in the sink underneath and passed them up to her.

'Could be,' agreed Hapgood. 'Might even be the two who talked to old Tasker this morning.'

The accident had been the talk of the village today. It had happened late last night, so they said, a bit before midnight. A man without a head. That gipsy had found him, that Lee, who lived with his daft sister just past Mr Chance's place. Some were already saying that Lee was involved – he'd certainly been robbing the body afterwards, because old Wally Pickles had been going home from the pub and seen Sergeant Mallory frisking Lee in the light of his Panda car headlamps, and the police didn't do that for no reason, did they? And the body had been lying there looking like a sack of old rubbish, in fact Wally hadn't realised it was a body until he'd heard the rest of the story that morning. Yes, everybody agreed, robbing a dead body sounded just like Lee. Look at the way him and his sister had messed up that bit of land they were squatting on, turned it into a right proper tip, hadn't they? What everybody had to do was to get a petition together, and get rid of 'em . . .

And right in the middle of that discussion, old Tasker Hobday had waddled in after leaving his mangy old dog tied to one of the benches on the forecourt. He had found the body's head. Jammed in one of those skid-lids. Lying in the stream. No, straight up, he really had. The police had talked to him and everything. He was a valuable witness.

'Come on, you lying old bugger,' had scoffed Hapgood, because nobody could spin a yarn quite like old Tasker.

'No,' had wheezed old Tasker, settling himself on a stool at the counter. 'Dead serious. The old girl found it. Swore me to secrecy, they did.'

'Who did?'

'The law did, o' course,' had retorted old Tasker indignantly.

For once the old chap was telling the almost ungarnished truth. And he had told it over and over to whoever would listen to him and was likely to buy him a pint for the hearing of it. Hobday had left for his hut at two o'clock, his eyes happily glazed and his gait more unsteady than ever. Not until he was halfway home did he notice that his collie wasn't with him, and he had to turn about and waddle all the way back again and untie her from the bench on the forecourt.

'If those two don't hang about, we can lock up early,' whispered Mrs Hapgood, leaning down unnecessarily low to take another glass from him and thereby treating him to a tantalising view down her cleavage; at which point all thoughts of Tasker's story slipped from his mind entirely. For this Mrs Hapgood was a recently acquired replacement for the old one, a mean, stringy woman, who had passed on to that higher place she'd always talked about. This one was twenty years younger than him, and had made him feel like a spring chicken all over again. Willowy below and buxom above, she was the kind of woman Maurice Hapgood had always dreamed about, and their rumbustiously gymnastic honeymoon in Marbella had left him completely washed out but sublimely content. She was talking lately about getting one of those water-beds.'

'I'll go and call time in the public bar,' he muttered.

'Don't be long,' she whispered, suggestively nudging his leg with her knee.

They both straightened, and, as they did, the bell tinkled over the saloon-bar door and two more raincoated men came in, another fair one and another dark one. And even though Hapgood glanced meaningfully at the clock on the wall, so that they would notice that it stood at two minutes to three o'clock and that they had arrived within a gnat's whisker of afternoon closing-time, they failed to take the hint. The fair one, a young Welshman, ordered a pineapple juice, and the other a half of draught Guinness. And before they even joined the other two over by the fireplace, Hapgood had guessed they were two more coppers, and, to his disgruntlement and deep disappointment, they looked like settling in for the afternoon.

FOUR

CHIEF INSPECTOR PRICE, THE NEWLY arrived fair one, sipped at his fruit juice while Detective Sergeant Rodgers, the newly arrived dark one, sat hunched over his glass of Guinness. Apart from the four of them, and a woman drying glasses behind the counter, the bar was empty.

'Twenty-one A, Jubilee Walk, Dave,' said Roper to Price. 'Take a Scenes of Crime Officer with you.'

'What are we looking for?'

'Not sure,' said Roper. 'George and I couldn't find any records of the work he was doing, no case-files, no anything. I doubt you'll have to take the floorboards up, but there's got to be something there that'll give us a lead to what Pope was up to.'

'More than being a private eye, you mean?'

'Could be,' said Roper. 'From a bit of telephone conversation we heard, it might just be he'd put the finger on somebody, and it could be that same somebody who strung that piece of wire across the road. And if you can turn up any photographic negatives or prints they might be even more useful.'

'He probably did all his own photo-processing,' explained Makins. 'And we couldn't find any pictures.'

'Perhaps he passed them on to whoever hired him to take them,' proposed Price. 'That's what these private investigators usually do, isn't it?'

'Depends how honest they are,' said Roper. 'But Pope was a bad apple when he worked for us. Perhaps he hadn't changed. And you, Peter,' he said, now addressing DS Rodgers, 'I want you to track down a television repairer called Lennie something-or-other. He's probably got a workshop or an electrical shop somewhere near Pope's office. He might even be a mate of Pope's. Then find out where the Six Ways service station is and pay it a visit. Ask for a Mr Banks and find out how well he knew Pope and what work he did on Pope's motor-bike. You never know, you might pick up a few more leads.'

When Price and Rodgers went on their way at twenty-past three Roper and Makins went no further than the counter. The woman had gone, and the man who had served them earlier was draping a glass-towel over the pump handles.

'Sorry, gents, I'm shut,' he said pointedly, while they were still several paces short of his counter.

'Mr Hapgood?' said Roper.

'That's right.'

'We're police officers, sir.'

'Oh, aye,' said Hapgood, without surprise, glancing only cursorily at Roper's warrant-card before sliding it back across the counter. 'Whatever you want, I hope it won't take long because I've got an appointment to keep.'

'Just a few minutes, sir,' said Roper. 'The name of Pope mean anything to you?'

Hapgood shook his head. 'Not a thing,' he said. He was an unprepossessing man, somewhere in his late fifties, weasel-faced and balding, and plainly impatient to be off to his appointment.

'Any customers come in here last night wearing motor-cycle leathers? Big feller, six feet or so? Red helmet?'

Hapgood only shook his head again.

'How about your bar staff?'

'There's only me and the missus; except at weekends.'

'Perhaps we could have a word with Mrs Hapgood then, sir,' said Roper, to Hapgood's patent and further

38

irritation. 'It could be that she saw him.'

'I doubt it,' said Hapgood.

Roper waited. Hapgood waited.

'We really would like a word with your wife, sir,' said Makins.

Hapgood glared at him, and finally turned and disappeared through the arch beside his till. He was gone for several minutes.

'She's on her way,' he said surlily when at last he reappeared.

While they waited, Roper taxed him again about the leather-clad man, but Hapgood obviously hadn't seen him, nor the motor-cycle that Hobday said he had seen in the car park by the gents' toilets last night.

Mrs Hapgood was more helpful. Lavishly painted, dark haired and pneumatically bosomed, even in her slippers she was several inches taller than her wisp of a husband. She seemed unaware that her frilly white blouse was buttoned on the skew and that the back of it was hanging out over her skirt.

Some ten minutes before closing-time last night, both the till in the public bar and the till in the saloon had run out of small change more or less simultaneously, and she had gone upstairs to the office to fetch down a couple of bags of coppers to right the matter. On her way out of the office she had felt a momentary draught and realised that the upper half of the sashed window was still open. She went back in to shut it.

'And that's when you saw this man?'

'Yes,' she said. 'That's right.' She stood with an arm tightly threaded through one of her husband's for moral support, although it was he who looked more in need of it. 'He was all in black and he'd got one of those helmet things on. He was talking to somebody in a car.'

'What sort of car? D'you remember?'

She didn't know, but thought its colour had been light; grey or green or something like that. She couldn't be

39

certain because the only illumination in the car park had been from the back windows of the saloon and public bars. They only switched on the car park floodlights at the weekends when it was really busy. There had been only two or three other cars out there last night.

'Was the light on in the office, Mrs Hapgood? When you saw him?'

'No,' she said. 'I'd switched it off on my way out the first time.'

Which meant that, in the dark herself, she could have seen the man in the car park fairly clearly. She had got the impression that he was tall. He'd had one arm on the roof of the car and was leaning in at the driver's window. She had briefly thought that he might be up to no good, and watched for a moment in case he was a car thief; but then, as her eyes had become accustomed to the dark, she saw that there was someone sitting in the car and that the two of them were talking together. At that point, thinking no more of the incident, she had come downstairs and recharged the tills with change.

'Did you happen to see his motor-cycle?'

'No,' she said. 'Sorry.'

'How about the car? Big or small, was it?'

She shrugged. 'Difficult to say.'

'Might you have seen it about here before?'

'Couldn't say really. But it was sort of glittering at the front. Twinkly, you know.'

'Mr Craven in last night, was he?' asked her husband, in the manner of an aside that had just sprung to mind.

'Didn't see him,' she said.

'What about this Mr Craven?' asked Roper.

'Nothing particular,' said Hapgood. 'He comes in here sometimes on his way home from London. Lives down the way a bit. He's about the only bloke I can think of round here with a grey motor with a lot of chrome on the front. A Merc. Like him; a bit la-di-dah.'

'But this Mr Craven didn't actually come into the pub

last night.'

No, he had not. Both seemed certain.

'Know his address?'

'Furzecroft,' said Hapgood. 'Bungalow. Big place, it is. About half a mile down the road past Mrs Wicks'. There's a sign on the gate. You can't miss it. But he doesn't get back from London much before half-eight as a rule.'

George Makins wrote the address in his pocket-book.

'And there's a couple called Lee we'd like to have a chat with. Know where we can find them?'

'Same direction,' said Hapgood, both his face and his voice now registering blunt disapproval. 'Follow the fence of Downlands Farm till you get to the end where the trees start, just this side of Elsie Wicks' place. They're hidden away in there somewhere. And a right mess they're making along there and all.'

'They're gipsies,' explained Mrs Hapgood. 'Been nothing but trouble since the day they arrived. They say they're brother and sister, but well . . . you know,' she added darkly.

The Lees took little finding, their old grey motor-coach standing in a clearing not more than thirty feet back from the road. There was a young woman in jeans and a yellow tee-shirt pegging washing on a line strung between a couple of trees, and the only mess that Roper could see was a black plastic sack doing service as a dustbin leaning against one of the rear tyres. The young woman, her slim back to them and damp washing draped over her shoulder, was humming away happily to herself in the pale afternoon sunshine.

But then Roper cleared his throat to herald his and Makins' approach and she started round on a heel, her eyes huge and wide, snatching her washing down from her shoulder and clutching it to the front of her yellow shirt.

'It's all right, my dear,' said Roper, raising a placatory hand, but otherwise standing stock-still in the face of her

41

obvious alarm. 'We're police officers.' Slowly, carefully, he reached into his jacket and produced his warrant-card, holding it out to her at arm's length. She backed a pace, only to be stopped short by a wet towel hanging from her washing line.

'You go away,' she demanded breathlessly, clutching her washing tighter. 'Go on, you go away.'

'Miss Lee, is it?' said Roper softly.

She nodded, swallowing, still poised for flight.

'What's your first name, my dear?'

'Annie,' she said, her cautious dark eyes still flicking from one to the other of them.

'Is your brother about, Annie?'

She shook her head vehemently. But then, slowly, her expression changed to one of happy and absorbed interest.

'You goin' to be lucky,' she said.

'Is that right?' said Roper.

Still hugging her armful of washing, she shuffled closer. Thinking she might at last want to look at his card he held it out to her, but her smiling gaze appeared to be fixed at some point beyond his right shoulder. She stopped a yard away.

'You goin' to be lucky,' she said again, more insistently. 'You just 'ad a swallow fly down on your shoulder. They're lucky, swallows. When you get a swallow fly on your shoulder, that's a real lucky sign.'

Mallory had cruelly described Annie Lee as having wood between her ears. What Roper saw more was a true free spirit, one of the lucky ones whom the world passed by and left untroubled.

'It's your brother we'd like to talk to, Annie. Any idea where he is?'

Her face clouded again. 'You 'aven't come to move us on, 'ave you? We always be gettin' moved on.' Her dark eyes fixed him in abject appeal. 'This be the best place we ever bin. An' we don't steal or nothin'.'

'No, Annie,' Roper reassured her. 'We certainly haven't come to move you on. We've come about the accident that happened last night. Do you know about it?'

She shook her head.

'Your brother's what we call a witness, you see,' Roper explained patiently. 'We only want a word with him.'

Alarm fleeted across her face again. 'You're not takin' him away again are you?'

Roper opened his mouth to reply, but was cut off by a warning shout of, 'Oy, you two! What you doin' with her!' and the rapidly approaching rattle of a bicycle that came to a skidding stop beside him with a man, obviously Lee himself, straddling it.

'Go on,' he said, jerking a thumb over his shoulder in the direction of the road. 'Shove it!'

'Police,' said Roper, lifting the card he still hadn't put away, and holding it close enough for Lee to make out every word and full stop. Makins had moved in swiftly to Lee's other side and taken a firm grip of his handlebars.

'Piss off,' said Lee.

'Get any lippier than that, old lad,' Roper warned him grimly, 'and you're nicked.'

'For what?'

'Obstruction, for a start,' said Roper. He put his card away. 'Now let's begin again, shall we? Your name Hughie Lee, is it?'

'What if it is? I still don't want no truck with you lot. And if you want us out of here, you'll have to get one o' them Court Orders. And you,' he said, pointing at his sister. 'Don't stand there cuddlin' all that wet washin', it'll bring that cough o' yours back. Go an' 'ang it up.'

'Somewhere we can talk, Mr Lee?' asked Roper, as the girl turned away.

'Depends what it's about,' Lee replied, still truculent. 'If it's about movin' on, we'll go in our own good time. I know what me rights are, see.'

'It's about the accident out there on the road last night.

The local beat-officer found you going through the victim's pockets, so he tells me.'

'Well, I bloody wasn't,' retorted Lee. At last he dismounted his rattletrap of a bicycle and tugged the bottom of his trouser-legs from the tops of his socks. 'Robbin' the dead, that'd be, wouldn't it?'

'We'd still like to talk about it, Mr Lee,' said Makins.

'Suit yourself,' said Lee, shrugging, less belligerent now. 'S'pose you'd better come inside. Just don't talk too loud in front of her, see. She's easy scared.' He slouched towards the coach, pushing his bicycle which he leaned against the front wing before climbing the two wooden steps standing on the grass beneath the dooorway. Roper and Makins followed him inside. Everything looked fresh and clean and bright. All the windows were open, each of them hung with floral-patterned cotton curtains, and at the rear end of the vehicle was a sleeping-bunk with another curtain, partly closed, along the side of it. Just inside the door was a red-topped kitchen table bolted to the floor and opposite that a bagged out old sofa also bolted to the floor, its back and arms draped with vividly coloured embroidered covers. A pile of folded bedclothes wedged underneath it showed that it also did duty as another bed. On the floor beside the table something with an inviting odour was simmering away in a saucepan over a camping-gas burner.

'Take a seat, if you want,' said Lee, grudgingly pulling out a chair from under the red table and gesturing at the sofa.

Roper sat gingerly at one end of the sofa, feeling a spring pushing against his behind, and Makins sat at the other end.

'How long have you and your sister been here, Mr Lee?'

'Three or four weeks.'

'And before that?'

'All over. The last place we was long at was Hereford. Before that it was Birmingham. Went up there from Cornwall.'

'You keep on the move then?'

'Have to,' said Lee. 'People gets funny ideas 'bout folks like us.'

'Got a record?'

'Would 'ave,' said Lee. 'If your people got their way. It's not for the want of their tryin'. 'Specially that bloody Mallory.'

'What about him?'

'Comes here a lot. Nights, mostly. Usually got some story 'bout somethin' bein' nicked. Has a good look round to see if it's 'ere.'

'Does he indeed?' said Roper, lifting a surprised eyebrow. 'Bring a search-warrant with him, does he?'

'I've never seen one. But I don't never make no trouble 'cause o' Annie.'

'What d'you do for a living?'

'Anything,' said Lee. 'Diggin', hedgin', bit o' gardening. Whatever I can pick up. Don't live on Social Security, neither. All I get I earn honest.'

'You've got a few nice things lying about,' Roper observed, his eyes having taken in several good pieces of china, twinkling glassware, brassware, two glittering copper kettles and a Victorian silver tankard that would have cost him a week's salary at an auction.

'We didn't nick 'em, if that's what you're thinkin',' Lee retorted gruffly. 'Our old Daddy's, they were.'

'Do a bit of totting as well, do you?'

'Used to,' said Lee. 'But it ain't worth a candle any more.'

'The people round here say you leave the place untidy.'

'Well, they're bloody liars,' said Lee. Which was probably true. Roper had still to see the mess around the coach that Maurice Hapgood had spoken of.

'And that girl outside, she's really your sister, is she?'

'Course she is,' retorted Lee, momentarily angry again. 'Our old Daddy give her to me when she weren't more'n five minutes old. Took her down to the river and baptised her together, we did. That's why she's the way she is now.

45

Slipped out of the old man's 'ands, she did. Nearly drowned. He never forgive 'imself for that. The 'ospital tried to tell us she were dead, but the old man wouldn't 'ave it, made 'em go back and try agin. She's 'appy enough though. There's no harm in 'er.'

'You don't look much alike.' Apart from their twenty year disparity in age there were other equally obvious differences between them. He was fairer skinned and lighter haired, grey eyed, square-faced. His sister was finer boned and swarthier, her face pointed and sharp-chinned.

'He married twice. First time 'e got me. Gorgio woman she was, but she never did take to the life. Stuck it for eighteen years, she did. When she upped sticks and went the old man married again. That's when 'e got Annie. She's pure blood.'

'She told me she saw a swallow sitting on my shoulder.'

'P'raps she did,' said Lee. 'There's no sayin', is there?'

'Got the sight, has she?'

'None of your business if she has, is it?' countered Lee, at which juncture his sister came up the steps and he drew his feet back to make way for her. 'You could be makin' us and the gentlemen a nice cup o' tea, if you like,' he said, as she passed him. 'You'll find a packet o' milk in the saddlebag o' the bike.' She turned and went out again.

'What were you doing on the road last night, when Sergeant Mallory spotted you?'

'I thought somebody'd dumped a bag o' rubbish in the road. I was goin' to shift it. Thought it was dangerous, lyin' there the way it were.'

Annie Lee came back with a carton of milk. She stopped by her brother and he opened it for her.

'But it wasn't a bag of rubbish, was it?'

Lee shook his head. 'It were a bloke,' he said. 'A bloke in a leather suit. Didn't 'ave an 'ead. Looked like it'd bin cut off.'

'And you were going through his pockets.'

'Told you before. I don't go in for thievin'.'

46

'Sergeant Mallory says you were crouched beside the body.'

'For about three bloody seconds,' retorted Lee. 'I'd only just bent down and Mallory turns up. I didn't 'ave time to take anythin' even if I'd wanted. Anyway, he made me turn out me pockets, an' he didn't find anythin', did he?'

'Some wire and a pair of pliers,' Roper reminded him.

'What's wire and a pair of pliers got to do with a bloke lyin' dead in the road?' enquired Lee scornfully.

A lot, Roper had decided several hours ago; but he forebore to tell Lee that just yet.

'On your way back from setting a few snares on the heath, were you?'

'I might 'ave bin.' Lee took a rubber tobacco pouch from the pocket of his jacket. With a Rizla-paper trapped between two fingers he teased out sufficient tobacco to roll himself a cigarette. Crouched beside him, his sister was taking the simmering saucepan off the gas burner and replacing it with a kettle she had just filled from a plastic container. If she had heard any of the muttered conversation between her brother and Roper she showed no signs of it.

'How long had you been out?'

"Bout an hour,' said Lee. 'When that Mallory turned up I was just on my way back 'ere.'

'Did you hear anything? While you were on the heath?'

Lee shook his head, his eyes downward as he concentrated on rolling his cigarette.

'See anything?'

'It were dark, weren't it?'

'Headlights?' suggested Makins. 'You must have seen a few headlights going along the road.'

'Well?' prompted Roper, when Lee didn't answer, and seemed to be concentrating unnecessarily intently on the shaping of his cigarette.

'Don't remember,' said Lee woodenly, sticking out the tip of his tongue and running it along the gum of the

47

cigarette-paper, still with his gaze resolutely down.

'Did you hear a motor-bike?'

'Can't say that either,' said Lee, popping the cigarette between his lips and feeling around his jacket pockets for matches. 'All I know 'bout's what I found in the road.'

'He was an ex-copper,' said Roper. 'Name of Pope.'

Lee's right hand, a match pinched between its thumb and forefinger, stilled an inch from the box. The moment passed.

'Never 'eard of 'im,' grunted Lee. 'Don't mean nothin' to me.' His hand moved on, the match flared and lit his shadowed face; but by that time it was too late and the flicker of recognition that might have sprung to his eyes was gone.

'I'd say our friend back there has got something on his mind,' said George Makins, when he and Roper were on their way back to the car and safely out of earshot. 'When you dropped Pope's name, he practically froze on the spot.'

'I know,' said Roper. 'I noticed.'

'You done somethin' bad, 'aven't you?' she accused, dumping a mug of tea down at his elbow so hard that the tea inside all but slopped over the rim.

'Course I 'aven't,' he said.

'So why d'you 'ave that owl on your shoulder when you come back in last night? And why d'you tell 'em all those lies?'

'I didn't tell 'em no lies.'

'You 'ad lies all round you,' she retorted fiercely. 'I seen 'em.'

He drew her down to sit on his lap. 'Look, girlie,' he said. 'I found a bloke lyin' in the road last night. I should've minded me own business, and I didn't. There ain't no more than that to it.'

'So why d'you lie?' she argued, wrestling free and

48

standing angrily over him. 'They'll be back. You see if they don't. That old one had your mark. I see it in his face.'

'You don't always see right. Not always.'

'Most I do,' she said. 'And he's got a bit o' sight, too. He knows things.'

"E's just another bloody copper,' he sneered. 'Just like all the others.'

'Not that one,' she said. "E's all right. 'E come with a swallow. Saw it perch on 'is shoulder. So just you take care.'

FIVE

AT FIVE O'CLOCK IN THE evening Roper was in the chill
and aseptic gloom of the mortuary and tapping on the
glass window of the examination room. Wilson, the
pathologist, sitting on a high stool by the workbench on
the far side of the room, glanced up from the notes he was
making and gave a cheery salute. His green-overalled
woman assistant was feeding instruments into an autoclave
by the sink and in the middle of the room one of the
attendants was hosing down a perforated stainless-steel
table.

Roper went in. He had never been enamoured of
mortuaries. They made him all too aware of his own
fragile mortality.

'Just getting a cup of tea organised,' said Wilson. 'Fancy
one?' A man of steadfast and remarkable good humour,
he stuck out his hand.

'No, thanks,' said Roper, as Wilson's warm hand closed
around his.

Wilson smiled, well aware of Roper's distaste for the
ambience. 'It's being served in the anteroom,' he
persuaded. 'Not in here.'

'Two sugars,' said Roper.

'Organise that, will you, Henry,' Wilson called to the
hosing attendant. 'One more tea, with two sugars.'

The attendant turned off the nozzle of his hose and
went out into the passage. Wilson turned back to the
bench. Lying on it, in two pieces, was Pope's red crash

helmet. It had been removed with a circular saw, cut into exact halves, fore to aft, like a chocolate Easter egg.

'Whatever did it decapitated him between his first and second cervicle,' said Wilson, looking out at Roper over the tops of his horn-rimmed spectacles. 'I doubt the poor fellow knew anything about it.'

'We reckon someone strung a length of wire across the road.'

'Feels about right,' said Wilson. 'He must have been steaming along at a hell of a rate of knots.'

'Like?'

Wilson puffed his cheeks thoughtfully. 'Seventy or eighty,' he said. 'Thereabouts.'

'He couldn't have died of anything else beforehand?'

'A cover-up job, you mean?' Wilson shook his head. 'I doubt it very much. He died a reasonably healthy man, apart from smoking too many cigarettes. His last meal was tomato soup and wholemeal bread. And about half an hour before he died he'd drunk several pints of beer, which means he was probably driving with more than the legal limit of alcohol inside him. I hear he was one of yours.'

'Regrettably,' said Roper. 'But he dived before we could push him.'

They went along to the cold-room together in order for Roper to make sure he was investigating the death of the right man. Another attendant hauled the drawer open and Wilson lifted the white cover down as far as Pope's broad pale chest. Apart from several layers of thick cotton bandages, wrapped around his throat from its base to his ear-lobes, he looked surprisingly intact.

'Staples and a few twists of surgical wire,' explained Wilson. 'He's who you thought he was, is he?'

'Definitely,' said Roper. A few years older, the beard a little greyer, it was Gerald Pope all right. A mean-looking bully-boy in life, his death had done nothing to enhance his charm.

*

By six o'clock Roper was back in his office at County, his desk a litter of photographs, some of them taken by CI Brake's sergeant at the scene of the crime, for crime it had surely been; others, Polaroids, taken by Wilson during the course of his autopsy this afternoon and which showed the headless body and the disembodied head in all their colourful and gruesome detail. Centre-stage at the moment though, spread on Roper's blotter, was an Ordnance Survey map of the stretch of road that ran west out of Appleford village. Marked with red ballpointed crosses to indicate the sites of various finds – the body, the head, the Honda motor-cycle, the signpost and the tree to which the ends of the murder weapon, namely a length of wire, had been secured – it brought some sort of order into what this morning, on the road itself, had looked like total chaos.

It seemed now that Pope's body, and perhaps his head too, had travelled on under their own momentum some twenty feet beyond the wire stretched between the signpost and the tree. With its rider snatched cleanly from it, the motor-cycle, kept upright by its own forward momentum and the gyroscopic effect of its wheels, had continued to travel onward a further two hundred and ninety-three metres, veered as it had slowed and started to dither, mounted the verge and plunged into and behind the shrubbery where Brake's officers had finally located it that morning.

Those, certainly, were facts. But only some of the facts, the basic mechanics. More complex was the human involvement that had brought those mechanics about.

If Pope had indeed been the intended victim, which as yet was still only an assumption, then the killer must have been watching him uncommonly closely, and, not only that, must have known not only where he *was* but where he was *going* to be a few minutes hence, namely astride his

52

motor-cycle and gunning it in the general direction of Dorchester. The stringing of the wire must have been precisely timed. Stretched across the road too soon and there would have been a chance of a heavier vehicle smashing straight through it, albeit suffering damage of some sort in the process. According to Mallory the road was only lightly used after seven o'clock in the evenings, but even then the wire would have to have been swiftly strung and equally swiftly taken down again, or Pope would not necessarily have been the only casualty. Ergo: it had been absolutely vital for the killer to know to within a minute or so when Pope was going to be passing. And, even then, an element of chance had been involved. In the distance at night one oncoming motor-cycle looked and sounded very much like another, and there had to be a probability that Pope might have been overtaken by a car, or that a car coming in the opposite direction would have broken the wire before Pope himself reached it.

But, on the other hand, from Appleford village to a mile or so beyond where the body had been found, the road was perfectly straight, thereby lessening that element of chance. If the wire had been first lashed to the silver birch tree, it could have been left lying loosely across the carriageway until the very last moment – namely the sighting of Pope's single headlight – then lifted and pulled tight by someone standing by the signpost, quickly lashed around it and made fast. And as quickly snipped away again when it had served its purpose, the work of a moment. With all the shrubbery round about the villain could have dropped from sight in a fraction of a second.

And out here in farming country wire was always at hand. Fencing wire, baling wire, and in Hughie Lee's case brass picture-wire for making rabbit snares out on the heath. Even if Roper knew the kind of wire that had been used, tracing its source would be nigh on impossible, unless, of course, he was lucky enough to turn up the particular length of wire in question.

A motive as yet could only be guessed at, although given Pope's alleged track record, and the line of business he had chosen after leaving the Force, motives probably abounded. There were plenty of good honest private investigators earning their crust legally, but there were bad apples too, working as Pope had, out of shabby offices and with only their names and telephone numbers on their notepaper and those numbers otherwise ex-directory so they couldn't be traced by anyone except the authorities. How they got sufficient work to make a living was anyone's guess, but certainly guessable was that a lot of that work was of the kind that the real professionals wouldn't touch.

DS Rodgers was back at six-thirty. One of the best leg-men at County, he had worn down a lot of shoe leather this afternoon and evening, but the effort had paid off. By dint of walking from one Dorchester television and electrical retailer to another, he had finally tracked down Lennie, the owner of one of the voices on Pope's answering machine.

His full name was Leonard Arthur Martin and he ran his one-man operation out of a lock-up garage on the southern outskirts of Dorchester. Some of his work was legal, but it had been Rodgers' considered opinion that a lot of it was not. Mr Martin's speciality was the repair of video recorders, and Rodgers had glimpsed, before Mr Martin had hastily closed his storeroom door on them, a pile of six such items still sealed up in their Japanese manufacturer's cartons, and since all six cartons were identical with each other—

'He's fencing 'em for somebody,' suggested Roper.

'Probably,' said Rodgers. 'And he was definitely on the wary side.'

On his way out of Dorchester, Rodgers had called in at the police station to have a word with one of the local DCs. It transpired that Mr Martin was already the subject of a close scrutiny and already had two prison convictions for receiving. Tomorrow, he would be the subject of another official visit.

That aside, Lennie Martin had talked, albeit reluctantly, of Gerald Pope. They had met by chance one lunchtime in a pub in Dorchester some six months before. Pope was newly divorced and looking for digs in the town. Lennie Martin had known of some. A woman friend of his, also divorced, was looking for a lodger. Martin introduced Pope to her and Pope had moved in with her the next day. But she and Pope hadn't hit it off, and after a couple of months the two of them had quarrelled about Pope's laxity in paying the rent and she had thrown him out. For a few weeks then, Pope had bedded down in a corner of Martin's lock-up while, so he told Martin, he looked around the town for business premises, although he had never told Martin what his proposed business was.

During those few weeks, just before last Christmas, Martin and Pope had spent most of the evenings drinking together. At about that time too, Pope had found himself a new woman. Martin had seen them together a few times, and to the best of his knowledge she and Pope had still been knocking around together within the last few days. Martin didn't know her name but thought she was a waitress in one of Dorchester's many tea shops and restaurants.

A few days before Christmas, Pope had collected his gear from Martin's lock-up and moved into his business premises in Jubilee Walk. He had borrowed Martin's van to do so. Over the Christmas and New Year holiday, Pope had more or less dropped from sight and when Martin saw him again Pope was sporting a bruised cheek and a split lip.

'Did he tell Martin how he came by 'em?'

'His ex-wife's new boyfriend,' said Rodgers. 'Apparently they all met up in the pub by accident on New Year's Eve; Pope got stroppy and the boyfriend waited outside for him in the car park afterwards and duffed him over.'

Which, if it was true, indicated that a word or two with the erstwhile Mrs Pope and her new paramour might not come amiss.

Of late, however, Martin had spoken to Pope hardly at all, except on the occasion Pope had brought his portable television in for repair. That had been a week ago, and despite several messages left on his answering machine Pope had failed to respond. Martin had suspected that Pope was short of cash again. Some weeks he had a walletful, other weeks none.

Unlike Martin's lock-up workshop, the Six Ways service station proclaimed its existence with a framed entry in the Yellow Pages; and Mr Banks, its owner, although not as knowledgeable as Lennie Martin, had been pithily forthcoming about Gerald Pope.

Pope, according to Banks, had been one of his more frequent customers, calling in at least twice a week for petrol, so much so that Banks had got to know him, not well but enough to idle away a few minutes of conversation with him whenever he called in. From these conversations, Banks, a trusting man, had formed the impression that Pope was a reliable sort, so that when, some five weeks ago, Pope had wheeled in his motor-cycle with a flat rear tyre, Banks had readily agreed to effect the replacement for him and to make a rush job of it. Pope had called in two hours later to collect the machine. Banks at the time had been out to lunch, and Pope had persuaded Banks' office-girl to let him take the machine away on the understanding that he would return the next day and pay by credit-card, which he had been unable to do at the time because he'd left his wallet in his office. The girl, recognising him as a familiar face, and one she had seen talking amicably to her boss, had foolishly agreed to Pope's request.

And still Mr Banks was waiting for his money and Pope had obviously taken to buying his petrol elsewhere. All Pope had ever let slip was that he lived in Dorchester, and armed with that Banks had been able to track down his telephone number from Directory Enquiries but, as is the legal requirement, the operator had declined to give him Pope's address.

And since Pope never answered his telephone in person, all Banks had ever spoken to, and been frustrated by, was Pope's answering machine.

Which was why Mr Banks was still a very angry man.

At seven o'clock Roper and Makins were on their way to have a chat with the ex-Mrs Pope. Still living in the house she had shared with Pope on the outskirts of Blandford Forum, and with the telephone number unchanged, she had not been difficult to find.

She showed them into her sitting-room.

'What's he been up to now?' she asked disinterestedly. 'Knocked somebody else about, has he?'

'He's dead, Mrs Pope,' said Roper, coming to the nub of the matter at once. 'A traffic accident down in Appleford late last night. I'm sorry.'

He expected her to show some sign of shock – or even grief – but obviously all her emotions for Pope had been used up years ago and her only change of expression was a surprised lift of her eyebrows. She was a mean-looking woman with a spiteful mouth. Perhaps Pope had made her that way, but in any event she plainly didn't give a damn that he was well and truly out of her life forever.

'Well, thanks for letting me know,' she said, with a casual shrug, as if it had just been pointed out to her that her slip was showing. 'Can I get you a cup of tea or something?'

'No thanks, Mrs Pope,' said Roper.

'Rainey,' she countered. 'Not Pope. I've been using my own name since the divorce.' Which was not the only change she appeared to have made. There was an estate agent's SOLD flag strapped to the gatepost outside. And the heels of a pair of man's shoes half-hidden under the telephone seat in the hallway had also not escaped Roper's attention on his way in.

'You'll appreciate we have to ask you a few questions,' said Roper. 'We won't keep you long.'

'I don't know anything about him any more,' she said. 'The last time I saw him was a couple of minutes past midnight on New Year's Day. I haven't seen him since, and I can't say I want to. I don't even know where he was living.'

'Dorchester,' said Roper. 'He had a couple of rooms he was renting as an office. We think he was sleeping there too.'

'An office?' she said. 'Doing an honest job of work at last, was he?'

'A private detective agency,' said Roper.

'Yes,' she said scornfully. 'That sounds about right. I guessed it'd be something a bit fishy.'

'Do you know if he had any enemies?'

'Plenty, I should think,' she said, still unable to keep the scorn out of her voice. 'Me and my new chap for a start. If it hadn't been for Stan not wanting to make trouble, Gerry would probably be doing three months right now for aggravated assault. Gerry put his boot in Stan's face, you know; but then he always was a bit of a thug.'

Which was not quite the story as Lennie Martin had told it. According to Martin it was Pope who had been the victim. Stan was one Stanley Docker, Mrs Pope-Rainey's current, and probably live-in, man friend. She had urged him to go to the police and report the incident but he hadn't wanted to do that.

Like most ex-partners with an axe to grind, once launched on her complaints against her ex-husband they came pouring out of her one after the other. The marriage had been a mistake from the very beginning. There had been other women, booze, lies, the unsocial hours he worked, his moody silences. Long before the divorce had been finalised he had, unbeknown to her, put the house up for sale; but the house was half hers and she

58

had dug her heels in and swiftly taken it off the market again. And in the time since, when she had been forced to agree to the sale or pay his half of the value of the property, he had phoned her every Friday evening to see if she'd found a potential buyer. A sale had finally been agreed that very afternoon.

And Roper, seated now on the sofa beside Makins as he listened to her endless, vindictive diatribe, watching her thin face and the way her mouth twisted whenever she mentioned Pope's name, soon became aware that her feelings towards her ex-husband were ones of virulent hatred. It even occurred to him that she might wilfully have delayed the sale of the house to keep Pope poor for a little longer; and from that passing thought sprang another. The house was worth about eighty thousand, half of which was Pope's. And if Pope had no living relatives, there would be no call on his ex-wife to share anything with anybody. And there were many who had murdered for a devil of a lot less than forty thousand pounds.

And now the house was sold and Pope was coincidentally and conveniently dead. The connection didn't seem a likely one, but it wasn't impossible.

'There's the question of a formal identification of your ex-husband's body, Mrs Rainey,' Roper said, as he and Makins were about to leave.

'Not me,' she said. 'He's nothing to do with me any more. You'll have to find somebody else to do that.'

They left soon after eight o'clock. It was dark now and raining again, and the investigation was no further forward than it had been this morning.

It was the Scenes of Crime Officer, who had spent the afternoon and evening in Pope's office with Price, who provided the springboard for the first leap forward.

Price returned to County at nine o'clock, under his arm the leather-bound blotting pad that had decorated Pope's desk. The SOCO had spotted a telephone number hastily

59

pencilled on the pad's upper right-hand corner. Lightly written, and smudged almost to extinction, even under the bright light of Roper's desk lamp it was only just readable; which was perhaps why Roper himself hadn't noticed it when he and Makins had been sniffing around earlier in the day.

'Tried ringing it yet?'

'Not yet,' said Price.

Roper asked for an outside line and tapped out the number. The only certainty was that it was somewhere in London. The phone at the other end rang three times, then came a click and the second of silence that precedes the switching in of an answering machine.

'This is Craven, Heilbron and Partners,' a carefully cultivated and mellifluous female voice proclaimed. 'The office is closed until nine-thirty tomorrow morning, but if you wish to leave a message or place an instruction, please speak after the tone. Thank you.'

Roper put the phone down again and wrote 'Craven, Heilbron' and the number on his jotting pad. It might be worth trying the number again tomorrow.

'Nobody there?' asked Price.

'Answering machine,' said Roper. 'And it sounded very upmarket. Not Pope's style at all.'

The rest of Price's search had turned up nothing except an expensive pair of binoculars hanging among Pope's clothes. He and the SOCO had stripped all the drawers from Pope's desk and filing cabinet, tipped them over and looked underneath, and behind, had taken all the clothes out of the steel cupboard he used as a wardrobe and ransacked the pockets, laid all his bedding on the floor and unfolded it, swung all the cupboards and cabinets away from the walls, lifted the edges of the carpet, and generally left no stone unturned.

They had found absolutely nothing to point them anywhere in particular. If Pope had ever kept records of his business dealings, then he must have been keeping them somewhere else. Although all the signs led to the conclusion that he had nowhere else. Except that Lennie Martin had told DS Rodgers that Pope had had a current woman-friend, but even then it was fairly evident that he had not been living with her.

'When the story breaks in the newspapers tomorrow, perhaps she'll come forward,' said Price hopefully.

'Not if she's married she won't,' said Roper.

Price left for home at ten o'clock, Roper half an hour afterwards. As far as he was concerned, it had been a fruitless day. Of suspects there were as yet only two. Mrs Pope née Rainey was one. And she had had a motive of sorts. The other was Hughie Lee, the gipsy, who had been caught crouched over the body late last night and who had later been found to be in possession of a coil of brass wire and the necessary pliers to cut it with. Roper also remembered the moment when he had mentioned Pope's name to Lee, and how Lee's fingers had briefly stilled over his matchbox. Of the two, Lee was the likelier suspect, but what could his motive have been and how could he possibly have come into contact with Pope in the first place? Certainly not through Pope's connection with the police because all Pope's police service had been worked out here in Dorset and, if Lee was telling the truth, neither he nor his sister had been anywhere near Dorset until three weeks ago, by which time Pope had long since been a civilian again. But Lee had clearly recognised Pope's name, so there had to be a connection somewhere, however frail that connection was.

It was only when he had arrived home in Bournemouth and was closing his garage door that a sudden flash of remembrance came. When he had written the names Craven and Heilbron on his jotter a couple of hours ago he had thought little of it. But now he did, and suddenly realised the possible significance of the name Craven.

That was the very name that the landlord of the Hanging Man had proposed for the driver of the car that

61

his wife had seen from their office window last night. The driver she had seen talking to the man in the crash helmet – who might just have been Gerry Pope.

SIX

FOR THE SECOND MORNING IN succession Roper broke his journey at the edge of Appleford Heath, today because he had noticed Mallory's Panda car parked half on the grass near where the Lees were camping.

He pulled in a few yards beyond and ratchetted on the handbrake, climbed out and walked back. The Panda was empty, the driver's door-window wound down a couple of inches and the ignition key still in the lock. Assuming that Mallory had left the vehicle in a hurry, perhaps in answer to an emergency call, Roper turned into the shrubbery and walked briskly towards the clearing where the bus was.

Or rather, to where it had been. For this morning there was no bus, only a black oily patch of grass and several black plastic sacks full of rubbish dumped among the bushes. And a woman in a hard-hat and tailored jacket sitting astride a chestnut hack and obviously sharing a private joke with a capless Sergeant Mallory, the two of them so absorbed in each other that neither was aware of Roper's approach. He recognised the woman as the dark one of the matching pair who had passed him yesterday morning on the road.

'Morning, Sergeant,' said Roper tartly, to Mallory's back. 'What's going on?'

Mallory swung round quickly, the smile he had been sharing with the woman dying on his face.

'I'd best be getting along,' the woman said, clearly recognising trouble when she saw it. She was still smiling.

She raised her crop to the visor of her hat and with a 'good morning' to Roper gave her hack a touch of rein and knee and turned it at a walk towards the road. Roper watched her go.

'Who's that?' he said, turning back to face Mallory as the clack of hooves sounded on the metalled surface of the road.

'Mrs Chance, sir,' said Mallory. 'Her husband's got the place next door.'

'I see,' said Roper weightily. 'And how about the first question I asked you? What the hell's gone on here? Where are the Lees?'

'They're gone, sir.'

'I can see that for myself, Sergeant,' snapped Roper. 'The point is, why did they go?'

'Scared, probably,' said Mallory.

'And what were they scared of? They were all right when I last saw them. Or did you happen to talk to them after I did?'

Mallory clearly had. His shifty gaze said it all. 'We should have nicked Lee,' he said surlily. 'He couldn't have gone anywhere then, could he?'

'When I want your advice, Sergeant, I'll ask for it. *Did* you pay Lee another visit after I'd gone?'

'I kept an eye,' Mallory conceded grudgingly.

'Don't play bloody semantics with me, laddie,' said Roper quietly. A patient man as a general rule, he hadn't taken kindly to Mallory from the start. 'When I say visit, I mean visit.'

'I paid a call on him last night,' Mallory finally admitted.

'And the bus was still here, obviously?'

Mallory nodded.

'And he wasn't likely to go anywhere without the bus, was he?'

Mallory shrugged. 'I suppose not.'

'But you still felt the need to have a word with him?'

Mallory didn't answer.

'Called just the once, did you? Or twice? Or three times? Make a nuisance of yourself, did you, Sergeant?'

'He was in that business with the motor-bike up to his neck.'

'Got evidence of that, have you? Know something I don't, do you?'

'No, sir,' said Mallory, casting his gaze downward at last. 'Not exactly.'

'So how many times did you call on the Lees after I'd gone? Exactly?'

'Three,' admitted Mallory, eventually. 'The first two times he was out.'

'Thought you'd have some fun and games, did you? Well, you've blown it,' Roper hastened on angrily, not waiting for Mallory's answer because there was really no need to hear it. 'I wanted a few more words with our Hughie and now, because you decided to play the heavy-handed copper, he isn't here, is he? So here's what you do: you go back to your car and get on the radio. I want to know where that bus is, but I only want to *know*. I don't want anybody nicked and I don't want the Lees harassed any more or even talked to. Just where the bus is. Got that? And next time lock your car when you leave it. And chat up your lady friends in your own time. Right?'

Makins held the lift doors open for Roper to join him.

'You look like someone who's just had his parking space pinched,' he observed, pushing the button for the third floor.

'The Lees moved out during the night,' said Roper. 'Bloody Sergeant Mallory put the skids under 'em.'

'Why the hell did he do that?'

'*Don't* ask me,' said Roper.

At ten o'clock, his wrath abated and his blood pressure back to normal, he put through another call to Craven, Heilbron and Partners in London, and the same mellifluous female voice answered him, although this

65

time in the flesh.

'I'd like to speak to Mr Craven, please.'

'I'm sorry, he's in a meeting. All the morning, I'm afraid. Would you like to leave a message. Or shall I tell him you called?'

'No. I'll ring back later,' said Roper. 'It's personal. Can you tell me what line of business you're in, by the way?'

There was a surprised pause. 'We're stockbrokers.'

'I see,' said Roper, himself surprised. 'Thank you. Good morning.'

'What did they say?' asked Makins, sitting at the other side of the desk and sipping at his coffee.

'Stockbrokers,' said Roper.

'What would Pope have been doing in that kind of company?'

'Not buying shares,' said Roper. 'That's for certain.' But there was certainly a connection somewhere. Mrs Hapgood might not have seen Craven's car parked behind the Hanging Man the other night, but it had to be more than mere coincidence that Craven lived close to Appleford village, and that his business telephone number in far-off London should have been scribbled on a blotting pad in Pope's poky office in Dorchester.

'I think it's visiting time again,' said Roper, standing up and unhooking his raincoat from his coatstand. 'Craven's place first.'

'But Craven's up in the City, isn't he? According to Hapgood he doesn't get home much before eight or nine o'clock at night.'

'True,' agreed Roper. 'But he's probably got a wife, and I'd rather talk to her first.'

It was only a ten-minute drive from County Headquarters to Appleford. The dullness of the early morning had given way to rain again. It looked settled in for the day and gave the vast expanse of the heath a grey and gloomy melancholy.

Makins drove on to the verge a couple of yards beyond a

66

five-barred oak gate set beneath a wrought-iron arch with the name Furzecroft worked into its white-painted tracery. The house that lay behind was an elegant sprawling bungalow, more like a red brick ranchhouse, with a double garage set among the trees over on the right. All of it looked as if it added up to a lot of money. And somebody was at home because there was a dark green Range Rover parked in front of the verandah and lights showing at one of the windows.

They closed the five-barred gate behind them and strode briskly along the driveway, a sudden bluster of wind from the heath driving the rain hard against their backs and gusting them along with it. The deep sheltered verandah was fenced with more decorative wrought-iron panels set in the brickwork, and a businesslike burglar alarm above the front door looked likely to deter even the most professional of housebreakers.

It was a plump, pink-cheeked girl who answered Makins' ring at the doorbell. Pink nylon-overalled, an aerosol of furniture polish and a duster clenched in her free hand, and her feet in a pair of white trainers with the tops of a pair of red socks showing at the ankles, it didn't seem likely that she was Mrs Craven; nor the Cravens' teenage daughter, if indeed there was one. The wings of her nose were chapped and raw.

'Yeah?' she said, sniffing wetly.

'Police, Miss,' said Makins, holding out his warrant-card.

She peered at it with red-rimmed eyes. 'Wassit about exactly?'

'The accident out on the road the night before last, Miss. We're looking for likely witnesses. Wonder if we might have a word with the householder, please. It shouldn't take long.'

'I'll go and see,' she said, sniffing horribly again. Leaving the front door open she slouched off back along the hallway and went into a room on the left. Faint voices then, hers and two other women, before she returned, hastily fumbling in her overall pocket for a paper handkerchief.

'You'd best cub in,' she said, the last couple of words muffled in the handkerchief.

'Got a cold?' enquired Makins amicably, as he wiped the soles of his shoes on the doormat and Roper followed him in.

'Had it for weeks,' she grumbled companionably as she closed the door behind them. 'Just won't go away.'

She led them along the hallway. Roper could almost feel the quality of the carpet through his shoes. Against the wall stood a highly desirable rosewood sofa-table, probably a Regency piece, a midnight blue Emile Gallé glass vase sitting at one end and a combined telephone, answering and fax machine at the other.

'The policeben, Mrs Craven,' the girl said.

'Do come in,' another woman's voice invited, but not Mrs Craven's. Mrs Craven was the willowy blonde in the red angora pullover and tightly-fitting black trousers. The other woman was the darkly beautiful Mrs Chance, last seen laughing with Sergeant Mallory, and looking as elegant off her horse as she did on it. She was dressed to leave, a sheepskin driving-coat draped over her shoulders like a cloak. Both were standing by a coffee table with a pair of matching cups and saucers and biscuit plates on it.

Mrs Chance raked the blond and baby-faced Makins with a bold and appreciative eye. 'Unless you want to ask me something too, I was just on the point of going home.'

'We're only making a few routine enquiries, Madam,' said Makins. 'It's about the accident along the way late on Monday night. We're looking for witnesses.'

'I'm sorry,' she said, shrugging. 'I can't help you.'

'I don't think I can, either,' the blonde chipped in. She was foreign, probably Scandinavian, a little nervous, and it was at that juncture that Roper realised that she was the other woman who had passed him on horseback early yesterday morning when he'd stopped to chat with CI Brake.

68

'Live locally, do you. . .?' Makins said, leaving the question mark hanging in mid-air, to Mrs Chance.

'Mrs Chance,' she said. 'About half a mile down the road. Downlands Farm.' She was still looking at Makins as if she wanted to take a knife and fork to him, much as earlier she had been looking at Sergeant Mallory. 'Vanessa Chance. And this lady is Mrs Craven.'

Mrs Craven twitched a smile. She stood with her arms tightly folded, her glance, whenever Roper caught it, an uneasy one. The spacious room, on two levels, ran the length of the house from front to back. Like the two women, the furniture was straight out of the Sunday supplements and the Lowry over the fireplace looked like the genuine article. Equally genuine was the Chiparus bronze of a dancing-girl on the stone shelf above the fireplace. The vast picture-window at the back let in too much of the miserable grey daylight so that the room felt sombre and chilly too. At the far end of the garden a weeping willow and a tall clump of reeds showed the course of the stream.

'Might your husbands have seen or heard anything?' asked Makins.

'What time did it happen?' asked Mrs Chance. She had taken a pair of driving-gloves from the pocket of her sheepskin.

'Some time between eleven and half-past,' said Makins. 'So far as we know.'

'My husband might have seen something,' she said. 'He was coming back from the village about then.' She slowly tugged on one of the gloves with a lot of finger-flexing, making the act faintly erotic, like a striptease in reverse, then the other.

'Mine was at home,' said Mrs Craven. 'About eleven he arrived, I think.'

'You can always ask them, can't you,' said Mrs Chance. 'Mine's home all day.'

'Mrs Craven?' asked Makins.

69

'Not until tonight,' she said, in her prettily fractured accent. 'He works in London. Nine o'clock would be best. Or even later.'

'Well, thanks for your trouble,' said Makins. 'Sorry about the interruption.'

'No trouble,' purred Mrs Chance seductively. 'You've brightened our little lives considerably. I'll show you out. You can call in on us any time you like,' she added, and even managed to make that sound like a sexual invitation of the most blatant kind. Mrs Craven, who had stood all the time with her arms tightly folded and hugging herself, seemed relieved to see them go.

Makins turned for the door, as did Roper, and there was a brief confusion as Mrs Chance went to step between them and Makins turned about again and almost bumped into her. 'The victim's name was Pope,' he volunteered hopefully, making it sound like an afterthought; although the loud dropping of Pope's name had been the prime purpose of their visit. 'I don't suppose that rings any bells, does it?'

It clearly rang nothing for Mrs Chance, but the name might have meant something to Mrs Craven. Roper, who had kept in the background – because it was a rare Detective Superintendent indeed who made door to door enquiries looking for witnesses to a traffic accident – and had uttered not a sound since entering the house, distinctly saw a stiffening of Mrs Craven's face and a bracing of her folded arms. It certainly wasn't a trick of the light.

'Never heard the name before,' said Mrs Chance. 'Sorry.'

'Nor me also,' said Mrs Craven, who still hadn't moved from her post by the coffee table and was plainly going to leave their showing out to Mrs Chance.

'You'll tell your husband to expect us this evening then, Mrs Craven?' said Makins.

'Yes,' she said, unmoving beside the coffee table and still

with her arms tightly folded, twitching another smile into place. 'Yes. Of course.'

Mrs Chance led them back along the hallway, a wake of expensive perfume trailing behind her. Out on the verandah she drew the door shut behind them.

'I wonder if you'd mind very much opening the gate for me, and closing it again behind me,' she said, smiling sweetly and addressing herself most specifically to Roper, whom she clearly regarded as Makins' silent underling. 'It would save me getting wet twice over.'

'Not at all, Madam,' said Roper, his face wooden. Mrs Chance was plainly used to having men tripping over themselves to do her bidding.

'Thank you,' she said, and as she clutched her coat about her and darted to the Range Rover they leaned into the rain and hurried back along the driveway. She overtook them in her car and waited a couple of yards short of the gate while Makins swung it open then closed it again after her. She drove off spiritedly, throwing up a dense cloud of spray, an acknowledging hand waving from her window.

'Well?' said Roper, settling himself into the passenger seat as Makins sorted out his ignition key.

'Mrs Craven was nervous about something. Hardly said a word, did she? And it looked as if she'd heard of Pope.'

Which was not unreasonable, given that her husband's office telephone number had been written on Pope's blotter. And despite the unlikelihood of Pope having the kind of spare cash that would have allowed him to indulge in a little speculation on the Stock Exchange, it wasn't totally impossible that he and Craven might have done some other business together. And, given that, Craven might have dropped Pope's name in conversation with his wife. But if he had, why had she been reticent about it?

'Where now?' asked Makins.

'Downlands Farm,' said Roper.

'Not much point, is there?' said Makins.

'We're supposed to be doing door to doors looking for

71

witnesses,' said Roper. 'Don't want to leave anybody out, do we?' Besides which it was only a few feet from Mr Chance's land that Pope's head had come to light.

Makins did a three-point turn and drove back towards the village, rain hammering on the roof of the car and the windscreen wipers sloshing noisily. Several cars travelling in the opposite direction had their headlights blazing and the view across the heath was almost obscured by the relentless downpour that looked as if it intended to go on for ever and ever.

The gate of Downlands Farm stood open, so that Makins was able to drive straight on to the access road, then across a wooden bridge over the stream, slowing briefly to squeeze past a driverless red tractor with a seed-drill hooked on the back of it. The tractor seemed not so much parked as hurriedly abandoned in the face of the weather.

The access road was macadamed, but in an acute state of disrepair and pocked with potholes. Like Mrs Wicks' bungalow, which Downlands Farm more or less abutted, the old farmhouse lay in low ground, grey and depressing and fortress-like in the rain. The green Range Rover was parked close to the front door.

'Same ploy as before?' asked Makins, hauling on the handbrake. 'Or are you back in charge again?'

'No,' said Roper. 'You do all the asking, I'll just listen. And make a point about finding out something about the Cravens if you can. Nice and subtle.'

'Right,' said Makins.

They climbed out, hastily slammed the car doors behind them, ducked their heads and ran. In the few paces to the Chances' front door they were drenched.

It was Mrs Chance herself who answered Makins' ring at the doorbell. 'Oh, hi,' she said, smiling her wickedly dazzling smile. 'That was quick. Come in out of the weather. Isn't it just *bloody*. I'll go and call my husband.'

Closing the door behind them and leaving them to wipe their shoes on the doormat, she went off down the passage

72

towards the back of the house. A quick look around told Roper that there was money here too, although unlike the Cravens' the money here was old, perhaps garnered over several generations of farming Chances. Everything at the Cravens' had been ostentatious, the artefacts probably purchased as investments with a view to selling them again when the market was right. The old mirrored coatstand here was put to everyday use, Mrs Chance's damp sheepskin coat hanging on it alongside a man's donkey jacket with waterproofed shoulders, a couple of pairs of green industrial wellingtons on the zinc-lined shelf underneath. An ornately carved oak chest, squatting on the stone floor opposite the coatstand, and probably dating from the Commonwealth, had a green telephone casually sitting at one end and a stack of telephone directories heaped untidily at the other.

There was a momentary draught as the distant voice of Mrs Chance bawled '*Nicholas!*', then a feeling of warmth again as her footsteps started back. She moved well, like a dancer, the ends of her hair and the hems of her slacks still wet from her dash to the Range Rover at the Cravens' house.

'Come and have a warm,' she said, shivering and briskly rubbing her hands together, as she led them into a sitting-room on the left where an inviting gas fire glowed redly. 'My husband's presently engaged in a labour dispute out in the barn, but he won't be a jiffy. Shall I take your coats or would you rather stand there and steam?'

'We'll steam,' said Makins. 'We're a little pressed for time. Thanks all the same.'

She stooped, and offered them both a cigarette from a polished mahogany casket lying on the coffee table. Both declined. She took one out for herself and Roper brought out his lighter and lit it for her.

'Thank you,' she said, smiling and exhaling smoke. 'Filthy habit, but I can't stop. Stupid, isn't it? Funny old business that accident, wasn't it? I rode down to the village earlier this morning and the woman in the newsagent's told me the poor man had had his head cut off. A piece of wire stretched across the road or something.'

Makins and Roper exchanged glances. The only way the news about the wire could have got about was either by inspired rumour or by Sergeant Mallory talking out of turn in the Hanging Man: the latter seemed more likely. Both the local newspapers and radio station had been requested to publish the news as a traffic accident and to make no speculations. So far they all had.

She was plainly disappointed when they offered neither confirmation nor denial of what was probably the juiciest bit of gossip to have fluttered through Appleford this year. She offered them tea – or coffee? – but again they both declined. She was certainly more sociable than Mrs Craven and Roper soon guessed that her constant vivacious chatter was a measure of her isolation in this lonely place. The dark and bright-eyed Mrs Chance was the only thing that seemed not to be part and parcel of Downlands Farm. Everything else fitted in as neatly as the pieces of a jigsaw puzzle – the lovely old furniture, the gilt-framed oil paintings on the walls, the Commonwealth chest in the hall, the worn but cosy-looking carpets. Mrs Chance was out of place here, a sleek, sophisticated townie, more at home in the bright lights than the farmyard; and probably married to the wrong man, although that was only another guess on Roper's part.

It took little to get her talking about Mrs Craven. Her name was Dagmar. She was Norwegian. She had been something to do with television over there, a presenter or something of that sort. Before that she had been a model. She and Martin had met in Oslo, married about eight years ago. Crazy about each other, the two of them were. And filthy rich, of course. Martin was something big in the City, a partner in a firm of stockbrokers. Ran a pair of Mercedes between them. His and hers. She spoke without animosity; but then, just as she was usefully launched on the subject of the Cravens, a door slammed noisily, probably snatched by the wind, and rubbery footfalls sounded on the stone flags of the hall.

'My husband,' she said, as a man turned in through the doorway. He was about thirty-five, gumbooted, cloth-capped and waxed-jacketed. His thin-lipped dourness looked permanent.

'How did it go?' his wife asked, presumably referring to the dispute in the barn.

'Badly,' he said curtly, then, just as curtly to Roper and Makins, 'What can I do for you two?'

'They're policemen, Nick. They've come about the accident outside on Monday night.'

'Don't know anything about it,' said Chance. 'Sorry.'

'Your wife happened to mention that you might have been on your way back from the village at about the time the victim was killed, sir,' Makins prompted helpfully. 'We're looking for witnesses, you see.'

Chance shot a glance at his wife that ought to have struck her dead on the spot. 'I wasn't anywhere near the village on Monday night.'

'Well, it's where you said you were going,' his wife retorted.

'I changed my mind,' he said. Switching his attention back to Makins, he said, 'If I'd seen anything I'd have come forward by now, wouldn't I?'

'The victim's name was Gerald Pope, sir,' said Roper, deeming it time to throw his weight in. 'Don't suppose you knew him, by any chance?'

There was a passage of silence. The name Pope, it seemed, had the power to cause a great variety of knee-jerk reactions in these parts. With Hughie Lee it had caused paralysis of his fingers, with Mrs Craven a locking of her jaw and folded arms, with Nicholas Chance a sudden inability to blink his eyelids, so that Roper knew, even before he spoke, that Chance was about to tell a lie.

'Sorry,' he said, shrugging casually. 'I've never heard of him.'

SEVEN

THEY TOOK AN EARLY LUNCH in the Hanging Man, choosing the public bar only because its back door had been open and was nearest to where Makins had parked the car. For the last hour the downpour had been ceaseless.

The only other occupants of the bar, at a few minutes still to midday, were four men hunched around a table near the dartboard and muttering fiercely to each other between mouthfuls of beer.

'Another few wasted hours,' observed Makins gloomily, taking a bite of his cheese roll and washing it down with a sip of shandy. Of late, George Makins had been observed to slip into such bouts of melancholy. Washroom gossip had it that it had something to do with a woman. She'd got her talons so deeply into young George that she'd made him go broody. Of late, too, he had become the owner of a portable telephone, and had been overheard to speak the words 'bridging loan' and 'mortgage' into it when he thought no one was around to overhear. So it all sounded pretty serious.

'Not entirely,' said Roper, more optimistically. 'From what Mrs Chance told us we seem to have latched on to the right Craven. Can't be all that many Cravens in the stockbroking business, can there?'

'I reckon that gipsy knew Pope, too,' said Makins. 'And I keep asking myself where he's got to.'

'Don't worry about it,' said Roper. 'If he stops with that

coach anywhere near civilisation, there'll be a complaint from some old biddy within the hour, whether its justified or not. He'll turn up.'

The voices around the other table grew louder. The subject of the angry conversation appeared to be Nicholas Chance, who, if Roper's intuition was working aright, was yet another resident of Appleford who was not entirely unfamiliar with Gerald Pope.

'We ought to get the Union in. They'll sort the bugger out.'

'Not any more, they can't,' a gruff voice retorted. 'Bunch of pansy-boys these days, they are.'

'He told me he was going broke.'

'Yeh, he told me that too. Lyin' bugger,' sneered another broad Dorset voice. 'Trouble is, what he's doin's legal.'

'Don't help me though, does it,' grumbled the youngest of the four, who seemed to be called Jacko and was clearly the epicentre of whatever the problem was. 'Three months wages in lieu of notice, and I'm lookin' for a new job on Monday. Two years I've worked for that bastard.'

'All that money his old man left 'im an' all.'

'I reckon that missus of his helped him get rid of that. I mean when did any of us see her doin' anything except gettin' in that Rover and drivin' off somewhere? Eh? Never bloody there, is she?'

'Probably got another bloke old Nick don't know about.'

'My missus saw her last Saturday afternoon in Dorchester. She was with that bloke who's got Furzecroft.'

'That Craven?'

'Aye, that's the one. Just coming out of a restaurant, the two of 'em were. All laughin' and gigglin', the missus said they were . . .'

All of which was probably only village scuttlebutt, and moved Roper not an inch towards finding the killer of Gerry Pope, but all the same it had been worth pricking an ear to. It sounded very much as if the fourth man, the young one, had been put off work by Chance because the farm wasn't doing well, or because Chance, or perhaps his wife, was pouring the money away faster than it was coming in and was trying to cut the wage bill. More interesting was that Mrs Chance might be fooling around with Craven while, at the same time, riding out and taking her elevenses with his wife.

They were back at County soon after one o'clock. At half-past, news came of the latest whereabouts of Lee and his sister. A Constable Stokes, prowling the lanes in his Panda car, had glimpsed a single-decked grey bus tucked among the trees on the northern edge of Wareham Forest. He had not yet been close enough to check its registration plates, but the bus was the right colour and had certainly not been parked there yesterday. Its precise location was just off the A35 and half a mile due south of the village of Bloxworth. A half-hour later, Stokes was patched back on the phone. The passengers in the coach were a man, dark and fortyish, and a young woman, somewhere in her twenties with waist-length black hair.

'Sounds just right,' said Roper. 'Well done, son.' So the Lees hadn't moved far, fifteen miles or so. More importantly they were still in the county. 'Stay close, but don't touch. And if they move on again, I want to know.'

DS Rodgers rang in at four o'clock. Since nine this morning he had been pounding leather around Dorchester again, calling in at every restaurant, café, sandwich-bar and public house in the hope of locating Pope's latest woman friend. One waitress in particular had seemed singularly reluctant to speak to him.

'A Mrs Barr. She works in the Blue Bird. It's a restaurant at the western end of town. She was definitely uneasy about something. And she's Irish.'

'But she didn't know Pope?'

'So she said,' said Rodgers. 'But I had a distinct gut feeling about her.'

'Like she wasn't telling the truth?'

'Just like,' said Rodgers. 'Can't be certain, mind.'

But Roper trusted Rodgers' intuition almost as much as he trusted his own, and if Rodgers' instincts told him that someone was lying then they probably were. Mrs Barr might have been merely nervous at receiving an unexpected visit at her workplace by a police officer, but Rodgers wasn't the sort to put the frighteners on anybody, except villains, and the call would have been as casually conducted as possible. Nobody ever got useful information out of door to door enquiries without putting a smile on first. But then she had been *Mrs* Barr, and who knew if there wasn't a Mr Barr somewhere in the offing and from whom certain dark secrets had to be kept. All of which, of course, was pure speculation, and if Mrs Barr had been Pope's lady friend she was fully entitled to keep that information to herself, frustrating though that fact was.

Most murder investigations were conducted on a catch as catch can basis. You found out who the victim was and talked to the people who knew him – wife, relatives, friends, workmates, neighbours and even his enemies – and eventually there was somebody you could home in on as being the likely villain. In this instance there was nobody to talk to. Pope's ex-wife hadn't seen him for months, according to her he had had no other relatives, his only known associate was the shady Lennie Martin, chance-met in a Dorchester pub, he had worked alone and his only neighbour was Mrs Cracknell to whom he paid the rent for his office each month.

In short, Pope had been a loner, and what Roper knew about him could be scribbled on the back of an envelope and still leave space to spare. He had been a police officer. He had been married and divorced, lived for a brief period with a woman who had taken him in as a lodger, spent a few weeks after that bedded down in Lennie Martin's workshop, then moved into 21A Jubilee Walk, where, on the strength of buying a few sheets of headed stationery, he had set himself up as a private investigator.

But, as always, it was what Roper didn't know about Pope that was more pertinent. Both the filing cabinet that had contained no files and the scarcely broached packet of headed notepaper showed that Pope had only just commenced his business. And if that was so, where had his money been coming from? According to the showroom whence he had purchased his motor-cycle, he had paid spot cash for it, at the same time paying, again in cash, a year's advance premium on a fully comprehensive insurance policy for it. All of which had made a very large hole in the better part of £6,000. Where had that money come from? Fifteen years in the Force would have given him a pension, but only just enough to keep body and soul together and certainly not enough to splash out on a high-class secondhand motor-cycle. And he'd been paying the rent for his office to Mrs Cracknell regularly.

He had expectations of course. When his wife finally exchanged contracts for the sale of the house he was likely to fall in for £40,000 or thereabouts, but expectations weren't hard cash. He might equally of course have borrowed the money on the strength of that expectation, but the bank in Dorchester, into which his police pension was paid, had lent him nothing; and with only a rented business address to send the bailiffs to, if he defaulted, it was hardly likely that he could have got a loan from anywhere else except at an exorbitant rate of interest.

All of which suggested that Gerald Pope might have had another source of income that no one knew about, and Roper would have been very surprised if it had been honestly come by.

At five o'clock he joined DS Rodgers in Dorchester, the two of them meeting under a rainswept awning outside a baker's shop, a few yards from the alley where Lennie Martin had his lock-up workshop.

Martin had been swooped upon this morning, but the visit by Rodgers yesterday afternoon had obviously alerted him and the lads from Dorchester CID had found only bare shelves and various items of equipment that were in for legitimate repair.

'Here he comes now,' said Rodgers, as a little yellow van with its indicator flashing sorted itself out from the traffic stream and turned towards the alley.

As soon as it had gone from sight, Roper and Rodgers opened their umbrellas and walked briskly after it. Too busy getting inside out of the rain, Martin didn't see them as he feverishly unlocked the padlock of the wicket-gate set in one of the garage's double doors, lifted a leg and stepped inside.

Roper and Rodgers collapsed their umbrellas and followed him in, the fresh draught behind him causing him to swivel quickly on a heel with an expression of alarm on his face.

'Oh,' he grumbled, recognising Rodgers and relaxing again. 'It's you bloody lot. I'd have thought you'd have had your noses blackened enough this morning. What d'you want this time?'

'Just a word, Lennie,' said Roper, holding out his warrant-card.

Martin took it truculently and tipped it towards the lamp that shone over his littered workbench. 'Superintendent, eh? This morning it was only a bleeding inspector. And he went away empty handed an' all.' He made a confident, all-encompassing gesture with Roper's card before he handed it back again. 'Look all you want. Nothing's changed here since this morning.'

'Like I said, Lennie,' said Roper. 'We've only come for a chat.'

Martin's eyebrows came together suspiciously. 'About what?'

'Gerry Pope,' said Roper.

'I've already told your boy here,' said Martin, with a jerk of his head towards Rodgers. 'He was just a bloke I met in a pub.'

81

'Want more, Lennie,' said Roper. 'We think he was done in.'

'But you said yesterday—' gasped a surprised Martin, words failing him as his astonished eyes flicked up at Rodgers. 'Bloody hell. You didn't say anything about him being *done in*.'

'That's just between us, Lennie,' said Roper. 'So we'd rather you didn't put it about.'

'Right,' said Martin, still looking dazed and perplexed, but plainly recognising an appeal to his better nature. 'Shtoom's the word. I'm burstin' for a cup of tea. How about you two? It's only mugs and bags, mind.'

'You're a gentleman, Lennie,' said Roper. He had something almost akin to a respect for petty villains like Martin. They shifted a few illicit video recorders, didn't knock old ladies about, put their hands up when their collars were felt and didn't carry their grudges about afterwards.

Roper perched himself on the high wooden stool in front of Martin's workbench and Rodgers made himself comfortable on an upended television set. Martin plugged in his electric kettle, sorted out three china mugs, and took a cheroot from Roper's offered packet.

'Which pub d'you meet him in?' asked Roper, striking his lighter.

'The Red Lion,' said Martin. 'Just casual. I heard him asking the barmaid if she knew anybody with a room to let. I chipped in and said I did, and we sort of went on from there.' He dipped his bald head to light his cheroot from Roper's lighter, blew smoke. 'Then a couple of weeks, he didn't pay the rent and she turfed him out.'

'Strapped for cash, was he?'

'Sometimes,' said Martin, moving away and reaching over the bench for a toffee tin, prising open its lid and taking out three tea-bags. 'Sometimes he had a walletful, other times he couldn't even afford a packet of fags.'

'Know how he got it, when he had a walletful?'

'I never asked,' said Martin, dropping a tea-bag into each of the mugs.

'Did he have a job?'

'More contacts, I think. He had a lot of contacts.'

'Ever shift anything for him?'

'Like his goods and chattels, you mean?' asked Martin, with a commendably convincing show of innocence.

'Come on, Lennie,' chided Roper. 'I'm a copper and you're a villain; we're almost on the same side.'

'A couple of times,' conceded Martin, eventually, and with some reluctance.

'Like what?'

'Compact-disc players. Those little portable ones. Two dozen.'

'Go well, did they?'

'Hot cakes,' said Martin. 'Kids mostly. But that's where the money is, these days, isn't it?' He turned away and switched off his boiling kettle and tilted it over each of the three mugs. 'Sugar?'

'Two,' said Roper.

'One,' said Rodgers.

'Understand he dossed down here for a while,' said Roper.

'A couple of weeks before Christmas,' said Martin. 'He brought in a camp-bed. Kept his clothes in that cupboard over there. Dropped me twenty quid a week for the privilege. Daytimes, he was mostly out and about on his bike; evenings we used to go for a bevvy together along at the Lion. Evenings when he wasn't meeting somebody, that is.' A waxed carton of milk was tilted over the mugs and he handed them around.

'Who did he meet?' asked Roper, sipping.

'A woman, mostly,' said Martin. 'So he said. She used to phone here at the workshop sometimes. All very furtive, it was. But whenever she phoned, he didn't go along to the Lion that evening. Like I told your lad, I think she was a waitress. Whenever she phoned there was cutlery and crockery rattling near where the phone was. And once, when I answered her, I heard somebody ask her who something was for and she said table six.'

'She ever give a name?'

'Never,' said Martin. 'It was just: is Gerry there. If I said no, she always said she'd ring back later. I did ask once for her name, so that I could pass a message on but she said he'd know who it was'd called. Married, I expect,' he added sagely, 'and Pope was her bit on the side.'

'Anything special about her voice?'

'Just that she was Irish,' said Martin. 'Definitely Irish.' He took down a swig of tea. 'Don't think she did him in, do you? One of those cream passionals?'

'Probably not,' said Roper. 'She'd be useful to talk to, though. When did she ring last?'

'Funny thing you should say that,' said Martin. 'Monday afternoon, about five o'clock. She hadn't rung here for months, not since he moved out. But Monday afternoon she did. She'd rung his office and left a message on his answering machine asking him to call her back. She told me she'd found a notebook of his. Something to do with his business. She thought it was important he knew where it was.'

'You didn't tell me that yesterday,' said Rodgers.

'You didn't ask, did you,' retorted Martin, burying his nose in his mug again.

Roper did the same, only then recalling that he had heard the voice of an Irishwoman on Pope's answering machine, asking him to ring her at work. At the time it had not seemed important but now, obviously, it was, because whoever she was she had clearly figured prominently in the last few months of Pope's life.

'You're sure she used the word notebook?'

'Definite,' said Martin, furrowing his forehead as he tried harder to remember. 'Little red notebook, that's what she said. She was worried in case he needed it and thought he'd lost it.'

Roper had known all along that Pope must have kept records of some sort. It had never occurred to him that those records might have been portable, something that Pope could have kept in his wallet.

'Did you ever see Pope with a little red notebook, Lennie?'

'A few times,' said Martin. 'Never saw inside it, mind. It usually came out when he wanted to use the phone.'

'Ever hear him talking on the phone?'

'He used to say they were private calls. He always took the phone into the storeroom and closed the door behind him.'

'How about this woman? Ever see her?'

'Only distant,' said Martin. 'Might not have been the woman on the phone, of course. But three or four times I saw him with the same woman. Talking. He was on his motor-bike and she was on the pavement, like they'd just met casual.'

'Think you could describe her?'

Martin sucked contemplatively on his teeth. 'Dark. Ordinary. Nothing special about her. About five foot six, I suppose. Twice I saw her she was in a light blue raincoat – with a belt. Nice hair, though. Long, you know. About thirty-eight to forty.'

It was a far better description than Roper had dared to hope for, and he wondered if it might fit a certain Mrs Barr who waited on tables in the Blue Bird restaurant. A shared glance with DS Rodgers told him it was likely.

'When did you last see Pope to speak to, Lennie?'

'Last week,' said Martin. 'Monday. When he brought his telly in. I checked it over and found the time-base circuit had gone on the blink. I tried to get in touch with him about it a couple of times, but all I ever got was his bloody answering machine.'

'How about before that?'

'About a month. But not to speak to. That was the second or third time I saw him with that woman. Before

85

that it was just after the New Year. Somebody had duffed him over. Black eye, split lip, a real going over he'd had.'

'His ex-wife's boyfriend, wasn't it?'

'So Pope said. He probably asked for it, mind. He was a dead mean bugger when he'd got a couple of beers inside him.'

'Did Pope ever tell you he was an ex-copper, Lennie?'

Martin all but gagged on a mouthful of tea. 'Bloody hell,' he spluttered. 'Him? He was a bigger crook than I *ever* was!'

Which was probably as good a character reference for Gerry Pope as any.

The ACC agreed with Roper. Somehow or another Gerald Pope's Irish lady friend had to be flushed out and made to come forward. A hastily concocted press statement, released just in time to be slotted into all the early evening television and radio bulletins, at last gave out the fact that the police now regarded Pope's death as suspicious, and pleaded for anyone who could account for his last few hours to make contact.

'Mr Docker?' asked Roper, holding out his warrant-card. It was seven o'clock in the evening and he and Rodgers were calling on the ex-Mrs Pope again.

'That's right,' the man said warily, taking the card and drawing back into the brighter light of the hallway to see it better.

'Who is it?' called Mrs Pope, from the kitchen.

'Police,' Docker called back over his shoulder. 'What d'you want exactly?' he said gruffly, handing the card back again.

'Just a word, sir,' said Roper. 'We're making enquiries into the death of Mrs Pope's ex-husband.'

'Going to a lot of trouble, aren't you?' grumbled Docker, opening the door wider and waiting while Roper and Rodgers wiped their shoes on the doormat. 'Considering

86

he only fell off his motor-bike.' Like Pope had been, he was a big, loutish-looking man, carpet-slippered and with his shirt gaping open and revealing an expanse of white undervest.

'Oh, it's you, Mr Roper,' said Mrs Pope's voice from the kitchen doorway. She was drying her hands on a towel. 'Can I get you a cup of tea or something?'

'We shan't be stopping long,' said Roper. 'But thanks all the same.'

'I'll be with you in a minute,' she said, turning away again. 'I'm just putting some potatoes in the oven.'

Docker ushered them into the sitting-room and went across to turn down the volume on the television. A cigarette burned in an ashtray on the arm of the chair in which he had obviously been sitting to watch one of the less intelligent game-shows.

'Who d'you want to talk to?' he said, collecting the smoking cigarette. 'Me or Dolly?'

'Both, really, sir,' said Roper. 'But perhaps you and I could have a quiet word together first. We understand that you and Mr Pope had a fight in a pub car park on the night of the New Year. That so?'

Docker shrugged his all-in wrestler's shoulders. 'He asked for it.'

'How come?'

'Dolly and me went from pub to pub to try and dodge him. He followed us on that bloody bike of his. Wherever we went, he turned up a couple of minutes afterwards. The last place, though, we thought we'd lost him. Then, about five to midnight, in he comes. He orders a beer, then walks across to where we are and sits down to join us and starts telling me what an old slag Dolly is. Talked in front of her as if she wasn't there. Well, we'd had enough by this time and decided to call it a day. All we'd wanted was an evening out and his ugly face popping up everywhere had put the kybosh on it. We got up and left. We walked round to the car park, and his bike was parked so close in front of my motor that I couldn't move it. I told Dolly to get in the car while I went back into the pub to fetch him out. But when I turned round, he was right behind me again.

'I told him to move the bike or I'd be moving it myself, and when I had I'd probably be driving straight over it. He told me he'd like to see me try. I got hold of the bike, he grabbed me and I thumped him. I mean you can only stand so much of that old nonsense, can't you. He hit me back, and we went on from there. I tripped over once and while I was down he tried to kick my bloody head in, and he would've if Dolly hadn't clobbered him with her handbag. I got up and then I really belted into him. Stupid really, but like I said, he asked for all he bloody got. When I'd flattened him, I shifted the bike and drove back here.'

'Drunk, was he?'

'It didn't show,' said Docker. 'But he was that sort; the more he had sloshing around inside him the steadier he got. And before you ask, all I'd had was four half-pints, and I left most of two of those behind trying to dodge him when we left the other places.'

'Ever see him afterwards?'

'Never,' said Docker. 'When I left him that time, I told him if I ever saw him within ten yards of Dolly again, I'd see to it he didn't walk for six months. If you want to know what he was really like, you should talk to Dolly.'

'Can you account for your movements on Monday evening, Mr Docker?' asked Roper. 'Between eight o'clock and midnight, say?'

'He was here,' said Mrs Pope, from the doorway behind him.

'That's right,' said Docker.

'All evening?'

'He got back here soon after nine o'clock,' said Mrs Pope – Roper still thought of her as Mrs Pope. She had advanced deeper into the room to stand beside Docker, her posture bristlingly defensive.

'You didn't go out again?'

'Only for a few minutes,' said Docker. 'I drove along to the local off-licence to get some cigarettes.'

'What time?'

'About twenty after ten.'

'And he got back here ten minutes afterwards,' said Mrs Pope.

'That right, Mr Docker?'

'As near as I remember,' said Docker.

'You're talking to him as if he's done something,' broke in Mrs Pope.

'Your ex-husband died in suspicious circumstances, Mrs Pope,' said Roper. 'We're having to explore a number of avenues. I'm sorry, but it's necessary. Which off-licence did you go to, Mr Docker?'

'Bannerman's,' said Docker. He was beginning to bridle now that it was sinking in that he might be suspected of being implicated in Pope's death. 'You can go along there and check, if you like. It's out of here, turn left, then first on the right. They know me.'

'What sort of suspicious circumstances?' asked Mrs Pope, breaking in again scarcely before Docker had finished talking. 'Yesterday you said it was an accident.'

'Your ex-husband was beheaded, Mrs Pope. We're pretty sure now he was murdered.'

She showed some emotion at last, taking a grip of Docker's arm as her eyes widened in horror. Docker looked equally stunned. It was too well done on both their parts to be an act. Docker's alibi would be checked with the off-licence as a matter of course, but Roper already guessed it would be a waste of time.

EIGHT

ROPER WAS BACK AT COUNTY soon after eight o'clock. George Makins followed him into his office while he was still hanging up his raincoat. There had been a response to the press release.

'Woman with a Northern Irish accent,' said Makins. She had rung at six-thirty and seven-thirty. Makins had taken that second call himself. He had tried to persuade the woman to talk to him, but she had insisted on speaking only to the most senior officer on the case. Makins had told her to ring back at eight-thirty. Like Lennie Martin, Makins had heard voices and clattering china in the background.

'Sound genuine, did she?'

'Sure of it,' said Makins.

Roper could only hope that she had been. Press releases were notorious for bringing prankster phone-callers out of their many closets and sending the police running every which way at once. But in this case there had only been the one caller. She had been Irish and a woman, neither of which had even been hinted at in the official statement. It was also likely that she was a waitress, which is what Lennie Martin had thought she was. Rodgers, too, in his tour of Dorchester's eating houses, had turned up an Irish waitress whose description fitted the woman that Martin had seen on several occasions with Pope. And, if all those ladies were one and the same, she was probably walking about with Pope's notebook in her handbag, and at the moment Roper would have given his eye-teeth to get a glimpse of that notebook.

His phone chirruped promptly at eight-thirty. He switched on his tape recorder with one hand and picked up the receiver with the other. At the end of the desk, sitting by another phone, Makins quietly tapped out the number of the Blue Bird restaurant.

'Good evening,' said Roper. 'Superintendent Douglas Roper here. How can I help you?'

There was a long silence, broken from time to time by the clatter of pots and pans, the kitchen sounds that Lennie Martin and Makins had heard. Makins gave a thumbs-down sign. The telephone line to the Blue Bird restaurant was engaged.

'Hello,' Roper said again, softly, striving hard to win her confidence before she lost her nerve and rang off again. 'Is there something you'd like to tell me about?'

There was a quick intake of breath. 'Are you the man looking into Gerry's accident?'

'I am,' he said. Makins was right. She was Northern Irish, softly spoken, but with an accent you could cut with a knife.

'I have something that belonged to him. A little book. It's got a lot of telephone numbers and things in it. I don't know what to do with it now.' A stifled sob came into her voice. He heard her swallow it. Another long silence followed. 'I'm sorry,' she said, sniffing. 'I'm very upset.'

'I'm sure you are,' he said. He left a pause hanging. In the background he could hear something like carrots being chopped on a board. 'Would it be better if we could meet somewhere and have a chat?' he suggested hopefully. 'I'm sure you could help us a great deal.'

There was another silence. He willed her not to ring off.

'I'll post it to you.'

'It could get lost in the post, couldn't it?'

'If I could have your address—'

'It really would be a great help if we could meet

91

somewhere,' he broke in, before she became too fixated on the idea of sending the notebook through the post. 'I'd like very much to talk about Gerry. Could we do that, do you think?'

'Look, I have to go,' she said. 'I'm at work. And I'm really very busy.'

'Give me your number and I'll ring you back.'

There was another long pause.

'No,' she said. 'No, I'd rather not.'

'Perhaps I could pick you up from work?'

'No,' she said. 'I couldn't do that either. I really must go.'

'Please,' he urged, before she could hang up on him. 'I'll meet you alone and I won't write anything down. I won't even ask you your name – that's a promise. Just Gerry's notebook and five minutes of your time. Wherever and whenever you like. It'll be just between you and me. You're probably the only person who can help us. Will you do that?'

Somebody in the background called for two steaks, one medium, one rare.

'I've got to go,' she said, a note of desperation in her voice now. 'I really have to.' There came another ringing clatter of plates. 'Tomorrow,' she said abruptly, just as Roper was about to concede defeat. 'The little alley where Gerry had his office—'

'I know it.'

'About ten o'clock. I have to go out in the morning and do some shopping. I'll meet you there. I'll bring the little book.' With a rattle and a click the line went dead. Roper swiftly depressed the cradle-button and tapped out the number of the Blue Bird restaurant.

The same soft Irish voice answered him, and he quickly passed the receiver to Makins.

'Sorry,' said Makins. 'I must have dialled the wrong number. So sorry.' He handed the receiver back to Roper who laid it on its cradle.

'Rodgers get it right, did he?'

92

'Ninety-nine per cent certain, I'd say,' said Roper. Again it wasn't a big step forward, but if the Irish lady didn't turn up in Jubilee Walk tomorrow morning at ten, Roper at least had a good idea where he could find her if he had to.

An hour later he and Makins were on their way back to Appleford, to see the stockbroking Mr Craven whose office telephone number had been scribbled on Gerry Pope's blotting pad. It had been raining off and on all day and with the dark the downpour had become relentless again, rattling like ball-bearings on the roof of the car and rolling down the windscreen like melting gelatine. It looked settled in for the night.

They came to Furzecroft. Tonight the gate under the scrollwork arch was open so that Makins was able to drive almost up to the front door and park behind a silver-grey Mercedes that stood close to the bottom of the steps.

They climbed out quickly and dashed the half-dozen paces to the steps and the shelter of the verandah. Other than a coach-lamp beside the front door and the faint glimmer of another light through its glass panel the house appeared to be in darkness.

Makins had to flatten his thumb three times on the bell-push before there was finally a response to the electric chime. The glimmer of light was suddenly a glow. A moving silhouette slowly obliterated it, paused to switch on the hall light, and resolved itself into the shadow of a man in a black dressing gown as it fell over the door in the instant before it was opened.

'Yes?' the man snapped irritably. 'What do you want?'

'Mr Craven, are you, sir?'

'I am.' He was a lean, self-assured man, a fluffy pink towel around his neck and its ends tucked into the collar of the dressing gown. His hair was damp and bare white ankles showed above a pair of heel-less leather carpet slippers. They had plainly disturbed him in his shower.

'Police, sir,' said Roper proffering his warrant-card and

93

introducing himself and Makins. 'We're making routine enquiries into the death of a Mr Gerald Pope.'

There was a moment of silence, too long a one. In the light from the coach-lamp Craven's face took on a sudden wariness, but it was quickly gone again.

'The name means nothing to me,' he said curtly, handing the card back again after cursorily scanning it. 'I'm sorry.'

'We found your name and telephone number on a pad in his office, sir,' persisted Roper, expanding fractionally upon the facts. 'It occurred to us that you might have done some business with him.'

'I see,' said Craven, sighing testily in the face of Roper's determined immobility. 'Well, you'd better come in, hadn't you. It's bloody freezing out here.'

He stood by while they wiped their shoes on the doormat, then led them into the sitting-room where Roper had spoken to Craven's wife and Mrs Chance that morning. An empty whisky tumbler and a sandwich plate with crumbs on it sat at one end of the coffee table.

'We did leave word with Mrs Craven that we'd be calling this evening, sir,' said Roper, to break the ice a little.

'I haven't seen her this evening,' said Craven. He stood belligerently by the fireplace, his hands stuffed into the pockets of his dressing gown and dragging it out of shape. 'She's out somewhere. What was that fellow's name?'

'Pope, sir,' said Roper. 'Gerald Michael Pope. He was the motor-cyclist who was killed along the way the other night.'

'Yes, I heard about that,' said Craven brusquely. 'But I still didn't know the man. You say my name and telephone number were on a writing pad?'

'A blotting pad, sir,' said Roper.

Craven stared meditatively down at his feet, his lower lip jutted, as if his name on a blotter, rather than a writing pad, made all the difference. 'No,' he said eventually. 'Nothing comes to mind. You mentioned something about business?'

'It was a London number, sir.'

'Ah, that's different,' said Craven, his mood subtly but

94

suddenly changing to one of helpfulness as he spotted the escape hatch Roper was offering him. 'If it was to do with my business, I can check that out in a few minutes. Join me,' he said, marching past them, out of the room and across the hallway to another room beside the darkened kitchen. He reached around the door frame for a light-switch, and they followed him in.

The room was a study, lushly carpeted, a reproduction antique desk in front of the floor-to-ceiling window, one wall lined with books and a metal computer console standing against another. Craven lifted the dust-cover from the computer and its keyboard and flicked a couple of switches. 'A modem,' he explained. 'Connects me straight through to the office computer in London. Shan't be a second.'

The screen glowed greenly. Roper and Makins watched as Craven expertly tapped out his office telephone number on the numeric pad on the computer keyboard; although what Roper was watching more keenly was the man. He found his sudden switch from lofty hostility to affability strange, to say the least. And that change had occurred when Roper had explained that the number on Pope's pad had been Craven's London number. Would Craven, he wondered, have been this helpful if that number had connected a caller here, to Furzecroft. Somehow he doubted it. And when he had mentioned Pope's name on the doorstep a couple of minutes ago, he was fairly certain that Craven had recognised it, and now he was even more certain because Craven was presently play-acting for all he was worth.

A procession of names scrolled brightly up the screen. Craven muttered them aloud as they appeared, frowning with concentration.

'Peters . . . Peterson . . . Pinto . . . Potter . . . No Pope, though.' He tapped a key and the list of names passing up the screen stilled with Pinto at the top and Potter at the bottom, together with details of their extensive shareholdings and their individual values at this afternoon's closing prices on the Exchange. Messrs Pinto and Potter were clearly gentlemen of some financial substance, and certainly way out of Pope's league. 'Perhaps he was just shopping around,' Craven suggested helpfully. 'We only keep records of actual buyers. And he made a note of my name because it's the first name in the partnership: Craven and Heilbron. Did he have money to invest, this Pope?'

'No, sir,' said Roper. 'Not that we know of. He'd just started up as a private investigator. He had an office in Dorchester.'

Craven spread his hands apologetically. He looked as authentic as a ham actor in a bad play. 'I'm sorry,' he said. 'The name still means absolutely nothing to me. And I've never had anything to do with private detectives. No need.'

Roper remained unconvinced. If Craven had known Pope he was not going to admit it until he was faced with some hard evidence, and that was as remote as it ever was.

Thursday morning at ten o'clock saw Roper slowly pacing the narrow sunless confines of Jubilee Walk. The rain had exhausted itself at last, although it was still glistening blackly on the pavements and lay in oily puddles in the gutters.

Twice during the last few minutes the same woman, in a pale-blue belted raincoat and towing a shopping trolley, had passed the High Street entrance to the alley. Each time she had cast a quick glance into it, met his eye and as quickly glanced away again, as if she were assessing his provenance and potential reliability before she plucked up the courage to approach him. He waited patiently, his warrant-card at the ready in his raincoat pocket. As she walked past the end of the alley yet once more, her shopping trolley trailing behind her, her glance at him this time was a longer, penetrating one. On her way back, at last, she turned in between the black iron bollards across the entrance and came slowly towards him, her empty shopping trolley rattling on the stone setts.

She was no scarlet woman, just another ordinary housewife out doing her shopping, trim and fortyish, with long dark hair and fashionably booted. All that distinguished her was her air of unease.

'Good morning,' he said, with a small but reassuring smile, bringing out his warrant-card as she stopped a couple of yards from him. 'I'm Douglas Roper. Thank you for coming.'

She came cautiously nearer, tucked her handbag under the arm that towed the shopping trolley and took the card from him. She read it carefully, matched his face with the photograph, then handed it back again.

'It's all right, isn't it,' she asked anxiously, 'if I don't tell you my name?'

'I'd like to know it, of course,' he said, 'but I certainly won't press you for it. You said you had something of Gerry's.'

'I do,' she said. 'His notebook.' She tilted her shopping trolley upright and reached into her handbag. What she brought out was a dog-eared, red-covered pocket notebook, the sort that Woolworth's sold in their thousands, its spine repaired with ageing Sellotape.

He took it from her, but didn't open it.

'Would you be able to tell me how you came by it?'

'He left it behind on Monday afternoon.' She spoke with the same breathless urgency as she had on the telephone yesterday evening. 'He made a couple of calls and left it beside the telephone, and I found it after he'd left and when I phoned to tell him, all I got was his answering machine. I did leave a message, but he never did reply, then I heard about him on the radio last evening and how the police were looking for witnesses because they were treating his death as suspicious and all that, you see. I was going to tear it up and throw it away somewhere because I couldn't keep it and didn't know what to do

with it, but then I thought, well, you know . . . if it wasn't
an accident then somebody must have done it to him and
he must have, well, been killed by somebody, and it might
have been somebody he'd been doing business with, you
see. Only he'd gone into private detecting, and you meet
some funny people in that business, he told me that a
couple of times, and I wondered if the person's name
might be written down in there somewhere.' Then, as
suddenly as she had started, she broke off, tears springing
into her eyes as she finally sank under the weight of her
emotions and plunged a hand back into her bag for a
fistful of crumpled paper handkerchiefs. 'I loved him, you
see. He meant the world to me. He was a good man. *Such* a
good man. You've no idea.'

Roper waited sympathetically. The essence of everything now was patience. Whatever kind of villain Gerry
Pope might have been there was one person at least who
mourned him.

'He was a policeman himself once,' she sniffed, dabbing
at her eyes and then at her nose. 'A sergeant, I think he
was.'

'Yes,' he said. 'He was. I knew him.'

'Really?' she said, looking up at him anew, her wet eyes
sparkling. 'I didn't know that.'

She had recovered considerably now that their common
knowledge of Gerry Pope had established a rapport,
almost an intimacy, between them. He sensed too that she
needed to talk to someone, a priest, doctor, a stranger
sitting beside her on a bus, anyone who would listen while
she poured out her troubles. She was certainly married. A
wedding ring bulged under her glove, and surely she
would not have met him so furtively and reluctantly if she
had been a woman living alone and with nothing to hide.
She was a woman with a secret and the weight of it was too
much for her, more so now that her lover was dead.

'You could probably help us a lot, you know,' he said,
exploiting what he was sure now was his emotional

98

advantage over her. A cold damp breeze blustered suddenly down the alley and lifted a discarded plastic carrier bag high over their heads like a parachute before it fluttered down again into a puddle.

'Oh, I don't know,' she protested, but she was weakening, he could see, and had recovered sufficiently to feel confident about stuffing her handkerchiefs back in her bag.

'There's a little coffee shop just around the corner,' he said. 'Ten minutes. And a cup of coffee might buck you up a bit. How about it?'

She glanced back up the alley whence she had come, anxiously deliberating. Then she looked up at him dejectedly with her red-rimmed eyes, and said, 'Yes. All right. But only ten minutes. Then I must do my shopping. Really I must.'

The coffee shop was a tourist-trap of low beamed ceilings and oak settles. At this time of the morning they were its first and only customers, and their coffees were brought by a teenage waitress who seemed not to care whether she served them or not. The windows ran with condensation.

Mrs Barr, for surely that was her name, dipped into her handbag for a packet of cigarettes and took one out. Roper lit it for her. Belatedly she offered him one too but he declined in favour of one of his own cheroots.

'Can I ask you where you met him?' he said, drawing a glass ashtray closer and setting it between them.

'Birmingham,' she said wistfully. 'About two years ago. Although it wasn't a meeting exactly. We had a little café, my husband and me. Gerry came in, early in the morning it was, about nine o'clock. He stayed till lunchtime, looking out of the window. Started with an egg and bacon breakfast and spent the rest of the morning drinking coffee. Gallons of it. Once he asked if he could use the loo, then he came back again and ordered more coffee. Watching, he was, that's what my husband said, and he didn't much like the look of him either, said he looked as if he was lying in wait for somebody. So when I served him again, I sort of made a joke out of it and asked him if he was waiting for his girlfriend. You have to be careful about asking questions like that, you see, in case you upset them. I have to be honest, he looked a bit suspicious to me, too, and I was a bit scared. But he was all right. He was a policeman, he said. And he showed me his identity card, like the one you showed me just now, with his picture on it and everything, so I knew it was all right, except that he wasn't a Birmingham policeman. I know that because we were always getting detectives in asking about people they were looking for. They had cards like that too, only with a different badge.

'Anyway, he told me that the Birmingham police had called him in because no one up there would know his face. He said the police did that sometimes. An undercover operation, he said he was doing ... surveying?'

'Surveillance?' suggested Roper.

'Yes,' she said. 'That's what he said he was doing. A surveillance. Looking out for somebody. Somebody the Birmingham police had been after for months.'

She paused for breath, took a sip of her coffee, rolled ash from her cigarette against the rim of the ashtray.

'Did he catch whoever it was he was looking for?' asked Roper.

'Oh, I don't know, but when he left it was in a bit of a rush. One minute he was there and the next minute he was out in the street. All that was left was a five-pound note under his saucer. Went across the street so fast he was almost run over. We never saw the going of him after that. It was lunchtime by then, you see, and we were getting busy.'

'Do you think he was watching a particular place? A shop or something?'

'There wasn't much in particular to watch,' she said,

with a weary lift of her shoulders. 'It was a proper beaten-up old place. Scheduled for demolition, most of it was. When the electrical factory along the way closed down because of the recession, we just gave up and moved out. Most of our lunchtime trade came from there, you see. It got to a point where we weren't even making enough to pay the rent. And the whole place was turning into a slum anyway. I hated it.'

'But he must have been watching something, if you say he sat for three hours just looking out of the window.'

'Well, like I said, there wasn't anything in particular to watch,' she said, over her cup. 'There was an old secondhand shop one side of us and a church hall on the other; and the hall was locked up. Had been for years. It was one of those mission places.'

'How about opposite?'

'Hardly anything,' she said. 'A sort of car workshop place. Did accident repairs and re-sprays. And next to that was a tyre shop. Eyesores, they were, both of them. I was glad when we had to move out, I really was. It's like Heaven down here compared with that awful place.'

'And when did you meet up with Gerry again?' asked Roper.

'About a fortnight before this last Christmas,' she said. 'Here in Dorchester.'

She and her husband had finally moved out of the café, and the flat over the top of it, last August, and even as the pantechnicon was being loaded with their furniture and chattels the bulldozers and demolition workers were already beginning their assault on the accident-repair workshop across the street. With what little money they'd had, they had moved south, and lived for a couple of months with a married sister she had in Bristol while her husband looked for work. But there had been no work, and certainly not enough money left to start up another café.

'So he bought one of those mobile snack-bars, those

101

things like ice-cream vans, you know. Weekdays he works the laybys and weekends he does the football matches.' Her tone had become one of barely disguised distaste. Plainly she considered a mobile snack-bar to be the very dregs of the catering business; or, more than likely, she was indulging in a little hate-transference and her real distaste was for her husband.

'Your husband never knew about Gerry, of course,' he said.

She shook her head.

'Sure?'

'Certain,' she said. 'If he knew, he'd kill me. I'd thought about leaving him for ages. Gerry and me had even started looking for a place.'

'Gerry just sort of turned up again, did he?'

'Where I work,' she said. 'He came in one lunchtime and we recognised each other. And we just got talking. You know. It went on from there. It wasn't deliberate or anything. It just happened.'

She was beginning to become emotional again and Roper gave her a breathing space.

'Would you like another coffee?' he said.

'Please,' she said, and he attracted the attention of the waitress who was diligently examining the state of her fingernails and seemed surprised to find that she still had customers.

'You obviously saw Gerry on Monday,' he prompted, when the waitress had gone back behind the counter.

'The afternoon,' she said. 'We mostly met Mondays. I get Mondays off till the evening. It's sort of shift-work, you see.'

'What time did he leave? Do you remember?'

'Half-past four. About.'

'And you said he made a couple of phone calls before he went.'

'He phoned the same place twice,' she said. 'The first time the person he wanted to speak to wasn't there, so he rang back a while after.'

102

'You didn't hear any of the conversation when he did get through?'

'No,' she said. 'I didn't. I was in the kichen and he was in the sitting-room. And he'd closed the door.'

They drew apart as their coffees arrived and the waitress added their cost to the bill.

'They were long-distance calls,' she said, remembering, as the waitress went away again. 'To somebody in London, I think.'

'Did he tell you that?'

'Yes, I'm sure he said London. And he gave me two pounds to pay for them. He was always very good like that.'

'Did he often make calls from your place?'

'No,' she said. 'Not often. Just now and again.'

He pushed the sugar bowl closer to her. She had, he had observed, kept her gloves on even though the café was warm. Perhaps, in her highly-wrought state, she had forgotten to take them off; or perhaps she was still trying to hide her wedding ring, although there was little point to that now. She was, he thought, a decent enough woman and not the kind given to casual affairs; and she had clearly been fond of Gerry Pope, however misguided that affection was.

'Did he say where he was going after he left you?'

'His office, so he said. He had an appointment. A client, a new one. Something to do with debt-collecting. Gerry would have got a commission on that. Ten per cent. He'd only just started in business, you see. He was prepared to take on anything.'

'Did he say when he'd see you again?'

'This morning,' she said. 'I usually called in to see him when I was doing my mid-week shopping. Just for a chat and a cup of coffee. You know.'

He didn't tax her any more. She asked him when the funeral was likely to be; she would have liked to send some flowers, anonymously, of course, and she became

103

distressed again when he was unable to tell her. She left the café before him, and he made it plain that he would not follow her.

'You will try and find out who killed him, won't you?' was her parting shot as she stood and gathered up her bag. 'I have to ask because I'm probably the only person who cares.'

'We'll do our best,' he said, rising and shaking her proffered, and still gloved, hand. 'I can't say more than that.'

'Thank you,' she said.

He gave her five minutes' start, paid the bill and walked back up the alley past Pope's office, then around the High Street to a side-turning where DS Rodgers was waiting in the car at a parking meter.

'Recognise her? he asked as he strapped himself in.

'Mrs Barr from the Blue Bird restaurant,' said Rodgers. 'Definitely.'

Roper's first port of call back at County was Chief Inspector Brake's office. Brake was in his shirtsleeves and elbow-deep in the quarterly accident statistics.

'Gerry Pope ever do any Duty Elsewhere, Charlie?'

'Like what?'

'An undercover surveillance job up in Birmingham? About two years ago?'

'Never,' said Brake.

NINE

RODGERS PHOTOCOPIED EVERY PAGE OF Pope's red notebook, and for the next hour he and Makins busied themselves at their telephones in the CID room.

In his own office, Roper thumbed through the tattered original. The names and addresses and telephone numbers had clearly been collected over a number of years. A lot of the earlier entries had been slashed through with either pencil or ballpoint. Prominent at the back end of the book was Lennie Martin's name and his home and workshop telephone numbers. The telephone number of the Blue Bird restaurant was also there, and bracketed with another number beneath which was more than likely Mrs Barr's home number. The Six Ways service station and the name of Mr Banks, its proprietor, had a page to itself.

More cryptic were the several entries that were simply sets of initials followed by one, and sometimes two, telephone numbers. These all had a page to themselves, beneath each of them a list of dates pencilled in at monthly intervals and becoming more crammed together as the space on the page was used up. Some went back a few years. More interestingly, none of the lists of dates had been instituted *after* Pope had left the Force, so whatever they referred to, and whoever the people concerned were, Pope had come across them while he was still a serving officer. There were five such lists, but three of them had been cancelled with a single pencilled stroke across the page. It was reasonable to suppose that those cancellations had taken place at some time around the last date shown on the appropriate page.

On one of the uncancelled lists the initials at the head of the page were MRC, and the first date, at the head of the list, was 19 February 1990, roughly two years ago, at about the time Pope had first met Mrs Barr in Birmingham.

What caught Roper's eye then, and made his skin prickle, was the uppermost of the two telephone numbers under the initials. It was the London number of Craven, Heilbron and Partners. He was still drawing the same breath when he stretched an arm and drew his telephone closer. He asked for an outside line and dialled the second number.

He waited for half a minute or so before a breathless woman's voice said, 'Hello?'

'Sorry to trouble you, Madam,' he said. 'It's the engineer at the telephone exchange. You reported a problem on your line about an hour ago?'

'No,' she said in a faint but unmistakable foreign accent. 'Not me.'

'You're not Mrs Jones, then?'

'No,' she said. 'Sorry. My name is Craven. You must have the wrong number.'

He apologised, and hung up.

So Craven had known Gerry Pope; so why was he so reluctant to admit it?

Makins and Rodgers came into his office together at a few minutes to midday.

'How did it go?' asked Roper.

'They were mostly people he'd had business dealings with,' said Rodgers.

'And a couple of suicides,' said Makins.

Roper shot an eyebrow.

Makins shuffled through the photocopies resting on his

knees. 'The first one's only hearsay,' he said. 'I phoned one of the numbers that Pope had crossed out.' He found the sheet he was looking for and passed it across the desk to Roper. It was one of the pages with a set of initials, a telephone number and a list of dates, the whole cancelled with a single diagonal slash. The initials at the top were DCW.

'Don't know what the first two initials stood for,' said Makins, 'but the man's name was Weston. He died about thirteen months ago. The woman who's got the house now bought it off Weston's widow. According to the neighbours, Weston went out in his car one day and didn't come back. He left his car in a short-stay car park in Charmouth, took a short walk and jumped off the cliffs. Nobody ever found out why.'

Roper ran a fingernail down the list of dates on the photocopy and counted backwards on his fingers. The last date entered under the DCW initials was fourteen months ago, roughly a month before Mr Weston had committed suicide, and perforce been cancelled in Pope's red notebook.

'Who's the other one?'

'Jobling, Mrs,' said Rodgers. He too sorted out one of the photocopies on his lap and handed it across to Roper. 'Mary Gwendoline. I spoke to her husband. She overdosed on tranquilisers washed down with vodka and orange. Last Christmas Eve. The old fellow's still pretty choked up about it.'

Roper checked the list of dates under the heading MGJ. Mrs Jobling had been deleted by Pope some time after 31 November last, almost exactly a month before she had downed her overdose.

Mr Jobling had come home from work on the afternoon of Christmas Eve and found his wife sprawled across the bed. According to the doctors she had been dead for at least three hours. The reason for her suicide was still a mystery.

'How about the other three?' asked Roper.

'Not a lot,' said Makins. 'One was a disconnected line, one didn't answer, and Peter spoke to a woman who agreed the sets of initials belonged to her husband but she'd never heard of Gerry Pope.'

'How about the one that didn't answer?'

'The exchange said the number was in Appleford village,' said Rodgers.

'Martin Craven's home number,' said Makins. 'According to the exchange.'

'I rang Mrs Craven myself,' said Roper. 'About an hour ago. She'd probably gone out in the between time.' Which was all to the good. Mrs Craven was likely to mention two unusual telephone calls to her husband; one she might forget.

'How about the disconnected line?'

'That was in Dorchester,' said Makins. 'The initials were JBR. According to the exchange, his name was Rubery. He asked for the phone to be disconnected on the fifth of February. Said he was moving house.'

Roper reached across the desk, and Makins handed him the photocopy of the page referring to Mr Rubery. The last date under his initials and telephone number was 9 January last, again almost a month, to within a few days, before Mr Rubery had moved house.

'What do we do now?' asked Makins.

'Not sure,' said Roper, needing a few more moments to think. At long last a pattern was beginning to show itself. There were five sets of initials accompanied by a list of dates in Pope's notebook. And of the owners of those initials two had committed suicide, one had moved house and one of the others was the stockbroking Mr Craven; and the last date under his name was almost exactly a month ago.

He pondered some more. The dates could probably signify meetings, appointments. Between Pope and the owners of the initials. And supposing they were meetings? They clearly took place at monthly intervals. Which meant

108

that Martin Craven ought to have had an appointment with Pope sometime early this week – like last Monday night in the car park of the Hanging Man in Appleford village. And Pope had not been able to record that meeting because he'd left his notebook behind at Mrs Barr's that same afternoon.

'Dave Price back from court yet?'

'He rang in,' said Makins. 'He reckons on being back about half-twelve.'

'Good,' said Roper. 'Now here's what we do after lunch . . .'

Roper walked up the front path of the neatly-kept semi-detached house on the outskirts of Weymouth. Dampness still hung in the air and an occasional stiff breeze from the south west carried the kelpy tang of the nearby sea in it. It was coming up for three o'clock in the afternoon.

'Superintendent Roper, Mr Jobling,' he said, showing his warrant-card to the tall, stooped, balding man who answered his ring at the doorbell. 'I rang earlier.'

Jobling hooked on a pair of reading glasses that hung around his neck on a black cord, and took the card. Unlike most folk he examined it meticulously. 'Yes,' he said, handing it back again. 'Do come in, won't you.'

The hall smelled of stale pipe tobacco and was darkly sombre in the dreary light of the afternoon. A cat sat washing its ears on the stairs.

'Would you care for a cup of tea?' asked Jobling hopefully, ushering Roper into his sitting-room. His movements were the brisk busy ones of a man not used to company but who needed to make the most of it now that it had arrived. 'I was just making one for myself.'

'Be most welcome, sir,' said Roper. 'Thank you.'

Jobling went out to his kitchen. Roper took off his raincoat and draped it over the back of one of the armchairs beside the hissing gas fire. The room had a

109

lonely feel, an emptiness, perhaps because there was too much furniture for one man to use, and too many little feminine knick-knacks lying around that Jobling probably hadn't the heart to part with.

He was back so quickly that he had clearly prepared the pot of tea and laid out the crockery well beforehand, the brass-handled wooden tray covered with a lace-edged cloth, the way his wife would probably have done. 'Do sit down, won't you?' he said, as he bent and set the tray on the coffee table in front of the fire.

Roper lowered himself into the armchair where his raincoat was. The other, more worn, facing the window and with an open book lying on the arm, was too plainly Jobling's regular seat. On the other arm was a glass ashtray with a briar pipe lying across it.

'Sugar?'

'Two, sir, please.'

Jobling brought the cup and saucer across to him, his shaking hand causing the cup to jiggle about noisily in the saucer. He was somewhere in his late sixties, probably retired, his clothes too large for his gangling frame as if he had suddenly lost a lot of weight, which he probably had.

Roper apologised for breaking into his afternoon.

'Not at all,' said Jobling, easing himself gingerly into his chair, carefully balancing his cup and saucer but still managing to slop some tea into the saucer. 'I'm glad of the company. Sometimes I don't see anyone to talk to for days at a time.' He took a sip of his tea and shakily lowered his cup back on to its saucer. 'You wanted to talk about my wife, I believe.'

'Yes, sir,' said Roper. 'If it won't upset you too much.'

'It won't,' said Jobling. 'Things pass. You know? I miss her greatly, of course, but one has to go on and do one's best. No, I don't mind talking about her at all. I think about her all the time, in fact. One does, you know. They never really go away.' He was a softly spoken, educated man, courtly, perhaps a retired headmaster or something

110

of that sort.

'Did your wife ever give any hint of what she intended to do, sir?'

'No,' said Jobling. 'I knew she wasn't well, of course, and very dispirited, but it never occurred to me that she would do anything like that. Never.'

'How wasn't she well, sir?'

'Terribly depressed,' said Jobling sadly. 'Changed – virtually – overnight. I eventually persuaded her to see her doctor, several doctors in fact. One suggested she saw a psychiatrist, but she dug her heels in over that. She got to a point where she wouldn't even leave the house. And she cleaned ceaselessly, dusting, vacuum-cleaning, window cleaning. I tried to get her to stop, but she wouldn't. Housework became a sort of obsession. Sometimes during the night, I'd wake and find her gone. More often than not she was downstairs frantically cleaning something.'

Things had gone from bad to worse. She had been prescribed tranquillisers, then stronger tranquillisers, then sleeping tablets, but all any of them did was to slow her down. And as the time had passed she had developed an agoraphobia so restricting that even the back garden had become a place of terror for her.

'Was she ever hospitalised?'

'No,' said Jobling. 'We all tried to persuade her, but she wouldn't go. I began to wonder towards the end if she wasn't becoming insane. They were quite terrible, those last few months, and I had to do most of my work at home to keep her company and look after her. Quite terrible.' Jobling broke off, his face pale and drawn as he took momentary cover behind his trembling teacup. 'She was so happy,' he said. 'Before.'

'Had she had any problems? A bereavement? Money troubles?'

'None,' said Jobling. 'Absolutely none.'

He told Roper that he was a solicitor, with a shared practice here in Weymouth; although since the death of his wife he had gone into partial retirement and only went into his office a couple of days a week.

'Can't concentrate, you see. I'm thinking of giving it up altogether now.' The old man smiled distantly. 'I intend to start work on the garden when the weather gets better. She used to do all that. She loved the garden.'

'Did anything particular happen to trigger her, last Christmas Eve? Anything at all you can think of?'

Jobling shook his head. 'They asked me that at the time. There was nothing. It was simply a culmination of all that was troubling her, I think. She just could *not* go on.'

Jobling set down his cup on the tiled hearth beside the gas fire and rose to his feet. Skirting the coffee table and Roper's armchair he went to a needlework box under the bay window. Roper heard a drawer being opened, then shut again. He reappeared at Roper's side, extracting with his long bony fingers a folded sheet of cream notepaper from a matching envelope. From the reverent way he handled it, the sheet of cream paper was clearly among the more treasured of his possessions, and Roper guessed what it was even before it was in his hand.

There were only six pathetic words on the sheet of paper, the wandering, disjointed handwriting showing all the despair of a woman at the end of her emotional tether:

Forgive me. I love you. Gwen.

'There was nothing else?'

'Nothing,' said Jobling. He took back the note, folded it carefully the way it had been and slid it into its envelope. He stood it beside the chiming clock on the shelf above the fireplace and returned to his chair.

'You said your wife went into this decline more or less overnight, sir,' said Roper.

'Literally,' said Jobling, reaching down into the hearth for his cup and saucer. 'After the accident.'

'Accident?'

Jobling sipped at his tea. 'Oh, it was nothing.' He lifted his shoulders deprecatingly. 'A bent bumper and a crumpled front wing. I didn't even bother to claim it on the insurance.'

'Was any other vehicle involved, sir?'

'Definitely not. She skidded in the rain one evening and drove the front of the car into a grass verge. As I said, it was hardly anything. But it worried her enormously; God knows why, but it did. She never drove again.'

The glimmer of a possibility came. Roper drained his cup, set it on its saucer and leaned forward to stand both on the coffee table.

'Can you remember exactly when Mrs Jobling had this accident, sir?'

'Yes, I can,' said Jobling. He rose once again, this time standing his cup and saucer on the mantelshelf, and left the room. Roper heard a wooden drawer slide open, the rustle of papers. Alone for a moment, he took out his pocket-book and checked the topmost date on the photocopy folded inside it. 12 July 1990. When Sergeant Pope had been working with the County Traffic Division. He tucked the photocopy quickly away as the drawer in the next room was slammed shut again and Jobling padded back in his carpet slippers.

'I always keep bills,' said Jobling. He gave another of his forlorn smiles. 'Gwen was always saying what an old fusspot I was about keeping records.'

Roper took the invoice from him. It had been made out by a crash-repair contractor here in Weymouth. One new front fender, and one near-side front wing replaced and resprayed, for the sum of £380. The invoice was dated 14 July 1990, and two days after the first date in Pope's notebook under Mrs Jobling's initials.

'Can you remember how long the car was in the repair shop, sir?'

'If it's important, I can tell you exactly.'

'Please,' said Roper, and Jobling padded off again to the back room. This time he was quickly back again, one of his fingers down the spine of a desk diary for a bookmark. He held it open so that Roper could read the relevant entry: 'Made appointment with Grace and Stokes for car repair. They will collect 8 July.'

The entry had been made on the sixth.

'And the accident your wife had, Mr Jobling, when was that?'

'The night before,' said Jobling. 'That would have been the fifth, wouldn't it?'

'I'm sorry to drag up old memories, sir, but can you remember what time Mrs Jobling got home that night?'

'Very late,' said Jobling. 'Almost midnight, I think it was.'

'Do you know where she'd been?'

'Osmington,' said Jobling. 'She'd spent the evening with a niece. She rang me just after eleven o'clock to say she was just leaving – she always did that so that I wouldn't worry.'

But Jobling had worried. Osmington was only a few miles along the coast and the journey that should have taken only ten minutes had taken her nearer forty.

Roper took out his pocket-book and wrote: '5 July 90. Osmington – Weymouth 23.30 hours approx. Any RTA?' And thanked God for orderly men like Mr Jobling who kept meticulous diaries.

Jobling watched him, a little puzzled now. 'With the greatest respect,' he said, 'you still haven't *really* told me why you're here. And why you should be so interested in my wife after all this time.'

'I'm investigating the death of an ex-police officer, sir. No, it's nothing to do with your wife,' Roper hastened to assure him. 'It happened only last Monday night; but your wife's initials and your home telephone number were in a notebook of his we found.'

'I don't understand—'

'Nor do I, sir,' said Roper. 'Yet. D'you know if this accident your wife had was reported to the police?'

'There was no need,' said Jobling. He was back in his chair and hugging the diary, still perplexed. 'As I said, no one else was concerned in the accident and my wife was only rather shaken up. As I recall, she didn't even go to see the doctor at that time.'

'Look, sir,' said Roper, hastening again to reassure as Jobling's perplexity began to change to justifiable concern. 'This business had absolutely nothing to do with Mrs Jobling. She's just one of several people he'd recorded in his notebook: perhaps she'd committed a parking offence or something like that. As I said, sir, the man was a police officer.'

'Yes,' said Jobling, greatly relieved. 'Yes, of course. I hadn't thought of that. I remember now, she did earn herself a couple of parking tickets.'

Some time had passed. Roper was on his second cup of tea and Jobling had lit his pipe. This coming Sunday would have been the Joblings' forty-fifth wedding anniversary. There had been no children, merely a tribe of nieces and nephews and god-children, one of the latter living in Montreal. In the coming summer he was flying over there to visit her.

'If I could ask you a personal question, sir,' said Roper, who had listened patiently throughout this digression and felt it was time to return to the matter in hand. 'Did your wife have any private financial resources? Something she could have spent without your knowing about it?'

'Why, yes, she did, as a matter of fact,' said Jobling, his brow furrowing again. 'How odd you should ask that.'

'Odd, sir?'

'Oh, it was only a small amount,' said Jobling. 'About five years ago my wife was bequeathed a little nest-egg by an elderly aunt. I think it was about two and a half thousand pounds. We didn't need the money so my wife invested it in a building society. She thought it would make something to fall back on when I retired. I was her executor, of course, and apart from a few small bequests to our nephews and nieces, keepsakes mostly, everything was left to me.'

115

But when Jobling had looked into his wife's financial affairs after her death he had been unable to find any record of her investment in the building society. He had contacted the society in question only to be told that the account had been closed since the previous November.

'So all the money had gone?'

'Apparently,' said Jobling. 'They told me it had been gradually withdrawn, mostly in amounts of a hundred and fifty pounds.'

'At monthly intervals?'

'Why, yes,' said Jobling. Unable to contain his curiosity any longer, he exclaimed, 'Look, old chap, I really *must* know what all this is about. If I thought my wife had been engaged in anything untoward—'

'She wasn't, sir,' said Roper, breaking in. 'I'm sure she wasn't. If you could bear with me a little longer, I'd be grateful. You told me your wife was agoraphobic, sir. And to draw this money out she would have to have attended the building society office in person, wouldn't she?'

'She could go out if I was with her,' said Jobling. 'And if we did we took the car so that we could get back quickly if she had an attack. We did go into the town once in a while – and she did always leave me for a few minutes, now I come to think about it. I suppose she could have drawn out the money then.'

'Could your wife have spent this money on herself?'

'I never saw anything she bought, if she did. She certainly bought herself no new clothes in her last couple of years. I wish to God she had. Now you *must* tell me why you're *really* here. You owe me that, at least.'

'I do indeed, sir,' said Roper. 'And I only wish that I could be as frank as you've been, but you'll appreciate that I can't, at least for the time being. But when I do find out what all this is about, you'll be the first to know. And that's a promise.'

TEN

AT FIVE O'CLOCK HE WAS back in his office. Price was holding the fort alone. Makins and Rodgers were still out.

'Any joy?' asked Roper.

'Some,' said Price.

A few loose ends were beginning to come together. Price had had a warrant sworn out during the course of the afternoon, and armed with that he had been able to find out the forwarding address to which Mr J B Rubery had had his telephone bill sent when he had quit his house in Dorchester back in February. Mr Rubery was presently living in Southampton, where George Makins was now. Together with a detective sergeant from the Hampshire Constabulary he was hoping to call on Mr Rubery later that evening.

DS Rodgers had phoned in about an hour ago. He had been over to Beaminster to interview neighbours of the late Mr Weston, who had leapt to his death from the cliffs at Charmouth. None of them knew very much, except that Weston had become a close and secretive man in the last few months before he had died. One neighbour, however, had been left a forwarding address and telephone number by Weston's widow. Mrs Weston was now living with her sister, also a widow, in Yeovil, in the adjacent county of Somerset. Rodgers had phoned her and made an appointment to call on her around half-past five that evening.

Price himself had also had a small success. A few

minutes ago he had at last made contact with the man to whose wife Makins had spoken earlier in the afternoon, and who had agreed that the initials in Pope's notebook were those of her husband but that she had never heard of Gerald Pope.

'RJB,' Price said, drawing his jotting pad closer. 'Mr Richard Bennett. Forty-two, Welbeck Drive, Swanage. And he got very uptight. Swore blind he knew nobody called Pope, nor ever had. I asked him if I could call on him later this evening, and he told me he was going out with his wife. Very tart, he was – until I told him Pope was dead.'

'And?'

'He could hardly keep the unsurpassed joy out of his voice. Still swore he'd never heard of him, mind. But I reckon he had. How did you get on with Jobling?'

'Tell you in a couple of minutes.'

Still with his raincoat on, Roper walked briskly along to Brake's office. Brake, in civilian clothes, was just on the point of going home.

'Won't keep you, Charlie,' said Roper. 'I'm looking for records of any traffic accidents your lads might have handled on July five, nineteen-ninety.'

'All I keep up here are the bare details. The nitty-gritty'll be down in the archives.'

'The bare details'll do for now,' said Roper.

Brake hung his driving-coat back on his coatstand and went to his array of filing cabinets. From one he took a file, riffled through its pages.

'There were four,' he said. 'One jack-knifed lorry on the A31 at Winterbourne Zelston. Driver seriously injured. Fire Brigade tender clipped a private vehicle on the A354: no serious injuries. Collision between two private cars on the A31 at Bloxworth. No serious injuries. Hit and run on the A353, just outside Osmington. Somebody knocked a motor-cyclist off his bike and did a runner. No serious injury. That's the lot.'

'That last one, at Osmington,' said Roper. 'What time of day did it happen?'

'Twenty-three twenty,' said Brake, turning back a page.

Which in more everyday language was twenty past eleven at night, and just about the time Mrs Jobling would have been travelling the A353 on her way back to Weymouth after spending that evening with her niece.

'And who was the attending officer?'

Brake's fingertip ran along the line of typing. 'Sergeant Pope,' he said.

'I bloody *knew* it,' said Roper, as the daylight dawned at last.

At five-thirty, the two of them were closeted among the archives down in the basement.

'The victim's name was Darren Mark Newbold,' said Brake. 'Aged nineteen, from Osmington. The treble-nine call was logged in at twenty-three twenty. Pope got to the scene at twenty-three twenty-seven and the ambulance arrived at twenty-three thirty-three. According to Pope, by the time he arrived the only person in the vicinity was Newbold; and he was lying unconscious on the verge with his bike a couple of yards away.'

'Somebody must have made the treble-nine call,' said Roper.

'Female. Didn't give a name. She said she'd knocked a man off a motor-cycle, gave the location of the phone, asked for an ambulance to come quickly, then hopped it. According to Pope he found the receiver dangling in a phone booth about fifty yards up the road from the accident. She panicked, probably, and just took off.'

'How about Newbold?'

'Concussion and a sprained wrist.' Brake turned forward a couple of pages. 'Signed himself out of the infirmary the following lunchtime.'

'But he was concussed when Pope turned up.'

'Flat out, face down,' said Brake. 'So it says here.'

'And no witnesses at all?'

'Nary a one,' said Brake.

DS Rodgers was back from visiting the widowed Mrs Weston at Yeovil soon after seven o'clock.

Mrs Weston had told a story similar to Mr Jobling's. She and her husband had been happily married for the better part of thirty years. Both had been pillars of the local amateur operatic society, they had taken their holidays together, bred a trio of daughters, all of whom had made a modest success of their lives, and paid their mortgage well before the appointed time. In short, the Westons had been a happy and united couple and had been heading towards a smooth and untroubled retirement together.

Until two years previously, when Mr Weston had suddenly suffered a change of personality. He had become sullen and morose and secretive, more or less overnight, as Mrs Jobling had, and for the first time in their lives the Weston's were frequently overdrawn at the bank, not seriously so but sufficiently to make the manager write to Mr Weston on several occasions.

Unlike Mr Jobling, Mrs Weston had kept no records, but she did recall that her husband had been concerned in a minor traffic accident at about the time he had suffered his personality change. He had driven one of their daughters home one night, quite late, as Mrs Weston recalled, and on his way back had collided with a tree while trying to avoid another car that had been turning heedlessly out of a side-road.

Then had come a strange turn of events that Mrs Weston had never quite understood. The car had only suffered slight damage but had never been repaired. Her husband had closed the garage doors on it that night and had never sat behind its wheel again. Instead, he had bought himself another car, a small Fiat that he kept parked in the street, and it was in this that he had driven to Charmouth that day and parked in the short-stay car park before he committed suicide. Mrs Weston had sold both vehicles after her husband had died, and a young man further along the street had been delighted to pick up a secondhand Ford Escort with bent radiator grill and cracked windscreen, but only twenty thousand miles on the clock, for £400.

'How about the accident?' asked Roper, to whom everything that Rodgers had so far told him sounded like an exact repetition of Jobling's story.

'He never talked about it,' said Rodgers. 'She got the impression he might have been hiding something, but every time she tried to get him to talk about it, he clammed up tight.'

'Check the first date in Pope's notebook that refers to Weston,' said Roper. 'Then ask Brake's sergeant to look you out the RTA files for the couple of weeks before, especially where Pope was the attending officer.'

'What am I looking for?'

'Hit and run accidents,' said Roper.

Rodgers was soon back. Hit and run accidents were blessedly rare, but there had been one five days before the first date referring to Mr Weston in Pope's notebook. It had happened late at night; the call had been logged in at a quarter to midnight and Sergeant Pope had been the attending officer. The victim, a cyclist, had been knocked from his bicycle – he had had no lights – and suffered minor concussion, a dislocated shoulder, a broken finger and facial bruises. He had been back at work within a week.

'Whereabouts was it?' asked Roper.

'The B3163,' said Rodgers. 'A couple of miles east of Beaminster, where the Westons used to live.'

It was beginning to smell more and more like blackmail, Pope the villain of the piece and the initials in his little red notebook his victims, the dates the occasions they met him and paid their dues, although in Mrs Jobling's case, since she was an agoraphobic, he might have made house calls when her husband had been out. It was little wonder that she had become sleepless and neurotic, always knowing it would soon be time for her tormentor to come up her front path again. In the end she had taken her life rather than face any more of it. And so, it seemed, had Mr Weston. All of which, as yet, was only theorising, but it was more than likely that Hit and Run Pope had not earned his nickname honestly, but had carved it for himself with cold deliberation.

At nine o'clock he decided to call it a day, and was unwinding his legs from under his desk when his phone chirruped.

'Roper,' he said.

The caller was George Makins, along at Southampton. Mr Rubery, late of Dorchester, had just arrived home from work and Makins was phoning from Rubery's flat.

'He wants to talk to somebody,' said Makins. 'It's about a traffic accident. It happened a couple of years ago. A hit and run, he tells me. He thinks she was a schoolgirl, and that he killed her. He wants to make a clean breast of it.'

'How soon can you get him here?'

'About an hour,' said Makins.

'I'll wait for him,' said Roper.

His full name was James Bernard Rubery, aged thirty-two, by profession a plasterer. Broad shouldered, bomber-jacketed, shaven-headed and with both wrists emblazoned with exotic tattoos, he looked like a young man who was desperate to get a lot of dirty water off his chest. He sat white-faced on the edge of Roper's visitor's chair, his hands clasped tightly between his knees, the coffee that Makins had fetched from the machine for him so far untouched. Brake's night-sergeant was also in attendance and had formally cautioned him, but Rubery was in a hurry to talk and had brushed the caution aside.

'It was January,' he said. 'Couple of years back. I was

going home from work. Late. About nine o'clock. And this girl on a bike, she just sort of came out of a side-turning. And I hit her square on. She came straight along the bonnet, hit the screen and rolled off. I can still hear the thump now. Terrible it was.'

'Can you recall exactly where the accident happened, sir?' asked Brake's sergeant.

'The road between Tincleton and Stinsford,' said Rubery.

'And you're sure about the time?'

'Nine o'clock, like I said. Might have been ten minutes either side. I don't remember exactly.'

'What sort of car were you driving, Mr Rubery?' asked Roper.

'Ford Capri,' he said. 'But it wasn't knackered or anything. Everything worked and it'd only passed its MOT a couple of days before. I'd had the brakes serviced and everything. I still run it. You can give it the once-over, if you like.'

'How fast were you travelling? Remember?'

'About twenty, I suppose. Honest,' he protested, meeting Roper's and Brake's sergeant's doubtful eyes. 'Half the road was coned off for repairs and it was snowing hard. You can check if you like.'

'Did you get a chance to use your brakes?'

'Not a lot. Twenty, thirty feet, near as I remember. She was just there, in the headlights. And what with the cones and the snow – and there was a scarifying machine parked beside the road, too – I didn't have anywhere to go, did I? Except straight on. It really was her fault, guv'nor, I swear. She just wasn't looking where she was going.'

'How far d'you reckon you travelled after you hit her?'

'Not far,' said Rubery. 'I slammed on everything. About twenty feet, I suppose. Then I stopped and she slid off the bonnet.' He closed his eyes and shivered. 'I still bloody dream about it.'

'What did you do then?'

123

Rubery lifted his hands and hugged himself, his hands tucked under his leather armpits. 'Nothing,' he said. 'My mind went blank. I thought of making a run for it, I was that scared, see. Then this car came along behind me and pulled up in front, then backed so I couldn't go anywhere. The bloke gets out and comes back to where the girl is. He crouches over her for a bit, then comes round and taps on the roof. I opened the window and he stuffs this card in at me. And he was only a bloody off-duty copper, wasn't he. Says the girl's dead, doesn't he? Asks me if I've been drinking. I said I hadn't, and he made me breathe straight up his nose, and he said I had and if I liked he'd drive me along to the local nick and he'd give me a breath test.'

'And had you been drinking?'

'One. Just one. Just a pint. With the lads when we packed up work. And that's the truth. But he said it smelt more like three or four and I was in dead trouble. Well, I got really scared then, because coppers can say what they like when it's one to one, can't they, and I can't work without a car, it's contract work, see, and I have to travel about a lot. Then he asked if I'd got a wife and kids, and I said I had; and he thought a bit and said I'd better shove off because if he nicked me I'd likely do three months for manslaughter. I said what about getting an ambulance or something, and he said he'd do that, there was no hurry now, was there? "Just eff off," he said. "Before I change my mind. I'm going to give you the best break you're ever likely to effin' get." They were his actual words. Honest.' Rubery looked pleadingly at Roper, then to Makins who was still catching up on his note taking at the end of the desk. 'I really am telling God's truth.'

Roper had little cause to doubt him. Rubery looked the sort who'd started life as a hooligan, met the right girl and settled down to work for all he was worth to keep her. And men who were desperate to tell the truth usually told all of it.

'So you went,' he said.

'Yeah,' said Rubery miserably, his face cast down. 'I went.' He was silent for a few moments. 'I don't think I really knew what I was doing. When I woke up next morning, I thought of turning myself in, but it was a hit and run by then, wasn't it? And you can do a couple of years inside for those, can't you. Specially if you've had a drink inside you. I tell you, I really was dead scared. Couldn't do my work properly or anything.

'Then about a week went by. And he rang me, this copper did. Told me the girl was DOA at the hospital and perhaps we'd better talk about it. Told me to meet him in this pub; we was still living in Dorchester then. And I did and he said he was having a bit of trouble keeping his mouth shut because some car had come along just as I'd driven off and the driver had taken a note of the first three letters and two of the numbers on my registration plate, so things were getting a bit dodgy for both of us. He asked me for a hundred quid, not for him, a sweetener for the other bloke, that's what he said. So I went to the bank the next day and drew it out. Cash, it was. He said it had to be cash.'

Things had gone from bad to worse. The demands for cash had become a regular monthly occurrence. In January this year the sweetener had been upped to £150. But that had been the last payment that Rubery had intended to make, because in the previous October, unbeknown to Pope, he had decided to shake off his tormentor by putting his house up for sale and moving his wife and family from Dorchester to Southampton, which he finally managed to do in early February. He had given his forwarding address only to those organisations with whom he would have bills to settle on his old property, and had more or less gone into hiding from then on.

'He didn't catch up with you?'

Rubery shook his head.

'Know his name?'

'He never mentioned it. He was just a face I recognised.

125

Big bloke with a beard. Used to turn up on a motor-bike. I had to duck out from under him, you see. I was having to work all the hours God sent to pay him, and the missus was wondering where all the money was going to, and I was having to lie to her too. Then tonight, your bloke,' he said, looking up at last and nodding towards Makins, 'and the other bobby turned up, and I was glad to let it all out in the open. Except now the missus knows I killed a little girl.'

'We don't think you did, Mr Rubery,' said Roper. 'All you did was knock her out for ten minutes and write off her bicycle. Which makes her a very lucky girl and you a very lucky man.'

'Oh, my God,' murmured Rubery, as first astonishment and then sublime relief overwhelmed him. He closed his eyes and tilted back his head, then slumped forward, his face pressed in his hands. And hefty and macho though the young man was, he broke down completely then, hiding his face with one hand while the other fumbled in the pocket of his jeans for a fistful of grubby paper handkerchiefs. Even Brake's hard-nosed sergeant was looking sympathetic. Makins took away Rubery's cold cup of coffee and went off to fetch him a hot one.

And, watching Rubery, Roper could only wish that he had been able to break similar news to Gwen Jobling and the late Mr Weston of Beaminster. He waited for Rubery to compose himself again. In the hour or so it had taken Makins to bring Rubery from Southampton Roper had not been idle himself. A half-hour down in the archives with Brake's sergeant had finally brought to light another night-time hit and run accident. It had taken place on the road between Stinsford and Tincleton around eight days before the first entry for Rubery in Pope's notebook. Interestingly, the attending police officer had been not Sergeant Pope but the local beat-sergeant in a Panda car. He had been called to the site in response to a treble-nine call. The call had been made by a man who had used a public phone booth which had been a mile up the road from where the accident had occurred and who had disappeared by the time the beat-officer and the ambulance had arrived on the scene. It seemed fairly safe to assume now that the absconded caller had been Gerry Pope, himself almost as guilty as Rubery, since he must have driven off and left the injured girl too. And from what Rubery had said, it was obvious that Pope had been in mufti and had come upon the accident by sheer chance, and had thus been able to keep his official nose out of the accident altogether.

Rubery blew his nose, dabbed at his eyes and drew himself up in his chair.

'Sorry about all that,' he said, sniffing as he dabbed at his nose with the ball of handkerchiefs. 'But I've had a couple of years of sheer bloody purgatory over all this business. It was getting to the point where I was going to have to spill the beans to somebody anyway.'

'There is one more thing I'd like to know about, Mr Rubery,' said Roper. 'How did he make the arrangements to meet you each month?'

'He phoned the night before,' said Rubery. 'Telling me a time and a place. The place was usually some out of the way pub that had a car park. We used to meet there and I'd hand over the cash, he'd tell me to stick around for a few minutes and then he would drive off on his motor-bike.'

'So that you wouldn't see where he went?'

'I don't know,' said Rubery. 'Probably.' He stuffed his handkerchiefs back in his jeans and sat upright again. 'I suppose you're going to charge me?'

'Not here and now,' said Roper. 'That'll be down to the Traffic Division.'

'Do time, will I?'

'I doubt it,' said Roper. 'Can't promise anything, of course.' It would be a hard judge who sent Rubery down. With hindsight, it was Rubery who had suffered more than the girl he had knocked from her bicycle.

'He told you all about it, did he? That copper?'

'He's dead, Mr Rubery,' said Roper, carefully watching Rubery's reaction.

There was hardly any. 'Can't say I'm sorry,' said Rubery. 'The lousy bastard.'

'Would you mind telling us where you were last Monday night?'

'Got home about eight o'clock.'

'Stay there?'

'Usually do,' said Rubery. 'You can check with the missus, if you like.'

But Roper decided it wasn't worth the effort unless something new turned up; and at eleven o'clock Makins was driving a slightly more sanguine Mr Rubery back to Southampton.

Chief Inspector Price had already done an hour's work when Roper turned in at eight o'clock on Friday morning. Price was sitting in his own office with a borrowed tape recorder and was playing back the tail end of the tape that had been in Pope's answering machine.

'On to something?' asked Roper.

Price wound the tape back a few inches, then replayed it. Pope's voice came first. '. . . I don't give a shit . . . Just be there.'

'. . . For God's sake . . . the banks are shut now, aren't they?'

At which point Price switched the machine off again.

'I think that's the voice I've just been talking to,' he said. 'Richard Bennett, the bloke I spoke to last night. He wouldn't say much over the phone, but he wants to come in here this evening and talk to somebody. He'd have come in this morning, only he's got an appointment up in London.'

'Who phoned who first?' asked Roper.

'I phoned him,' said Price. 'I thought I'd catch him early before he left for work. I asked him if there was a chance he'd like to change his mind about knowing Gerry Pope.

128

He hummed and hahed a bit, then decided he did. He'll be in this evening around eight o'clock. If I was reading him right, he sounded relieved.'

'Found a matching accident report?'

Price slid a photocopy across his desk. The accident report, from the archives, was another of Sergeant Pope's. It referred to a hit and run accident on the B3390, a few miles south of Affpuddle, which had occurred six days before the first date under Mr Bennett's initials in Pope's little red notebook. The victim had been a pedestrian, his injuries severe concussion and a compound fracture of his right leg. The victim was only partly-sighted and hence had had no idea what had hit him. Neither the vehicle nor the driver had ever been found.

Which left only one of Pope's own possible victims outstanding, and that was Mr Martin Craven; and at nine o'clock, with Brake himself sorting through the masses of old paperwork, Roper finally turned up an accident report that fitted the topmost date under the initials MRC in Pope's red notebook.

A week prior to that first date there had been an accident on a side-road a few miles west of Wareham, at 22.40 hours on the night of 12 February 1990. The victim had been one Sidney Arthur Manley, aged sixty-two years. The incident had been aurally witnessed by a Mrs Mavis Baxter who had been out walking her dog. A few seconds before the accident, Mrs Baxter had been crossing the road in question when a pair of headlights had rushed out of the dark, the driver thumping his horn impatiently. The car had missed her dog by only inches. She was still drawing her breath on the grass verge when she heard a distinct dull thud, followed by a squeal of brakes and rubber. She had, alas, done no more until she had seen the sign Brake's men had erected near the accident site the next morning and which asked for any witnesses to come forward. The car, the only one she had remembered seeing at the time, had been 'grey and silvery', and had been travelling 'much too fast'.

Whoever had made the call to the emergency services had been a male, and the time of the accident had been based upon the time his call was logged. Mrs Baxter had been able to say only that the time had been somewhere between half-past ten and a quarter to eleven. On his reception into the accident bay of the hospital, Mr Manley had been recorded as dead on arrival. And the attending police officer, of course, had been the ubiquitous Sergeant Pope.

ELEVEN

AT MIDDAY ROPER AND MAKINS drove out to Appleford again, this time to interview Mr Craven. According to his wife, to whom Roper had put through a chance telephone call a half-hour before, Mr Craven was not at work today. He had driven into Dorchester and Mrs Craven was expecting him back soon after twelve o'clock. Of all the people Roper had spoken with so far, it had to be Martin Craven against whom the dice were most heavily loaded. However much he denied it, he *must* have known Gerry Pope. He lived within spitting distance of where Pope had been killed, the odds were about fifty to one on that he had been concerned in the only genuinely fatal hit and run accident that Pope had recorded in his little red book, and according to the dates in Pope's book Craven should have met up with Pope again a day or two either side of last Monday. And not investigating a run of coincidences like that would be like having a half dozen ragingly aching teeth and putting off going to a dentist.

The day was another grey depressing one, the heath drained of all its colour, the still air filled with a heavy dampness. According to the forecasters it would stay this way till Easter, and that was still a week away.

What first caught Roper's eye as they approached the Cravens' bungalow was Mrs Wicks' antiquated Volvo canted up on the verge outside with a Panda car drawn up behind it with its hazard-winkers flashing. Both were empty.

131

Makins parked on the heath side of the road. There was no sign anywhere of Mallory or Mrs Wicks, which caused Roper's first presentiment that all was not well.

They were about to climb the three steps up to the verandah when Makins took a grip of Roper's raincoat sleeve. 'Cop that,' he said, nodding towards the glass-panelled front door.

But Roper had already seen it. A distorted silhouette of a human hand pressed flat against the glass. Further behind the glass a black bulk near the floor straightened and resolved itself into a man.

Roper climbed the steps and rapped on the glass. 'Who is it?' called the voice of Sergeant Mallory.

'Roper, Sergeant.'

'Better come round the back, sir,' shouted Mallory.

Roper and Makins walked around the verandah. The door to the kitchen was open. Mrs Wicks was standing alone in there, her vast body trembling and her face much the same colour as the sky outside.

'You all right, Mrs Wicks?' asked Roper concernedly.

'Yes,' she said. 'Just a bit shaky, that's all. She's out there.'

'She?'

'Dagmar. Mrs Craven. She's lying in the hall. It looks as if she's had an accident.'

Roper went out into the hall. Mallory was still standing over Mrs Craven's prone body. Scattered around his feet were the myriad blue shards of what had once been the Emil Gallé vase that had stood on the sofa table against the wall.

'Dead, is she?'

'Just unconscious, I think, sir,' said Mallory.

With glass crackling under his shoes, Roper crouched beside the body and examined it for himself, his fingertips feeling for a pulse under Mrs Craven's ear. There was one, very faint, very slow. The blonde hair at the right side of her head was a mass of blood that had still to congeal. 'Somebody call you, Sergeant?'

132

'I was passing,' said Mallory, as Roper slowly rose to his feet. 'And Mrs Wicks flagged me down.'

'How long ago?'

'Couple of minutes,' said Mallory. 'I radioed for an ambulance as soon as I came in and saw her.'

Blood still seeped from the wound. It looked deep. She lay face down, saliva trickling from the side of her mouth, her body stretched out along the green carpet, her head on the coconut doormat, the flat of one hand against the glass of the door, near the bottom.

'You moved her?'

'No, sir. I only did what you did. Looks like she fell and caught her head on the corner of this table, and that glass thing got tipped over in the process.'

'Not to break into little pieces like that, it didn't,' said Roper. He ran his fingers along the edge of the table. He felt first, then saw, a scarred indentation on the wood. It looked recently done. Treated kindly, Gallé vases were crafted to last for ever, and one certainly wouldn't have smashed into fragments like that by simply falling three feet on to a soft carpet. At the corner of the table, the corner nearest the front door, was another mark, but he didn't touch it because it looked like human débris, a tiny fragment of skin with a broken hair still rooted in it.

If it had not been for the broken vase, the scene in the hall could easily be assumed to have been an accident. But the vase, smashed into little pieces the way it was, gave Roper a sense of disquiet. Certainly the vase had not caused Mrs Craven's wound, the table had done that, but in some way, and perhaps not a passive one, the vase had been involved. One way or another, he was sure that violence had been done here, and within the last few minutes.

'You don't have a cigarette, do you?' asked a desperate Mrs Wicks when he joined her in the kitchen. Still deathly pale, she was presently overflowing a high stool beside the chrome and plastic breakfast bar.

'Cheroot?'

133

'Whatever you've got,' she said, reaching out gratefully to pluck one from his packet. 'Thank you.'

He struck his lighter for her and held it to the wavering tip of the cheroot. 'How did you happen along, exactly?'

'I was bringing her ring back,' she said, opening her left hand to show him a diminutive cardboard box that she'd been holding so tightly it had left white depressions in the palm of her hand.

'Ring?' he asked, perching on the stool beside her.

'Her engagement ring. I'd put a new claw on it for her. I rang earlier and told her I'd drop it in on my way into Dorchester to do some shopping. But when I got here . . . well, you know the rest for yourself.'

'Can you remember what time you rang her?'

'About a quarter of an hour ago,' she said.

Roper shot his cuff to look at his watch. It was a quarter past midday now. 'And you definitely spoke to Mrs Craven?'

'Positive,' she said. 'Couldn't really mistake that accent, could you?' The colour was slowly returning to her face and she was beginning to relax a little.

'And you arrived here when?'

'Only a couple of minutes before you did. I saw the hand pressed against the door, did a quick turn about to nip back home to phone for an ambulance and fortunately met Sergeant Mallory on his way home for lunch. And that's about it. It all happened in a bit of a rush.'

So Mrs Craven had been fit and well at midday and unconscious by about ten past.

There came the muffled sound of a car pulling up at the front of the house, then the slam of its door. A couple of seconds later, Makins' voice shouted, 'Round the back, please, sir,' and whoever had arrived could be heard briskly drawing closer around the verandah.

It was Martin Craven, tweed-capped, red-faced and angry. 'What the *hell* are all you people doing in my bloody house,' he raged, stopping short on the doorstep as he saw

Roper and Mrs Wicks sitting in his kitchen. 'And what the hell's going on exactly?'

'There seems to have been an accident, sir,' said Roper, rising from his stool, as did Mrs Wicks beside him. 'Your wife's had a fall. She's out in the hall –' But even as he spoke Craven was in the kitchen and pushing past him and striding out along the hallway. Roper hurried after him.

'My God, what the hell's happened here,' said Craven, still blazing with anger, standing over his wife's outstretched body. Roper would have expected him to show some sign of shock or horror, but for the moment Craven seemed more concerned by the litter of broken glass around his feet. Then he crouched down by his wife and felt inexpertly around her throat for a pulse.

'Did any of you *think* to ring for an ambulance?'

'Yes, sir, Sergeant Mallory did,' said Roper. 'It's on its way. And please don't move your wife, sir,' he said, bending and gripping Craven's wrist as Craven went to roll his wife on to her back. Faintly, in the distance, could be heard the fluttering wail of an ambulance siren.

'Jesus, man,' hissed Craven, as Roper dragged him back to his feet. 'Take your bloody hands off me.' Teeth bared, breath sawing in and out, he snatched his wrist free. 'You know she's been bloody robbed, don't you?' He looked accusingly at each of them in turn, Makins, Mallory, then back to Roper. 'Her bloody engagement ring's gone. I wonder what the bloody hell else is missing.'

'Mrs Wicks has the ring, sir,' said Roper, sure he could smell whisky on Craven's breath. 'Your wife asked her to repair it. She brought it back this morning, and found your wife lying here.'

'And who did this?' demanded Craven, nodding down at the shards of blue glass sparkling on the carpet.

'I've no idea, sir,' said Roper, not astonished, because he had been in the job too long, but certainly surprised that Craven's concern for his possessions still seemed to be predominating over concern for the wife who was lying unconscious at his feet. A soft squeal of brakes outside was the ambulance arriving. Mallory hurried off towards the kitchen to bring the crew in around the back.

'So what happens now?' asked Craven.

'Well, sir, I suggest you go with Mrs Craven to the hospital. With your permission, my sergeant and I will have a quick look around here, then we'll follow you.'

'Why follow me?'

'We'd like to ask you a few questions, sir. Purely routine.'

'But you said it was a bloody accident,' argued Craven.

'Perhaps, sir,' said Roper. 'Or perhaps not. That's why we'd like to look around.'

'I see,' said Craven waspishly. 'Then I'll stay with you and drive along to the hospital afterwards.'

'Suit yourself, sir,' said Roper. He and Craven stood aside as the two ambulance crew came up the hall, the man carrying a stretcher, the woman a first-aid case and a stethoscope. 'That was a quick response,' observed Roper, to the man, as the woman crouched beside Mrs Craven and opened her case.

The man looked at his watch. 'A bit slow, actually,' he said. 'Fourteen minutes.'

Roper frowned down at his own watch. 'You sure about that?' he said. It was only twenty-one minutes past midday now. Less fourteen minutes would have made the call at seven minutes past twelve.

'Positive,' said the ambulanceman. 'It's logged on the docket in the cab. You can check if you like.'

Roper took a grip of Mallory's elbow and steered him into the sitting-room out of Craven's earshot. 'What time did you get here, Sergeant? Can you remember exactly?'

'When Mrs Wicks flagged me down it was eleven minutes past twelve.'

'Sure?'

'Certain,' said Mallory. 'And I radioed for the ambulance about a couple of minutes afterwards. I'd just done that when you arrived.'

136

Something wasn't ringing right. From what Mallory was saying, he'd put out the call for an ambulance some time after ten past twelve. The ambulance had responded to an emergency call that had been logged in at seven minutes past twelve. Roper checked Mallory's wristwatch against his own. They agreed to within half a minute.

'Who did you put your call through to?'

'County HQ, sir,' said Mallory. 'I've only got the one radio channel.'

So if Mallory had contacted County, that would have cost another couple of minutes while they in turn contacted the ambulance depot. Something surely wasn't right here . . .

'Do something for me, Sergeant,' said Roper. 'Go outside, radio County and ask 'em to get in touch with the ambulance depot. I want to know exactly what time they logged in the call that sent that ambulance here. And who made it.'

Mallory frowned vacantly, then turned and left the room in the direction of the kitchen. Roper joined Makins and Craven out in the hallway. Mrs Craven, her head swathed in a mass of cotton wool and bandage, was being turned over on to her back and lifted on to the stretcher.

'How is she?' asked Roper.

'Difficult to say,' said the ambulancewoman. 'She's had a fair old crack. Looks like a depressed fracture of the skull. Her pulse is definitely quickening up though, which is probably good news. You'll be coming with us, will you, Mr Craven?'

'Later,' said Craven. 'I've things to do here first.'

She lifted a surprised eyebrow in Roper's direction, but said nothing.

The bungalow was quiet again. Mrs Craven had been driven off to the hospital, Mrs Wicks had gone to do her shopping in Dorchester and would be interviewed later, and Sergeant Mallory had reported back on the result of his call to County. As Roper had suspected there had been two calls requesting an ambulance to attend Furzedown. One had been logged in at 12.07, the second, from County Police Headquarters, at 12.13.

'Where did the first call come from?' had muttered Roper.

'Here, sir,' Mallory had muttered. 'According to the records, Mr Craven made it himself, and gave this telephone number. Told the operator his wife had taken a fall and was lying unconscious.'

The two of them had been standing in the kitchen while Craven, in company with George Makins, had been making a brief tour of the bungalow to check if anything obvious was missing. Nothing was, and now Roper, Makins and Mallory were sitting patiently in the long sitting-room while Craven poured himself a stiff Scotch, the suede-topped tweed cap he had been wearing now discarded and lying beside the galleried silver tray upon which his collection of drinks stood on a handsome Edwardian sideboard.

'Not working today, Mr Craven?' asked Roper, when Craven had at last sat down opposite him and taken a sip of his Scotch.

'I decided to work at home today. According to the radio, the early morning trains were running badly.'

'But you weren't working, were you, sir? You were out in your car.'

Craven scowled angrily across the hearthrug. 'I don't remember who you are exactly,' he said.

'The name's Roper, sir. Superintendent, County CID.' Craven remembered him all right. He was just trying to cut him down to size. He was that sort. 'As I was saying, you were out in your car. Mind telling us where you went?'

'I had to go into Dorchester.'

'Because . . .?'

'I'd run out of printer paper for my computer.'

'And you bought some?'

For answer, Craven reached inside his driving coat and brought out his wallet. He took from it a folded invoice and held it out at arm's length. Roper rose and took it from him. The invoice was from a stationer's in Dorchester. It bore today's date. Roper made a mental note of the name of the shop and handed it back to him, then returned to his chair.

'What time did you leave for Dorchester, sir?'

'A few minutes after ten. You can verify that if you wish. When I left, the cleaning girl was out in the hall collecting her wages. She saw me go.'

'Do you have a name and address for this girl, sir?' asked Makins, who by now had taken out his pocket-book.

'Dawn something-or-other,' replied Craven. 'She lives in the village. I expect you'll find her details in my wife's address book. You'll find it in a drawer in the table in the hall.'

Makins rose and went outside. It had struck Roper that Mr Craven seemed more than ordinarily keen to establish his recent whereabouts. As a general rule it was mostly folk with something on their minds who did that, like villains, and errant husbands.

'Might she have stayed for a while, this cleaner?' asked Roper.

'Hardly,' said Craven, tipping back the last of his Scotch and generally making it plain that his wife was highly unlikely to socialise with a mere minion.

'Dawn Bracewell, sir?' broke in Makins, who had returned and was turning the pages of the address book. 'That ring a bell?'

'Yes, that's her,' said Craven.

Makins jotted Ms Bracewell's details in his pocket-book.

'Was your wife on any kind of medication, sir?' asked Roper. 'Anything that might have made her dizzy?'

'No, she wasn't. So far as I'm aware she wasn't on anything.'

'Mrs Chance didn't call?' asked Roper, recalling that Mrs

Chance had been taking coffee with Mrs Craven when he and Makins had called here on Tuesday morning, and wondering if their shared elevenses was a regular daily occurrence. He also recalled the little snippet of gossip he had heard in the Hanging Man about Craven and Mrs Chance being seen arm in arm in Dorchester, and wondered if it was true – and how relevant it might be to Mrs Craven lying injured in her hall.

But Craven didn't know whether Mrs Chance had called that morning or not, nor did he seem to care. He pushed himself out of his armchair to replenish his tumbler.

'Have a few drinks before you went out, Mr Craven?' asked Roper, to Craven's back. 'Or was that afterwards?'

'Are you suggesting I did that to her?' said Craven, intently pouring.

'Well, did you, sir?' asked Roper, still to his back.

Craven carefully capped his bottle before he replied. 'I thought you said it was an accident.'

'It's that Gallé vase you had in the hall, sir. I'm surprised it broke into little pieces like that.'

'Are you suggesting I hit her with it, for Christ's sake?' Only then did Craven turn and meet Roper's eye again. He sipped at his Scotch.

'No, sir, not exactly,' said Roper. 'I wondered if she tried to defend herself with it.'

'You're saying that someone else was concerned?'

'Suggesting, sir, that's all. What time did you get back from Dorchester, Mr Craven?'

Craven blinked. 'You saw me arrive here, for Christ's sake.'

'Yes, sir,' Roper agreed equably. 'So I did. But I meant the first time. When you made the 999 call for an ambulance to attend your wife.'

Craven's rising tumbler stopped an inch short of his mouth. 'Rubbish,' he retorted. 'I did no such thing.'

'The call was logged in at seven minutes past twelve, sir. The caller gave your name and telephone number.'

'Well, it bloody well wasn't me,' said Craven. He returned to his chair, but this time sat on the arm.

'So where were you, sir, at seven minutes past twelve?'

'Probably in the Cherry Tree,' said Craven. 'I stopped off for a drink.'

'And how far's the Cherry Tree from here?'

'About a mile,' said Craven. He jerked his head in the general direction of Dorchester.

'This pub have a public phone?'

'I wouldn't know,' said Craven. 'I've never had cause to ask.'

'Or perhaps you've got a car phone?' Because who was to say where that emergency call had in fact come from? Or, indeed, who had actually made it? For Craven to have come home, had a fight with his wife, perhaps even intended to kill her and made a hash of it, then swiftly driven along to the Cherry Tree in order to establish an alibi, could easily have been done in the few minutes between twelve o'clock, when Mrs Wicks had phoned, and seven minutes past when the emergency call had been made. And what publican ever knew to the minute what time a particular customer had walked into his bar?

'Yes, I do have a car phone, as a matter of fact. But I haven't used it for a week or more.'

'You didn't happen to use it between here and the Cherry Tree?'

'Now look,' retorted Craven, lifting his little finger from his tumbler and aiming it at Roper like a miniature pistol. 'Don't think I don't understand what you're bloody well implying. I had absolutely nothing to do with what happened out there to my wife.'

'I'm not suggesting you did, sir,' said Roper. 'But we don't think what happened was a straightforward accident. You see, the 999 call was made for an ambulance at seven minutes past twelve, and the caller was a man. So whoever he was, he must have known that something had happened here and therefore must have come inside the

141

house in order to find out. Sergeant Mallory didn't arrive here until twelve-twelve, so he couldn't have made the call, and you're telling us that you weren't here either.'

'And you suspect me.'

'No, sir,' said Roper. 'But from our point of view, as well as yours, it would be useful if we could eliminate you from any future enquiries.'

'It's quite simple, really,' said Craven, as if he were talking to a witless child. 'We simply wait for my wife to recover.'

'Yes, sir,' agreed Roper. 'So we can. But Mrs Craven might be unconscious for several days. The villain, if there was one, could be miles away by then.'

Craven, less rattled now at this appeal to his better nature, considered that at some length. He drained his tumbler, then set it on his knees, slowly rolling it back and forth between the palms of his hands. 'Yes,' he agreed at last. 'I do see what you mean. And it's possible I might know something. Something . . . well . . . disagreeable.'

'Disagreeable, sir?'

Craven sat for a few moments more like a man wrestling with his conscience, then said, 'I wonder if you and I might have five minutes alone, Superintendent. It's a private matter. I wouldn't ask otherwise.'

For the first time there was a note of solemn sincerity in his voice. Roper gave a nod to Makins, who rose and left the room. Mallory followed him and closed the door after them.

The tumbler continued to roll back and forth between Craven's hands. Then it stilled and Craven said abruptly: 'I think my wife has a lover. I have evidence. I wondered if it was him who called this morning.'

It sounded unlikely, but not impossible. But it did go some way to explaining Craven's lack of concern for his wife, if it were true.

'You say you have evidence, sir?'

Craven stood up and set his tumbler on the shelf above

the fireplace. He left the room, leaving the door open behind him. He returned, without his driving coat now and holding something that glittered in his hand. He closed the door quietly behind him and came across to where Roper sat. The something was a man's gold wristwatch on a black leather strap. He laid it across Roper's open palm.

'I found it on the shelf behind the shower curtain, one evening about three weeks ago,' he said. 'It certainly isn't mine.'

The watch was an Avia, with a gold bezel and a stainless steel back. It would not have come cheaply and whoever had left it here would certainly be missing it by now.

'Did you mention to your wife that you'd found it?'

'Hardly,' said Craven.

'And she never mentioned it to you, of course?'

'Of course,' said Craven. 'And if she had, it would have needed a hell of a story to convince me.'

Craven certainly sounded as if he was telling the truth, and if so it put an entirely different aspect on the matter of the attack on his wife. If there was another man then there might have been a lovers' quarrel and it might have been him who had made that first treble-nine call before hurriedly quitting the premises. And if that was what had happened it would be up to Mrs Craven to press charges when she recovered consciousness.

The telephone rang in the hall as Roper handed back the wristwatch. 'To be frank, sir,' he said, 'my sergeant and I were calling here to talk some more about Gerald Pope. I'd still like to do that, but perhaps later on this evening, if that's all right with you?'

Craven's mood changed immediately back to one of hostility. 'How many times do I have to tell you? I'd never heard of the bloody man until you called the other evening.'

'I think you had, sir,' said Roper, levering himself out of his armchair. 'How or why I don't know, but I intend to find out. Shall we say eight o'clock this evening?'

'Whatever time you like,' said Craven. 'But you can ask

me until you're blue in the face. I shall continue to tell you that I never knew him.'

There was a knock on the door. It was George Makins. The telephone call was from the hospital.

'They'd like a word with you, Mr Craven. They need to do some emergency surgery on your wife.'

'I'll see you at eight o'clock, Mr Craven,' said Roper. 'And if you do decide to go along to the hospital, I suggest you hire a minicab.'

'I intend to,' said Craven.

'Good, sir,' said Roper. 'I'll see you at eight o'clock.'

TWELVE

'OH, MY GOD!' EXCLAIMED MRS CHANCE, clapping both hands to her cheeks in horror when Roper broke the news to her. And it was news, that much was certain, because the best actress in the world could never have put on a display like that without a lot of rehearsals behind her. 'She's not dead, is she?'

'No, but she's concussed. They're carrying out emergency surgery on her now.'

Mrs Chance's hands had stayed at her cheeks, her eyes still huge.

'A car accident was it?'

'She was at home. It looked like a fall. We wondered if you might have had some kind of contact with her this morning. If you did, it would help us fix a time.'

Her dark eyes fixed him, narrowing, shrewd and hard suddenly. 'Time? Why should you want to fix a time? Martin's home today, isn't he? Why don't you ask him?'

'Mr Craven was out, Mrs Chance.'

Another expression briefly clouded her face. It looked singularly like suspicion, but passed so quickly that Roper couldn't be certain. Then she turned away to the wooden cigarette casket on the coffee table, flipped it open, stuffed a cigarette into her mouth and struck a lighter that had been standing on the shelf above the fireplace. With shaking hands she finally managed to bring the flame of one to the tip of the other. She took a couple of deep draws on the cigarette, then suddenly lifted her head and stared at Roper along her shoulder.

'There's something going on, isn't there?' she said. 'Or you wouldn't be here, would you? It wasn't an accident, was it?'

'We're not certain yet, Mrs Chance,' said Roper. 'But there's a possibility that someone else was in the house with Mrs Craven when it happened.'

'Like a burglar?'

'Even that, perhaps. Although according to Mr Craven nothing seems to be missing. When did you last see Mrs Craven, Mrs Chance?'

'Yesterday,' she said. 'The afternoon. We took a jaunt into Dorchester together.'

'Not today?'

'She phoned me about half-nine.'

'What did she have to say?'

'Nothing much. Just to say that Martin was at home today and we'd better call off our coffee date.'

'Mrs Craven have many friends?'

'Just me, I think. There isn't exactly a great social life in these parts.'

'How about male friends? Did she have any of those?'

She caught his drift quickly. 'A lover, you mean? No, I don't think so . . . Although . . .' She broke off, frowning and shaking her head. 'No, of course not . . . it's quite silly.'

'What's silly, Mrs Chance?' asked Roper, after a moment or so, when she seemed reluctant to continue.

'Look,' she said. 'It's probably nothing. Just something I've noticed.' And what Mrs Chance had noticed was that Mrs Craven had taken to driving out somewhere in the early afternoons two or three days a week.

'How long's that been going on?'

She shrugged. 'Oh, three or four weeks, I suppose.' Which was about the time Craven had found that wristwatch behind his shower curtain.

'But you never actually saw her with a man?'

'No,' she said. 'Never.'

'And she never dropped a hint that she might be seeing somebody?'

'No. She's not that sort.'

'But when we spoke the other day, Mrs Chance, you told us how well the Cravens got along together.'

'Well, yes,' she agreed. 'So far as I'm aware, they do. But whoever knows what goes on inside other people's heads? I'm sure she gets bored along there on her own sometimes – I get bored too. And I know for a fact that Martin works all the hours God ever made. At least I've always got someone to talk to here, even if it's only one of Nicholas's workmen coming into the yard to fill a bucket. Poor old Dagmar's got nobody.'

So perhaps there was some substance in that wristwatch and Craven's suspicions that it had been left behind by his wife's lover. But none of that was police business unless Mrs Craven succumbed to her injuries. If and when she recovered doubtless all would eventually be revealed.

Roper held back his last few questions, which were the prime purpose of his and Makins' visit to Downlands Farm, until the two of them were buttoning their raincoats preparatory to leaving. He dropped the first one casually.

'D'you happen to know if Mrs Craven's had a car accident during the last couple of years, Mrs Chance?'

She thought for a moment, then shook her head. 'No,' she said. 'If anyone's told you that they must be thinking of Martin. He certainly had one. Dagmar told me about it.'

'Happen to remember when it might have been?'

'About two years ago,' she said.

'Mrs Craven give you any details?'

'I don't think she knew any,' she said. 'Martin's car was suddenly left in the garage with its front dented, and he was using hers. Then he drove away with it one morning and the next day he'd got a new one.'

'What sort of car was it? D'you remember?'

'A Mercedes,' she said. 'They're all he ever drives.'

'How about the colour?'

147

'Sort of creamy-grey,' she said. 'Like the one he's got now.'

Dawn Bracewell, Mrs Craven's morning cleaning girl, was still nursing her atrocious cold. She lived with her widowed mother in a terraced cottage near the Hanging Man.

Dawn had last seen Mrs Craven at ten o'clock this morning, as near as she remembered. She had been to the village chemist to get something to ease the effects of her cold, then walked along to Furzecroft to collect her wages. She usually received them on a Thursday, but yesterday Mrs Craven had had no cash until she went to the bank in Dorchester in the afternoon. This morning she had given Dawn an extra pound, to compensate for her waiting overnight.

'But she's like that. Kind. You know.'

'Mr Craven in the house, was he?'

'He was going out. Went while I was there.'

She had not stayed long, ten minutes at most. She had heard Craven's car being driven away.

'You don't work Fridays then?'

'Do usually,' she said. 'But Mrs Craven rang me early and told me not to bother because Mr Craven was at home. He can't stand the noise of the vacuum cleaner.'

'How d'you get on with him?'

She wrinkled her raw, red nose. 'Don't see him much. Just Fridays sometimes.'

From the way she spoke, she appeared to have little liking for Martin Craven and reading between the lines it seemed that she had a great deal of sympathy with Mrs Craven for being married to him.

'But she is a bit dim,' she added. 'Just a bit. You know.'

'Dim?'

'Vague,' she explained. 'A bit helpless. You know. Although I expect he made her like that.'

'How come?'

'The way he talks to her all the time. Always putting her

148

down. Sort of arrogant, you know; like she was a bit of dirt under his feet. I can't think why she puts up with him.'

'Violent, is he?'

'Oh, yes,' she replied assuredly. 'He's got a temper all right.'

'I meant physically violent, Dawn,' said Roper. 'Towards Mrs Craven.'

'Oh, no,' she said, shaking her head as she was just about to bury her nose in a new paper handkerchief. 'I don't think he's *that* bad. Just a nasty piece of work. You know.'

'Ever hear them quarrelling?'

She blew her nose noisily. 'Sometimes,' she said. 'Like I said, he wasn't there all that much when I was.'

'How about this morning?'

'Doh,' she said. 'Dot this bording.' She sniffed horribly and cleared her throat. She plucked another tissue from her box ready for the next time. 'He didn't say anything when he went past us in the hall. Not even "see you later", or anything. He drinks a lot too. I know, 'cos I clean the glasses he leaves dirty on the sideboard – and I see the way the stuff in the bottles goes down from one day to the next. And I know it isn't her because all she drinks is coffee. Leastways, that's all *I've* ever seen her drink.'

Tasker Hobday sat over a half of bitter in the saloon bar of the Hanging Man. He rarely used the saloon – the beer was a couple of pence dearer in there than it was in the public – but he knew the detectives did and hoped they would again today. Because old Tasker was a man with much on his mind. There had been a lot going on in the village just lately, and more this morning, and he knew he'd seen what he'd seen and that somebody important ought to know about it.

'Think it's any of our business?' asked George Makins.

'Might be,' said Roper. 'Depends what Mrs Craven has to say when she's *compos mentis* again.'

The two of them sat by the fireplace in the saloon bar of the Hanging Man. It was coming up for half-past one. At quarter past they had called in at the Cherry Tree. The landlord recalled someone who fitted Craven's description, certainly his suede-topped tweed cap and his Mercedes, calling in at about five to twelve. He had ordered a double Scotch. A couple of minutes after Craven's arrival the landlord had had to go down to his cellar to see in his weekly delivery of draught beer. The delivery had taken about a quarter of an hour, during which time the barmaid who looked after the public bar had kept half an eye on the saloon bar through the serving-hatch between the two. Thus kept busy, she had not seen Craven leave the premises. The only certain thing was that when the landlord returned to the bar, at some time around ten past twelve, Craven was no longer sitting at the saloon bar counter.

Which proved nothing except that Martin Craven might have had the opportunity, and unless some evidence turned up to connect Mrs Craven's injuries with the murder of Gerry Pope, the affair along at Furzecroft was none of Roper's business, strictly speaking. Nevertheless the few enquiries that he and Makins had made had at least brought to light the fact that Martin Craven had been concerned in a traffic accident some two years ago, and at about the same time as Craven's first entry in Pope's red notebook.

'We've still got to prove the connection,' said Makins.

'Have faith, George,' said Roper, but Makins was right. Intuition was one thing, proof another, and those entries in Pope's book were proof of nothing, unless Craven could be forced in some way to make an admission. And he was only likely to do that if he was faced with some hard evidence.

'Excuse me, guv'nor,' a wheezy voice whispered at Roper's shoulder. 'You got a minute?'

Roper glanced up. It was a woolly-capped Tasker

150

Hobday, looking decidedly furtive.

'All the time in the world for you, Mr Hobday. Can I buy you a beer?'

Hobday shook his head, his eyes still flickering anxiously all around. 'I'll be out by the gents,' he whispered hoarsely. 'It's important.' And with that he waddled off towards the door to the car park.

After a puzzled glance at Makins, Roper went after him, but by way of the front door and the forecourt and then down the side of the building past a stack of empty beer crates. Hobday was lurking between the toilets and a white Ford transit van. He drew back out of sight when he was sure Roper had seen him.

'I don't want nobody to know I told you,' he whispered, when he and Roper were tucked well out of sight of the bar windows. 'Cause it might not be anything. But I saw something this morning, and Elsie was telling me about that Mrs Craven and about her having an accident and the ambulance coming for her and everything.' He glanced past Roper, then quickly behind him. 'Only I do Elsie's windows of a Friday. He didn't see me, of course.'

'Who didn't see you, Mr Hobday?'

'Mr Chance. Him that's got Downlands Farm. Cutting through the back of Elsie's garden, he was, like he didn't want anybody to see him. So I followed him a bit, and when he got to my hut he went round the back of it – I don't have windows at the back, see, then he went on past it towards Mr Craven's place. He was sort of creeping, like. Very suspicious I thought he looked. Then when Elsie came back from Dorchester she told me what had happened to Mrs Craven. I'm only putting two and two together, mind.'

'Remember what the time was, Mr Hobday?'

'No, I don't exactly. 'Bout ten minutes before Elsie went off to do her shopping, I suppose.'

'How far did you follow Mr Chance?'

'Not far. Couple o' hundred yards. I just wanted to make sure he wasn't going into my hut.'

'So you didn't actually see him go on to Mr Craven's property?'

'No,' said Hobday. 'Can't say I did. But it's suspicious though, eh?'

And perhaps it was. The time would have been about twelve o'clock, time enough and plenty for Chance to have got to the Cravens' bungalow, had a scuffle with Mrs Craven, telephoned the emergency services for an ambulance and been away again before Mrs Wicks and Sergeant Mallory had arrived on the scene. Why, and if, he had done so would remain a mystery until Mrs Craven recovered consciousness, but if that had been the actual scenario, then Mr Chance was going to be doing a lot of sweating over the next few hours.

'Did you see Mr Chance come back again?'

Hobday shook his head. 'Wasn't watching,' he said. 'Elsie'd asked me to get the windows finished before she came back. And I didn't think all that much of it until she did, and told me what had happened to Mrs Craven.'

'Have you seen Mr Chance go that way before?'

Hobday shook his head again. 'No,' he said. 'Never. That's why it struck me odd, see. I mean he really was creepin', like he was up to no good. Course, I could be wrong mind, and I don't want to make no trouble for anybody – that's why I didn't want to talk in the bar.'

'You did the right thing, Mr Hobday,' said Roper. 'Thanks for letting me know, and I'll keep it in mind. Just don't put it about to anybody else, though, eh?'

'Daren't,' said Hobday. 'I didn't even tell old Elsie.'

'Wise,' said Roper.

'What was all that about?' asked Makins, when Roper returned to the bar.

'The old boy saw Farmer Chance creeping through the bushes towards the Cravens' bungalow this morning. He reckons the time was about twelve o'clock. Might not mean anything, of course.'

'Reckon it does, though?'

'Let's hope Mrs Craven can tell us,' said Roper. He sipped at his beer and finished his roll, still mulling over what Hobday had told him and wondering if in the final analysis it would all lead back to the death of Gerry Pope. Martin Craven, whatever he said and however much he denied it, had surely known Pope. And from the signals his wife had sent out on Tuesday, she too had known Pope. Chance had sent out similar signals, and so had Hughie Lee. Which was a little clique of four people, all of them practically living on each other's doorsteps, who knew or were suspected of knowing a murder victim who had been killed within a quarter of a mile from where they each lived. And now, that very morning, one of those same people had become a victim herself and another had been spotted making tracks towards her property in circumstances that could only be described as suspicious. Why had Chance chosen to walk along beside the stream? If he had needed to see Mrs Craven on honest business why had he not simply walked or driven along the road and not skulked about in the shrubbery? The call for the ambulance had been made by a man. Which man? Nicholas Chance or Martin Craven? And supposing it had been made by Chance? Had it been Chance, too, who had inflicted those injuries on Mrs Craven? Had he intended to kill her? And if he had, then *why* had he?

Or had the caller been Craven himself? He had not been seen to remain at the Cherry Tree public house. Ergo: he had no alibi for the period in question. His lack of interest in accompanying his wife to the hospital had been callous to say the least. Had he intended to kill her, and botched it? Had he intended to kill her because of their common knowledge of Gerry Pope? Had she found out something about the events of last Monday night?

Hopefully Mrs Craven would recover, but until she did these questions would be part of life's great imponderables.

The only constructive move that Roper made during the course of the afternoon was to detail a WPC to sit outside Mrs Craven's room. She rang in at four o'clock to say that the emergency operation seemed to have been successful and that Mrs Craven's condition was being described as comfortable. Craven himself had put in an appearance at the hospital soon after one o'clock that afternoon and signed the obligatory consent papers. He had left soon afterwards and made no contact since. Some flowers had arrived in a florist's van at three forty-five. Their sender had been a Mrs Chance.

Roper treated himself to the rare luxury of an early dinner at home. He was back in the office at seven-thirty. According to a couple of notes on his message pad, Mrs Chance was telephoning the hospital every half hour to enquire as to Mrs Craven's condition. Craven had phoned only the once, at seven o'clock. Another message was from Dave Price. Mr Richard Bennett, owner of the initials RJB in Pope's notebook, was calling in at County for an interview at eight o'clock. Price would be conducting the interview in company with Chief Inspector Brake.

At ten to eight Roper and Makins were on their way back to Appleford.

Craven was no more amenable sober than he was with a couple of whiskies inside him. If anything, his denials that he had ever known Pope were even more vehement than they had been that morning.

'I insist on knowing what your damned game is,' he demanded. 'You keep calling here and asking the same bloody question over and over again.'

'It's no game, sir,' Roper assured him. He took from his briefcase the photocopy of Craven's page in Pope's notebook. 'I suggest you take a good look at this before you say any more.'

Craven all but snatched it from him. 'It's just a list of dates,' he said, having quickly scanned it and handing it back again.

'With your initials and telephone numbers at the top of the page, Mr Craven. Going to deny that too, are you, sir?'

'Of course I damned well don't,' snapped Craven. 'I'm simply saying I can't think how they got there or what connection I could possibly have with the man you say wrote them.'

'He was a police officer, sir,' said Roper. 'A sergeant. He was attached to the County's Traffic Division. He was mostly on motor-cycle duties, which means he was frequently operating alone.'

'And that should mean something to me, should it?'

'Yes, sir, I think it might,' said Roper. 'We've got two independent witnesses and one sworn testimony alleging that Sergeant Pope was guilty of a criminal offence, namely demanding money with menaces. They all concern hit and run accidents.'

'Good heavens, man,' blustered Craven. 'Do you think I could ever have been involved with one of *those*? I couldn't have lived with myself.'

Roper opened his briefcase again. This time he took out several photocopied sheets of an accident report.

'Gray's Lane, Mr Craven,' he said, reading the topmost sheet. 'It's a through-road between the southern end of the A351 and the A352. Ever used it?'

'I don't think I even know it. The other two roads you mention I use night and morning.'

'You work late?'

'I do,' said Craven. 'Eight or nine o'clock, sometimes later.'

'How about February twelve, nineteen-ninety, sir? Use them that night, did you?'

'My God,' exclaimed Craven exasperatedly. 'You surely can't expect me to remember that!'

'It might have been the only time in the last three years

155

you used Gray's Lane, sir,' said Roper, for whom Brake and his team had done a little more historical research during the course of the afternoon. 'It was a Monday, and the southbound carriageway of the A351 was subject to a diversion between ten o'clock and eleven-fifteen that night. An articulated lorry had shed its load. That ring any bells, does it, sir?'

And it did. It rang a thunderous peal, so loud that Roper could almost hear it himself. Craven had known all along what these persistent visits were all about, and he might go to his grave and continue to deny it, but he did know, his eyes said it, his body said it, but Roper wanted to hear it out of the man's mouth. If he was right, Martin Craven had killed a man called Sidney Manley, not a man in his prime but one with a dozen or more good years left to him. And really it was worse than that. There might, remotely, have been a chance for Manley, but, despicably, Craven had left him, worse in a way than cold-blooded murder because Craven had been left with an option and he'd chosen to ignore it.

'I've no idea what you're talking about,' said Craven, but too much time had passed between the question and the answer and Roper had been watching him so intently that he had almost been able to see Craven's mind working. Craven had killed Sidney Manley. He was lying and he would continue to lie. Men like Rubery and Weston had been unable to bear the weight of what they had done, and neither had poor Mrs Jobling. Craven could, and would, but one way or another Roper would have to find a way to drive him into a corner and wrestle the truth out of him. Mrs Chance had said that Craven's car had been involved in some kind of accident two years or so ago. The car in question had been sold on by Craven. Since, again according to Mrs Chance, the car had only been a few weeks old at the time, then it was reasonable to suppose that it was still on the road. It would be on record on the DVLA computer at Swansea. Given its registration

156

number and its present owner, it could be traced back to the day it first came out of its showroom.

But Craven, of course, and conveniently, could remember none of his cars' registration numbers except the one he was currently driving.

'But you always drive a Mercedes, sir. That right, is it?'

'For the last fifteen years, yes,' said Craven. The admission came grudgingly, and that the telephone out in the hallway should ring just then was clearly of overwhelming relief to him. 'I presume I can answer that?' he said.

'I don't see any reason why not, sir,' said Roper.

The conversation in the hallway was only brief. 'It's for you,' Craven said to Roper when he returned. 'A Detective Sergeant Rodgers.'

'Hello, Peter,' said Roper, out in the hallway. 'What have you got?'

'Just had a call from the WPC along at the hospital,' said Rodgers. 'Mrs Craven came out of the anaesthetic about half an hour ago. She's still a bit woosy, but she's just told the staff nurse she doesn't want Craven anywhere near her.'

'Did she say why?'

'Apparently not. But the staff nurse says she seems scared of him.'

'Can we interview her yet?'

'The doctor says he'd rather we didn't,' said Rodgers. 'He'd be happier if we could leave it until tomorrow.'

There could only be one reason, surely, why Mrs Craven did not want to see her husband. 'Get an overnight replacement for Docherty,' said Roper. 'I don't want anybody getting to Mrs Craven before we do. And if she does get a visitor I want the WPC sitting in with them. And thanks for letting me know.'

He returned to the sitting-room. Craven was still standing in front of the fireplace.

'That was a message from the police officer along at the

157

hospital, Mr Craven. I suggest you give them a ring.'

'She's not . . .?'

'No, sir. She seems to be sitting up and taking notice.'

'Good,' said Craven; which was not at all the reaction Roper had been expecting. 'Then if you've finished here – which I presume you have – I'll drive along to see her.'

'According to my information, sir, your wife has given instructions that she doesn't want to see you.'

Craven's eyes blazed angrily at him. 'That's your idea, isn't it? Don't think I didn't hear what you were muttering over the telephone out there. It's all part of this entrapment game you're trying to pull on me, isn't it? First Pope, then my wife. You're determined to get me for something, aren't you?'

'My job's to get at the truth, sir,' said Roper. 'One way or another, I'm certain you knew Gerald Pope and I'm determined to find out how and why.' He picked up his briefcase and buckled the flap. There was no more he could do here tonight, much as he would have liked to. And he was puzzled too over Craven's reaction to the news of his wife's recovery after her operation. The fact that Mrs Craven had barred her husband from visiting her in the hospital had led Roper to only one possible conclusion – which had been spiked only seconds afterwards by Craven's apparent unconcern that his wife would soon be fit enough to make a statement.

Craven had been watching him with narrowed eyes and a tightly set mouth. 'You haven't heard the last of this, mister,' he threatened. 'You've crossed swords with the wrong man.'

THIRTEEN

IT WAS RARE FOR THE ACC (Crime) still to be seated behind his raft of a desk at nine o'clock on a Friday evening. Martin Craven's retaliation had been swift. He must have telephoned the ACC within seconds of Roper and Makins leaving Furzecroft.

'He's complaining that you're harassing him, Douglas. That true?'

'Yes, sir, I'm harassing him,' agreed Roper. 'I'm sure Craven killed a man a couple of years back in a traffic accident. Pope knew about it and was blackmailing him.'

'What proof have we got?'

'Pope's notebook.'

The ACC wrinkled his nose disparagingly. 'Not enough.'

'We've managed to track down three similar instances, probably four. One of the drivers is spilling the beans to Dave Price and Charlie Brake right now. It's just a question of making Craven come up with the goods.'

'Perhaps there aren't any goods.'

'I'm pretty certain there are, sir,' said Roper. 'I think Craven could have met Pope at the Hanging Man in Appleford on Monday night. He might even have paid him, and the only reason Craven's dues weren't recorded in Pope's book was because Pope had left it behind at his lady friend's.'

'Still only wishful thinking on your part, Douglas; with the greatest respect.'

'According to Mrs Chance, Craven bent his car a couple of years back. He got it fixed and promptly sold it. And it was practically a brand-new car.'

'And this Mrs Chance, can she prove it?'

'I will,' said Roper. 'Eventually.'

'I admire your tenacity, Douglas,' said the ACC. 'Just take care, that's all.' His point made, he leaned back in his swivel-chair and stretched out his legs under his desk. 'How about Craven's wife? Any ideas about that one?'

'Not sure,' said Roper. 'Might have been Craven himself, although he's playing it pretty cool.'

'What about Hobday's sighting of Chance?'

'He didn't actually see him go on to Craven's property, more's the pity.'

'Why's it a pity?' asked the ACC, scowling.

'I think Chance knew Pope, too.'

'Too much thinking, Douglas, and not enough knowing,' said the ACC. 'I don't want to cramp your style, but I'd rather you kept clear of Craven until either his wife accuses him of attacking her or you get a clear-cut connection between him and Gerald Pope. And that's an order, Douglas. I'm sorry.'

With a plastic cup of coffee in his hand Roper stood at his office window and watched the rain sheeting down into the floodlit car park. A few minutes ago he had gone into the CID room and peeped through the Venetian blinds of Dave Price's office window. A haggard-looking Mr Richard Bennett, Pope's fourth victim, was still being interviewed.

But the man Roper wanted was Craven. Unlike Weston, Rubery, Mrs Jobling and Richard Bennett, everything pointed to the fact that Martin Craven had caused a death, perhaps two. And the only other person who had known about one of them was Gerald Pope. And Pope had run true to form and blackmailed him. If that connection could be proved beyond doubt then it was only a short step

160

thence to deducing that Pope and Craven had met in the car park of the Hanging Man last Monday night. And whoever had killed Pope must have known in which direction Pope would be travelling in the subsequent few minutes. That, really, was the nub of the whole business, that foreknowledge, that precision of timing.

And all that would be left lying in the sieve, bright and shiny as a gold nugget, was Martin Craven, whose meeting with Pope on Monday had not been recorded because Pope had left his notebook behind with Mrs Barr, and who must know that stretch of road as well as the face he shaved in the mirror each morning.

He turned away from the window as Price came in after a token rap on the door. Mr Bennett had bared his soul and was now on his way home.

'Get anything useful out of him?'

'Nothing we hadn't already guessed,' said Price.

In Bennett's case the victim had been an elderly man, the road a country lane a few miles south of Affpuddle, the time a few minutes after eleven o'clock at night. Bennett was a sales representative and had been dining a prospective client. He admitted to having drunk three glasses of hock and a brandy during the preceding three hours. He had also admitted that he had been travelling at some speed at the time. A few seconds before the accident he had noticed in his driving mirror that he was being hotly pursued by a motor-cycle with a flashing blue light. He had swiftly decelerated, glanced in his mirror again, glanced back through his windscreen and, to his horror, seen a man in a raincoat and holding a walking stick bathed in his headlights.

Bennett was still prepared to swear that he had only tapped the man and bowled him over. The police officer on the motor-cycle, a bearded sergeant, had diagnosed differently. After a brief examination of the victim he had told Bennett that he had killed him and that he was in a whole mess of trouble. As had Rubery, Bennett had

161

begged the sergeant to radio for an ambulance, just in case the man still had a chance, but the sergeant had retorted that it was too late for that and that he was going to throw every chapter and verse in the book at him, drunk in charge, reckless driving. Manslaughter too had been mentioned in passing.

Bennett, by this time deep in shock and frightened out of his wits, had desperately, foolishly – and criminally – offered the police officer the contents of his wallet, and to his immense relief the offer had been taken up. He was given thirty seconds to quit the scene. Which he did. So far as he had been aware the policeman had not even taken a note of his car's registration number.

But of course the sergeant had. A week later, late at night, Mr Bennett had received a telephone call. A problem had arisen. Another police officer, travelling in the opposite direction to Bennett, had stopped by the accident a few moments after Bennett had driven off. That officer had noted the make of Bennett's car as it had passed him and all three digits and two of the letters on his registration plates. So now there was somebody else to keep quiet. And, like Rubery, Mr Bennett had paid, and continued to pay.

'How much?' asked Roper.

'Eighty quid a month,' said Price. 'Pope put it up to a hundred last January. Said it was because of inflation.'

Bennett had made his last payment to Pope last Thursday, when Pope had monitored the telephone conversation they had had late in the afternoon – the conversation Roper and Makins had heard on Pope's answering machine. Bennett had paid Pope that night out of his firm's petty-cash box and replaced the money on Friday morning as soon as the banks had opened. Again like Rubery, Bennett had reached the point where he knew that his only way out of the cleft stick he had made for himself was to own up to causing the accident. Only in Bennett's case, he was determined to take the police

162

officer down with him; but all he had to identify him was the registration number of the motor-cycle the man was currently riding. Then, a couple of weeks ago, a friend of a friend of a friend – Bennett would admit to no more than that – had persuaded another friend who was a police officer to get Pope's name and address from the DVLA computer at Swansea. Such favours placed the offending officer's job on the line, but there were still a few who were prepared to take the chance.

The information on Pope had finally reached Bennett this last Wednesday morning. On that same evening, Price had telephoned him to tell him that Pope was dead, and only tonight had Bennett discovered that he had in fact killed no one.

'Where was he on Monday night?' asked Roper.

'Bristol,' said Price. 'He was entertaining a customer. Left there about ten past eleven. He says the man can vouch for him.'

So another potential suspect could be crossed off the list. If Bennett had been up in Bristol at eleven he could not possibly have been anywhere near Appleford for at least an hour after Pope had been murdered.

'Where did he meet Pope to pay him?'

'Pub car parks mostly. Always after dark. And when Pope left he always told Bennett to give him five minutes' start – or else.'

Which tallied so exactly with Rubery's account that it could only be the truth.

'Pope wasn't daft, Dave,' said Roper, when Price called into County late on Saturday morning to see if and how things were progressing, although the only likely progress that day was George Makins' questioning of Mrs Craven along at the hospital, and that was not going to take place until the late afternoon. It was Price's rest-day and he had only dropped in on the off-chance. In jeans and a floppy red pullover he was on his way to collect his two daughters

163

from their ballet lessons. 'He just squeezed them enough to get all the juice out and leave the pips behind.'

'He wasn't exactly getting rich on it though, was he?'

'We don't know what Craven was paying him yet, do we? A bloke who buys Gallé vases and hangs a genuine Lowry over his fireplace has probably got money coming out of his ears. Craven might even be where Pope's *real* money was coming from.'

'But can we prove it?'

'Not yet,' said Roper.

'Well, then,' said Price, impatiently hitching a shoulder. Price was not renowned for his spirit of optimism but rather his haste, which sometimes stifled his imagination. 'Craven's not the sort to come in here and confess, is he? You've got to remember, he could have *actually* killed somebody.'

'There's a way,' said Roper. 'There's got to be.'

The problem lay dormant for most of the afternoon, which Roper spent in Poole, not entirely stoically, trailing around the shops after his wife, Sheila, who always seemed to know precisely what she was looking for and was prepared to search even the unlikeliest nook and cranny for it. That day it was a suit of a specific grey and specific cut. It was almost three o'clock when she finally emerged triumphant from a fitting room with something completely different.

'That's not grey,' he grumbled. 'That's black.'

'I know,' she said. 'But it's a terrific bargain. It's been reduced.'

'To what?'

'Ninety-five.'

'Ye bloody gods,' he muttered. 'What the hell did it cost before? No, don't tell me.'

At four o'clock the question of Martin Craven shot to the surface again, unexpectedly and serendipitously propelled by the cheerful and bespectacled mother-figure of a waitress who came to take their order for afternoon tea. She had a South Midland accent that could only have been cut with a chain-saw. To Roper's recently attuned ear it sounded like music.

'And how about yow, sir?' she asked, ballpoint poised over her pad.

'What's all this about whisky-flavoured marmalade?' he asked, scanning the menu.

'It's roight,' she said. 'It's loovely. It's got real whisky in it. My 'ooby eats it boy the spoonful.'

'I'll try that, then, please,' he said. 'And a couple of slices of toast.'

'Roight,' she said, taking down his order with a couple of deft hieroglyphs.

'You sound as if you're from distant parts,' he said.

'Bromsgrove,' she said.

'Birmingham?'

'Yes,' she said. 'That's roight.'

With his newly sharpened interest he watched her flit back to the kitchen.

'What's the matter?' asked Sheila Roper.

'She comes from Birmingham.'

'So?'

'It's been happening all this week. I keep tripping over people who've either been to or come from Birmingham.'

'It's hardly the hind end of the world, is it?'

'Fancy eating out tonight?' he said, abruptly changing the subject.

'I thought you said we were broke.'

'I only meant buying-dresses broke. I didn't say we couldn't eat.'

'Beats the hell out of doing the washing-up,' she said.

Roper was showering when George Makins rang at six-thirty. Mrs Craven had spent the afternoon sleeping and Makins and a WDC had not been allowed into her room to see her until she had woken at six o'clock, and even then they had only been permitted to take a statement from her and not to question her.

'She says it was Craven,' said Makins. 'He came back just as she'd put the phone down on Mrs Wicks. She and him had a bit of a barney apparently. She'd asked him to collect some dry-cleaning in Dorchester and he'd forgotten. They exchanged words, she slapped his face, he gave her a shove and that's about all she remembers. He gets pretty violent sometimes, so she says.'

'How did the Gallé vase get smashed?'

'She didn't say, and I couldn't ask,' said Makins. 'She's still very vague about the whole business.'

'Pity,' said Roper. 'How about pressing charges?'

'She doesn't want to,' said Makins. 'She reckons it'd only make the situation worse. But she's still pretty firm about not letting him visit her, and she won't speak to him on the phone either. The only person she wants let in is Mrs Chance; she turned up about ten minutes ago with another truckload of flowers, but she didn't come in. What d'you want me to do now?'

'Nothing,' said Roper, bitterly disappointed. Craven seemed to be nimbly evading him at every turn. 'Except type up her statement and go home.'

The Blue Bird restaurant in Dorchester was a select little place, although as Sheila Roper observed trenchantly, after a searching examination of the menu, it might be *très chic* but it was also *très cher* into the bargain. The rear of the restaurant was a fake-Victorian orangery of glass, and what looked like lacey white ironwork but which was probably twentieth-century plastic. The tables were isolated from each other by trelliswork screens hung with flowering mimosas, and they were plastic too, but the food was good and the portions generous. Roper's taste-buds, however, were not at their most discerning because Mrs Barr was again on duty here tonight.

'Do you two know each other?' asked Sheila Roper, spiking up another sliver of sole meunière.

'Who's that?'

'That waitress. The dark one. She keeps on tossing you dark and meaningful glances.'

'She's Gerry Pope's late lady friend,' said Roper.

'Oh, I see,' she said shrewdly. 'And there was I thinking we were having a quiet Saturday night out for once. And all the time you've got your mind on business.'

'Not entirely,' he said. 'It depends how curious she is. If I'm lucky, she'll come across and ask how I'm getting on.'

'What if she doesn't?'

'Then we just pretend I haven't seen her.'

'So we're here by accident?'

'You've got it,' he said.

It was almost nine-thirty, and the two of them were on their cheese and crackers, when Mrs Barr could contain herself no longer.

'I do beg your pardon,' she said, a touch nervously, 'but I'm sure you were the gentleman I was talking to the other day – about Gerry. You're Mr Roper, aren't you?'

'That's right,' he said, smiling up at her with praiseworthy surprise. Her forename was Kathleen. She wore it on a blue plastic tag pinned to her dress. 'This is my wife.'

The two women exchanged hellos.

'I hope you don't mind my interrupting,' said Mrs Barr, still casting worried glances all round. 'But I was wondering how you were getting on. With Gerry's business, you know.'

'Not good,' he said. 'There's still too much we don't know. Like that trip he made to Birmingham, for instance. I thought you might be able to help us over that, but we didn't know where to find you.'

A customer caught her eye. 'I'm sorry,' she said. 'I have to go.'

'Two minutes,' he said. 'That's all I need.'

'I get a break in ten minutes,' she said. 'I'll try and come back.'

'We'll be here,' he said.

167

They finished their cheese and crackers, and dawdled over another coffee. It was almost ten to ten before she managed to get away and join them. Roper tried to persuade her to at least take a coffee with them, but apparently even sitting with the clients was a serious infringement of the house-rules and the manager had made this exception only because Mrs Barr had told him that the Ropers were people she had known in Birmingham, that they were passing through Dorchester and were never likely to meet up with her again.

'The day Gerry came to Birmingham. Can you remember exactly when it was?'

She frowned over that for a long time. 'No,' she admitted at last. 'I really can't. It was a few weeks after Christmas. That's all I remember.'

'How about the year?'

'The year before last. The year we moved out.'

'You said there was a yard opposite your café. It did car repairs.'

'Yes,' she said. 'There was.'

'Remember who owned it?'

'A man called Harry Pierce. He used to come into the café a lot.'

Roper took out his diary and noted the name. She was fairly certain it was Pierce, with an 'i', and not Pearce. She had only ever heard him called Harry, so his proper name was probably either Henry or Harold. She recalled the repair yard as always being a place of mystery. There was never a sign on the gates, and they were usually shut. Mr Barr had always suspected Pierce of being a crook. The police had called there on several occasions.

'When Gerry left the café you told me he crossed the road.'

'Yes,' she said. 'Then he just sort of disappeared. He went behind a lorry. I didn't see the going of him after that.'

That much, about a lorry, was new. All she'd suggested

last time was that Pope had more or less vanished into thin air.

'Perhaps he went off in the lorry?'

'Yes,' she agreed. 'He might have done at that.' To the best of her memory the lorry had been parked across the gates of the yard. The lorry – she vaguely recalled its colour as a scruffy pale blue – had called at the yard once or twice a week. She remembered the driver particularly.

'A sort of rag and bone man, he was,' she said. 'He used to drop in at the yard to collect their rubbish. Tyres and bits of old cars and things like that, you know. He used to call into the café too. I always used to fill a vacuum flask for him. Used to have a girl with him sometimes. Don't think we ever saw them after that.'

No, thought Roper, you wouldn't have, not if Gerry Pope had got to them. He still recalled how Hughie Lee's fingers had frozen over that matchbox when he had slipped Pope's name into the conversation. The Lees had been a spell in Birmingham too, brother and sister.

'Can you remember what the lorry driver looked like?'

'Just that he was dark and short. Not very talkative. Always paid in pennies and twopences, as if he'd had to go down his piggy-bank.'

'How about the girl?'

'Oh, honestly, I don't remember. I never saw her get out of the lorry.' Mrs Barr glanced fretfully down at her wristwatch. 'I really do have to get back to work now or the other waitresses'll be getting upset.'

'The lorry driver,' said Roper, as the last ray of hope shone brighter, reaching across to stay her with a hand over her wrist as she started to rise, 'could he have been a gipsy?'

'Yes,' she said, extricating her hand. 'Yes, I think he was. I really have to go now.'

'Satisfied?' Sheila Roper asked, as he slipped his diary back inside his jacket. 'That must be the most expensive interview you've ever conducted.'

'And worth every penny,' he said.

FOURTEEN

ON SUNDAY MORNING, CASUALLY DRESSED and alone, he drove out towards the village of Bloxworth and the northern perimeter of Wareham Forest. Some half-mile south of the village, he pulled in behind the Panda car that was waiting for him. Its young driver climbed out, carefully putting on his cap and squaring it.

Roper wound down his window. 'Constable Stokes, are you, son?'

'Yes, sir,' said Stokes, flinging up the kind of salute a man could only learn on a military parade ground. 'They're about two hundred yards further along the road. He's just come back from the village with the morning milk, so they're probably settled in for the day.'

'Behaving themselves, are they?'

'Good as gold, sir. Wouldn't know they were there. I think he's got a few snares scattered about, but I reckon it's best to leave well alone.'

'Too right, Constable,' said Roper, thinking what a pity it was that Sergeant Mallory hadn't done the same.

'They're behind those rhododendrons,' said the youthful Stokes, pointing. 'About thirty yards in. D'you want me to hang about, sir?'

'No,' said Roper. 'If Lee gets another whiff of a uniform he'll probably scuttle off again. But thanks, and well done.'

Stokes returned to his car. As he drove off, Roper climbed from his, closed and locked the door and started walking. The morning was a bracing one. There was still a

170

spring nip in the air but the sun was showing its face at last and the daffodils were beginning to open. He heard Annie Lee laughing long before he saw her. She was playing with a puppy, a fat little golden retriever that was skidding around on uncoordinated legs in pursuit of a ball she was rolling for it. On such a morning the scene was almost too idyllic to spoil and he waited at the edge of the clearing until she happened to look up and notice him. This time she showed no caution. She scooped up the puppy and brought it across to show it off to him.

"Ughie bought 'im for me,' she said proudly, pushing her nose down and affectionately nuzzling the puppy's velvety ears. 'It's my birthday present.'

'Got a name for him yet?' asked Roper, scratching under the puppy's appreciative chin. From the tail of his eye he saw Lee appear in the doorway of the coach.

'Sam,' she said. 'But when he's growed up I'll probably call 'im Samuel.'

'It's a good name, Sam,' he said. 'Nice and reliable.'

'It's bought,' said Lee, as he came down the steps. 'Bought legal. I've got a receipt.'

'I don't doubt it, Mr Lee,' said Roper.

'So what do you want this time?'

'Just a chat,' said Roper.

'About what?'

'Things in general,' said Roper, gently extracting a finger from between the puppy's playful but wickedly sharp teeth. 'Nothing you need to worry about.'

'Never leave us people alone, you lot, do you?'

'I'm not after you for anything, Hughie,' said Roper patiently. 'If I was, I'd have come here mob-handed.'

'How do I know you haven't?'

'Take a good look around,' said Roper.

But Lee didn't look anywhere. 'You'd better come inside,' he grumbled, already turning away.

Roper followed him up the wooden steps and into the coach. Lee sat down on the bagged-out sofa, Roper on the

171

chair at the end of the red-topped table.

'Cheroot?' said Roper, proffering his packet, as Lee reached out for his rubber tobacco pouch on the couch beside him.

Lee took one grudgingly, said nothing, and pushed his face forward as Roper struck his lighter.

'Got out of Appleford a bit sharpish, didn't you?' said Roper, around the cheroot he was lighting for himself.

'It was time to move on,' said Lee surlily, looking away.

'No, it wasn't,' said Roper.

Lee looked back again with his dark knowing eyes. Smoke surged angrily between his teeth. 'It were that Sergeant Mallory,' he said bitterly. 'He were scaring Annie. I'd have stayed put, but she don't like trouble. It upsets her.'

'How was he scaring her, Hughie?'

'I told you last time. Kept turning up nights and asking where I was. Two or three times, sometimes. As if he were after me for something. The other night he was sitting where you are now when I come back. Told me he'd 'ad a formal complaint about the mess we was makin'. Told me if I knew what was good for me I'd best move on or he'd slap a poachin' charge on me there an' then. An' he'd get somethin' called a place of safety order put on Annie, so's she could be put away somewhere. So I didn't argue. We just upped and went. Annie liked it back in Appleford an' all. An' that Mrs Wicks, she was a real good 'un. An' I was just gettin' a nice little gardenin' business goin' there. We weren't no trouble to nobody. It's always us the police come down on when something 'appens somewhere.'

'When was the last time?'

'Before we come down this way,' said Lee. 'Up in 'Ereford.'

'Get in trouble, did you?'

Lee raised his face and looked at Roper scornfully. 'I can't afford to get in trouble, can I? If I got put away there'd be nobody to look after Annie, would there be?

172

They took Annie in too. Kep' us there all night.'

'Can't lock you up without a reason, Hughie.'

Lee shook his head. 'There weren't no reason. Leastways, not a proper one. Annie found a little kid wanderin' about the trees near where we'd camped. About six, she were. Cryin' 'er eyes out. She were lost, see. Annie sorts 'er out – she's good with kids – an' this little girl says if Annie can show 'er the way back to the road she'll be all right, cause she knows the way from there. So Annie takes 'er out to the road, and this copper comes along in a car and asks what she's doin' with this kid – cause its mother's a neighbour of 'is and he's recognised 'er. Got very stroppy, 'e did, and o' course Annie's not very good at explaining things. Anyway, he takes the kid where she belongs in 'is car. A week later the kid went missin' again, only that time it were for good. An' they come to us first, don't they, and ask all these questions. And Annie, out the blue, says the little girl's gone for a swim in the river. An' that's where they found 'er next mornin'. Been dead several days, they said. So back they come to us and run us both in. Then, the *next* morning, some old bloke walks into the station and confesses 'e done it. So they 'ad to let us go, didn't they.'

'Fair circumstances, Hughie,' said Roper. 'Given those grounds, I might have run you both in myself.'

'Yeah ... well,' grumbled Lee. 'It don't matter what 'appens to us, do it? Just bloody gippoes, ain't we?'

'Where d'you come from before Hereford?'

'Birmingham,' said Lee.

'Police trouble again?'

'I weren't doin' anything illegal there either,' said Lee, letting smoke seep out from the side of his mouth. 'Our Daddy were alive then and he wouldn't have none o' that. Knock the shit out o' me he would've, old as he were.'

'So what were you doing?'

'Totting,' said Lee. 'Scrap metal mostly.'

'Cars?'

'Mostly cars. Some other stuff. Washboilers, all that. Lot o' copper in some o' those old washboilers.'

The girl had joined them, sitting on the floor in the doorway in the morning sunshine, still hugging her new toy. If she was listening it didn't show.

'Ever meet up with a bloke called Harry Pierce?'

Lee's eyes narrowed, weighing, measuring. 'I might have done.'

'Might or did?'

Lee stared hard back for another moment or two, then dropped his gaze to the cheroot he was rolling between a finger and thumb. 'Aye,' he said. 'I knew Harry Pierce.'

'Did crash repairs on motors.'

'Aye, he did. I used to pick up 'is scrap.'

'And that's where you met up with Sergeant Pope.'

Silence. A fly buzzed in the doorway.

'Come on, Hughie,' urged Roper. 'I sussed out you knew Pope the last time I sat here. All I want to know is how come.'

Lee took a long drag on his cheroot. 'He were a right bastard, that Pope,' he said.

'We were after him ourselves,' said Roper. 'Nobody likes bent coppers. Not even other coppers.'

Lee laid his wrist on his knee and contemplated his cheroot. The fly had come deeper into the coach and settled on the table.

'I'd just finished taking some stuff out of Harry Pierce's place,' said Lee. 'And he copped me. Told me to drive down the road a bit. Said I was in dead trouble.'

'Get in the cab with you, did he?'

'Aye, he did. I drove the lorry down the way and round the corner to a bit of waste ground. Then he climbed out and started going through the stuff in the back.'

'Did he find anything?'

'Aye, he did. A bumper, and a grill off a radiator. Really started coming on hard then, he did. Told me he was going to nick me for conspiracy.'

174

'Conspiracy with who? Harry Pierce?'

'He didn't say. Told me what he'd found was evidence of a serious accident somebody was trying to cover up. Told me I'd a lot of fast talking to do.'

'And you didn't know what he was talking about?'

'No. Course I bloody didn't. I was nearly wetting my bloody self, wasn't I?' Lee's hand rose and he took another draw on his cheroot. The hand was shaky now, probably in anger. Pope had obviously put the skids under Lee so hard that he'd never forgotten it.

'So what happened? He obviously didn't nick you.'

Lee picked up a glass ashtray that was sitting beside him. He held it out for Roper to tap the ash from his cheroot. 'He calmed down. If I played my cards right, he said, he could probably keep my name out of it. Then he took a picture. He laid the stuff he'd sorted out on the ground and took a couple of pictures. I just stood there. Then he asked me if I'd got any spanners.'

'Why spanners?'

'He wanted the number plate, the one on the fender. Said he wanted to take it away with him. Evidence, he said it was. Got me to unbolt it for 'im. Wrapped it up in a newspaper he'd got. Then he told me to sod off, and if he ever saw my face or the lorry in that part of Birmingham again I'd wish I'd never been born.'

'Did you tell Harry Pierce all this?'

'Not bloody likely,' said Lee. 'I never went back there again. Did what I was told, didn't I? Never did like trouble.'

'No chance you'd remember the details on the plate, I suppose?'

'Yeah, I do,' said Lee. 'I wrote it down, didn't I. In case he tried to fix something else on me.'

Which was more than Roper had ever dared to expect. 'Still got it?' he asked, feeling some adrenaline flowing at last.

Lee leaned forward between his knees and felt about

under the sofa. His left hand reappeared holding an old red Oxo tin. He prised the lid off, leafed through the untidy wad of papers inside and finally sorted out a creased scrap that looked as if it had been torn from the corner of an old brown paper bag. He passed it across to Roper.

'Can I keep this?'

'Not likely,' said Lee. 'It's all I've got.'

Roper copied the registration number into his pocketbook. The year letter was exactly right. 'Did you see the car it had come from?'

'It were a Merc. Harry and his lad were working on it in the shed at the back.'

'How about the colour?'

'Don't remember. Except it was light. Might've been grey.'

Mrs Chance had said creamy-grey, but descriptions didn't come much closer than that.

'And when did all this happen?'

'A couple of years back,' said Lee. 'A couple of months after Christmas I s'pose it was.'

'Pope tell you his name, did he?'

'Detective Sergeant Pope, he said he was. Said he was Birmingham CID. Flashed a card at me like that one o' yours. Got his picture on it an' everything.'

'Ever see him again?'

'Twice,' said Lee. 'Three times if you count the other night. Except I didn't recognise 'im that time.'

Roper felt the hairs rise on the backs of his hands.

'Tell me about the twice, Hughie. Lately, was it?'

The first time had been in Dorchester. About a month back. Pope had been with a dark-haired woman, the two of them standing at a bus stop. Lee had recognised him at once. He had half-recognised the woman too.

' – Sure I'd seen 'er before somewhere.'

'You probably did,' said Roper. 'She and her husband used to run the café opposite Harry Pierce's place.'

'Bloody 'ell, so she did. How did you know that?'

176

'Not a sparrow falls, Hughie,' said Roper. 'How about the second time you saw him?'

'Down at Appleford. On the heath. Week before last. An afternoon. Tuesday, I think. He was bird-watching.'

'What makes you think he was bird-watching?'

'He had these binoculars. Big ones. And a camera with a socking great tube on the front. And he was wearing one o' those army camouflage jackets.'

'Whereabouts was he on the heath?'

'About a quarter-mile from where we used to be. Near that posh bungalow place. 'Im and 'is motor-bike were tucked in the bushes. 'E were lying down. I almost tripped over the bugger.'

'Sure it was him?'

'Definite,' said Lee. 'I stood within a yard of 'im, and 'e looked up at me. Same bloke, same beard, same everything. I carry 'im about,' he tapped his temple, 'in 'ere. I don't think he recognised me, but then he wouldn't have the need, would 'e? But I remember 'im, though. Always bloody will.'

'Which way was he looking?'

'Facing the road. Towards the bungalow.'

Knowing what he did now about Gerry Pope, Roper considered him an unlikely bird-watcher. Pope had been, amongst other dubious endeavours, a private investigator and what private investigators spent most of their time doing was watching not their little feathered friends but other people, erring wives, wayward husbands. Pope had had his binoculars trained not on some thing but some body. And the only bungalow along that stretch of road was Martin Craven's. So Pope had probably been watching Furzecroft. And there had to be a reason for that.

Lee walked back to the road with him, his sister following, still cuddling her puppy.

As they reached the edge of the trees and came out into the sunlight, Lee muttered softly, 'Can you do something for us now?'

'If I can,' said Roper. 'It depends.'

Lee jerked his head in the direction of his sister who had stopped a couple of yards behind them. 'She keeps asking if we can go back to Appleford. She was real settled in there. It were only that Mallory.'

'It's not up to me to say, Hughie,' said Roper. 'And Sergeant Mallory's got a job to do. But unless you misbehave yourself, he won't be paying calls on you any more. I can promise you that much. Just keep your rubbish to yourself and don't let him catch you setting snares. All right?'

Lee nodded.

'Good,' said Roper. He turned to go, but then turned back again. He tugged out his wallet from his hip pocket and took out a ten pound note.

Lee declined to take it. 'Don't need charity,' he said. 'It's not my style.'

'It's not for you, it's for the dog. He needs a collar and a lead.'

"E wants a red one,' Annie Lee chipped in. "E told me.'

'A red one'd do nicely,' said Roper.

'She 'as to give you something for it,' said Lee. 'It's the way.'

Annie Lee felt around the pockets of her jeans. Finding them empty, apart from a crumpled linen handkerchief, she settled for a grip from her hair. Roper took it as solemnly as it was offered and clipped it down the fold of his wallet. 'Thank you,' he said.

There was a long silence while the girl continued to regard him with her dark and lustrous eyes. Whatever kind of muddle her mind was in, her eyes were as wise and as old as time. 'Whatever it is you're lookin' for,' she said, 'it's near where water is. Just you remember that.'

'Yes, I shall, Annie,' he said. 'Thank you.'

She watched him all the way back to his car, and the three-point turn he made in the narrow lane, and as he drove away and glanced into his mirror he saw her receding image still standing there.

At midday he had reverted to a smart suit and was back behind his desk at County Headquarters. A uniformed and surly Sergeant Mallory was sitting across the desk from him, George Makins was in the CID room checking up on the present whereabouts of the car that Martin Craven had had repaired up in Birmingham, and Chief Inspector Brake, who had been enjoying a quiet and sunny Sunday working in his garden when Roper had phoned him, would be back here on duty within the hour.

' – So you're denying all this, are you, Sergeant?' Roper asked tartly.

'Yes, sir,' replied Mallory. 'I was just following up complaints, like I'm supposed to do.'

'Who complained?'

'Several people, sir.'

'And you logged all these complaints, of course. And all the visits you made to the Lees.'

Mallory shifted uncomfortably in his chair, but didn't answer.

'So you didn't?'

'No, sir. Not exactly,' Mallory conceded at last. 'They didn't seem worth the paperwork. And Lee's lying. I never said I'd have his sister put away.'

'Yes, you did,' said Roper. 'You talked about a place of safety order. Lee's not the sort to pick up jargon like that out of the air. It could only have come from you.'

'If you're going to believe –'

'The truth, Sergeant. Or I'm logging this conversation in your pocket-book – in which case those stripes could be off your arm in about half the time it took to sew 'em on.'

'There was a lot of talk in the village.'

'I'm not interested in gossip, Sergeant. I want to hear about the complaints.'

179

'There was just the one,' Mallory finally admitted sullenly.

'From?'

'Mr Chance. I met Mrs Chance in the village last Tuesday afternoon, late. She told me her husband wanted to see me about all the rubbish that was getting blown over into his land from the Lees' place. I told her I'd see to it.'

'Did you see all this rubbish for yourself?'

'No, sir. I just took his word for it. And the Lees did leave two sacks of garbage behind when they decamped.'

'Perhaps you didn't give 'em time to get rid of 'em.'

Mallory shrugged. 'Perhaps not.'

'You've stopped a man earning his crust, Sergeant.'

'He was rabbiting on the heath.'

'You want to stop him feeding himself too?'

'No, sir.'

'Then just do your job,' said Roper. 'And if I get just the slightest puff of wind that you aren't treating somebody right I'll be down on you like a ton of bloody bricks. Do we understand each other?'

Mallory spent a moment more in sullen reflection. 'Yes, sir,' he said.

'Back to work then, Sergeant,' said Roper. 'I'm already investigating one dodgy copper and I don't want to find myself investigating another one. It's bad for morale.'

'Yes, sir,' agreed Mallory, looking relieved now that he had got off so lightly. He rose, his cap in one hand, and moved his chair back to the marks in the carpet where it had been.

'And I don't carry grudges, Sergeant,' said Roper, as a parting shot. 'So unless you put it about yourself, this conversation hasn't happened.'

'Thank you, sir,' said Mallory. He turned towards the door and as he went out Makins was standing aside for him in the passage with his notepad in his hand.

'Any luck, George?' asked Roper, as Makins came in.

'I think we've scored,' said Makins. 'I managed to track

180

down the current owner of Craven's old Merc. Name of Watson. Lives in Brierley Hill, near Birmingham. He bought it off a secondhand dealer in Walsall a couple of days after Craven dropped it into the showroom. And he knows for certain it was *our* Craven because he had the nous to photocopy the vehicle transfer document before he sent the original off to the DVLA. He's taking the photocopy to his nearest nick. I've phoned them and they'll fax it down to us as soon as Watson turns up.'

'Brilliant,' said Roper.

'It gets better,' said Makins, with more enthusiasm than he had shown in several days. 'Watson's a motor-mechanic with his own business. He'd had the car about a week and thought the exhaust was getting a bit noisy. So he put it up on his hydraulic lift and had a poke about underneath. He found the silencer box had a bloody great dent underneath it and the front end plate was coming adrift – as if it had been driven over something.'

And that still wasn't all. Mr Watson had replaced the damaged exhaust himself. And he had found, snagged up on one of the brackets he had had to unscrew in order to remove the original pipe, a short strip of partially charred navy-blue cloth with a metal buckle stitched into one end. From the description Watson had given, Makins had drawn the conclusion that the navy-blue strip might have been the wrist strap of a waterproof trenchcoat.

And what, among other things, the late Mr Sidney Arthur Manley had been wearing on the night he had become an accident statistic, had been a brand-new navy-blue trenchcoat, with wrist straps, one of which, according to the mortuary records, had been torn away. And it had not been found at the scene of the accident.

'Watson prepared to swear to this in court?'

'All of it,' said Makins.

FIFTEEN

MAKINS PULLED ON HIS HANDBRAKE outside Furzecroft and Brake's white Land Rover pulled in close behind him on the grass verge. It was two o'clock on the same Sunday afternoon. The fax from Mr Watson had landed on Roper's desk soon after one o'clock, Brake had been briefed on the unexpected turn of events by half-past, and the ACC, so reluctant yesterday to pursue Martin Craven but faced today with such a weight of evidence against him, had not only withdrawn his decree but given his blessing.

Craven was still in his dressing gown, his hair awry. What seemed to cause him most consternation was Brake's uniform and the array of metal stars on his shoulder-boards, plus the beefy, uniformed sergeant who was accompanying him. Roper effected the introductions.

'It's about my wife, I take it?'

'No, sir,' said Brake. 'I'm from County Traffic Division. I think you might be able to help us with certain enquiries we're making.' As Makins remarked later, if it hadn't been for the floor stopping it, Craven's jaw would have dropped from sight. To give the man his due though, one had to be quick to notice it. 'It was a road accident, sir. A fatal one. Couple of years back.'

'Then I know nothing about it,' said Craven. 'Sorry.' He tried to smile. It came out glassy, as if his dentist had his fingers hooked in his mouth.

'We've got some new evidence, sir,' said Roper. 'We'd

like to talk about it. We'll wait for you to get dressed if you like and we can do it over at County Headquarters. It's up to you, sir.'

But a visit to County was clearly the last thing Craven wanted.

'It can't wait till tomorrow?'

'No, sir,' said Brake.

Craven led them into his sitting-room. In the two days since his wife had gone into hospital he had managed to turn it into a tip. A lesser mortal would have apologised for the mess, but Craven wasn't that sort. All he did was to gather up several days' supply of newspapers from the chairs and dump them on the coffee table amongst the other detritus of dirty plates and mugs and glasses. Prominent on the table was an empty Scotch bottle with its cap off.

'I presume my name has been put forward by mistake as a witness,' he said, remaining standing as the others arranged themselves in the spaces he had cleared.

No one answered. Brake made a stagey business of opening his briefcase and picking through the papers inside it, finally extracting one.

'You are Martin Ryall Craven are you, sir?' asked Brake. Makins had gleaned Craven's middle name from the faxed vehicle transfer form. Brake had spoken it as if he'd been reading it straight from the accident report on his lap.

'I am,' said Craven. 'Now look –'

'If you'd just bear with us, sir,' said Roper, cutting in.

'The accident was a couple of miles west of Wareham, sir,' said Brake, reading now. 'February twelve, nineteen-ninety. About ten-thirty at night. The victim was a Sidney Arthur Manley. He was found to be dead on arrival at the hospital.'

Craven said nothing this time, his hands fidgeting in the pockets of his dressing gown.

'We've reason to believe the car was a grey Mercedes, sir,' said Brake. 'And you drive one of those, don't you, Mr Craven?'

'Now I do,' said Craven.

'And *then*, sir,' said Roper. 'You've driven a Mercedes for years. You told me so yourself.'

'You're trying to say the car that knocked him down was mine?' Craven's outrage was no more successful than his earlier glassy smile had been. 'My God, how preposterous.'

'We've also managed to track down the vehicle in question, sir,' Brake pressed on resolutely. 'It was purchased from a secondhand dealer in Walsall shortly after the accident. A couple of weeks after the current owner bought it, he had cause to look at the exhaust. There was a strap from Mr Manley's raincoat sleeve caught up in one of the exhaust brackets. The gentleman in question is prepared to testify to that in court.'

'And you're still saying it was my car?'

Brake brought the fax of the vehicle transfer form out of his briefcase. He held it out. Craven stepped forward and took it and tilted it towards the window.

'But you've only got this fellow's word, for Christ's sake.'

'No sir, we've got more than that,' said Roper, which all but stopped Craven in his tracks there and then. 'Sergeant Pope took a number of photographs –'

'Who the hell's Sergeant Pope?'

'We've already been through all that, Mr Craven,' replied Roper.

'Photographs of what, exactly?' retorted Craven. But it was only empty bluster now.

'Parts of that same Mercedes, Mr Craven. A front fender, complete with registration plate, and radiator grill. Pope laid them out on some waste land just around the corner from Harry Pierce's yard and took photographs. He also took the number plate away with him. You do know who Harry Pierce is, don't you, sir?'

Even now it was still only a shade short of a longshot, and if Craven denied it the way he had denied everything else so far there wouldn't be a cat's chance in hell of ever really proving it. For the next few minutes everything hinged on bluff, not on what Roper and Brake knew but what Craven was led into believing they did. But already he was showing what in the lingua franca of the interview room were known as the buy-signs: from the shape of his dressing-gown pockets his hands were bunched into tight fists, his face was beginning to look sweaty and his hitherto cold and penetrating stare had lost a lot of its voltage.

'Yes,' he said, hanging his head. 'It was Pierce I went to.'

'Thank you, Mr Craven,' said Roper.

'Does anyone have a cigarette?' asked Craven, after Brake had formally cautioned him. In the last couple of minutes Craven had become grim and drawn, all his old arrogance gone. Roper almost felt sorry for him, except that a few years ago Craven had run a man down in his car and hadn't had the guts to stay and help him.

Only Brake had any cigarettes. Craven scrabbled one clumsily from the pack and Brake struck his lighter for him.

For a while the stage was Brake's. Craven still recalled the accident with exceptional clarity; like Pope's other victims, now that he had been cornered, he was desperate to get it all off his chest, right down to the minutest detail. He admitted that he had been drinking for most of the afternoon prior to the accident and had been in no state to be driving at all. He even recalled the woman walking her dog, and swerving hard to avoid her. A few seconds later he had struck and run over Manley.

'I stopped. I got out. All one side of his face – God, it was horrible . . . I couldn't think what to do . . . I thought he was dead . . . Then I saw his fingers moving . . . and he started to make noises, words, I suppose, but he couldn't get them out.' Cigarette ash fell on Craven's lap but he was too absorbed in telling his story to notice it. 'I knew my chances were nil so far as the law was concerned, not in the state I was in. And I thought if I called an ambulance I could get away before it arrived. Which I did. I used a phone box a half-mile or so down the road. I didn't give my name of course.'

'Any idea what speed you were doing when you hit Mr Manley, sir?'

'None,' said Craven. 'Forty or fifty, probably.'

'About eighty,' corrected Brake. 'We measured the skid marks.'

'I'm sorry,' said Craven.

'Bit late for that now, isn't it, sir,' said Brake.

Some time had passed. With the yellow-covered Accident Report book resting on the arm of his chair, Craven had drawn a sketch of the scene as he remembered it and then written in his own words his account of the accident. When he had finished, he signed his name at the end of his account with a tired flourish, together with that day's date. He passed the book and ballpoint pen over to Brake, who countersigned it under Craven's signature. Brake's sergeant did the same.

'Who put you on to Harry Pierce, Mr Craven?' asked Roper.

'A colleague in the City,' said Craven. 'I told him I wanted some bodywork repairs done by someone who wouldn't ask too many questions.'

'And Pope? How did he come into all this?'

'Apparently he passed me as I was driving away from the accident and he was on his way to it. He noted my number. I didn't know that at the time, of course. I did remember seeing a policeman on a motor-cycle but we passed each other so quickly I didn't think he'd noticed me.

'Two or three days went by, I used my wife's car in the meantime, then my contact rang me and said this chap in Birmingham would do the job for me, but it was strictly cash on the nail, and if I got the car into his workshop by nine o'clock in the morning I could collect it at lunchtime.

I said okay.'

'How much?' asked Roper.

'Fifteen hundred,' said Craven. 'And that included all the damaged parts going to a crusher.'

'You didn't ask him to look under the car?'

'I didn't think of it.'

For a few days after the trip to Birmingham, Craven had thought that he had got away with it. Then, late one night, he had received a phone call from a man who had given no name. He had claimed to be a police officer who was investigating the death of a Mr Sidney Arthur Manley. He had also claimed to be in possession of the crumpled registration plate of Craven's Mercedes. Worse was to come. The man had then gone on to tell Craven that a laboratory examination of the plate had revealed traces of blood that were identical with Manley's, incontrovertible proof, in fact, that the victim had been run down by Mr Craven's car; but if Craven would meet him the next day there might yet be a way of Mr Craven keeping himself out of a whole mess of trouble.

They had met in a pub in the City at lunchtime on the following day. Craven, as arranged, had been wearing a grey suit and had carried a copy of *The Independent* tucked under his arm. The other man, darkly bearded, had been wearing a black leather bomber jacket and jeans and been carrying under his arm a long slim parcel wrapped in brown paper.

The brown paper parcel had contained the number plate.

'He told me there was another man involved, someone at the laboratory who was still holding back on the paperwork. And if I could come up with a reasonable amount of cash, the paperwork could be lost from the system as easily as the number plate.'

'How much?' asked Roper.

'Two thousand,' said Craven. 'Cash. He waited outside the bank while I drew it out.'

'And you still didn't know who he was?'

'I asked him for some kind of proof that he was what he said he was. He showed me a police identity-card. Kept his thumb over his name of course. But I saw the crest on it and knew he was from down here.'

Once again, Craven had thought that that had been the end of it. But of course it had not. A month later he had been summoned to another meeting with the bearded man. The technician at the Forensic Laboratory had been proving difficult. He wanted more money. He still had the paperwork in his possession and intended keeping it, and naturally there was a price for his silence.

'How much?' asked Roper, yet again.

'Six hundred,' said Craven. 'A month.'

'The price ever go up?'

'No,' said Craven. 'It stayed at six. Any more and I couldn't have paid it. I told him that.'

'When did you make the last payment?'

'Monday,' said Craven.

'In the car park at the Hanging Man?'

'Yes,' said Craven. 'I drew the six hundred out of the bank at lunchtime. But stupidly I'd spent a fair bit before I came down from London, and all I had to give him was five hundred and a few. He told me that if he didn't get the other hundred by Friday he'd cut my legs from under me. And the price would be going up too.'

It all fitted in too well with the rest of the Pope saga to be anything but the truth. Pope had glimpsed Craven driving past him a few minutes after he had run down Manley, remembered Craven's car number and put two and two together. It would have been easy for him, using his authority as a traffic-sergeant, to obtain Craven's name and address from the DVLA computer over at Swansea on some pretext or other, suspected stolen vehicle or something of that sort. He might have spent a few days then watching Craven's house, might even have taken official leave in order to be able to do so. In any event, he had certainly followed Craven to Birmingham, sat in Mrs Barr's café for three hours until he had seen Hughie Lee about to drive off with Pierce's weekly load of scrap, then rushed off to beard Lee and unbolt Craven's old registration plate. It could be said that Pope's pursuit of Craven had used up a lot of luck; but, on the other hand, when Pope had been a police officer, no one had ever complained of his lack of diligence.

'What did you do with the registration plate, Mr Craven?' asked George Makins.

'I hid it in the garage,' said Craven, lamely. 'I couldn't think what else to do with it.'

A more practical man than Craven would have cut it into little pieces with a hacksaw. Roper and Brake stood by in Craven's garage as, still in his dressing gown, he opened a step-ladder between his wife's car and his own, climbed it, reached up and took down a brown paper package that was tucked behind a rafter. He blew the dust off it before bringing it down and giving it to Brake. Brake ripped the paper away from one end.

It was the registration plate, still buckled after its impact with Sidney Manley.

'Did you kill Pope on Monday night, Mr Craven?' asked Roper.

'No,' said Craven, flicking dust from the ladder off the skirt of his black dressing gown. 'I thought about it often enough, but I didn't.'

'What time did you arrive at the Hanging Man on Monday?' asked Roper, when they had returned to the house and seated themselves again.

'I couldn't tell you,' said Craven. 'Not exactly. Shortly before eleven, I suppose.'

'And Pope was already there, was he?'

'He always was.'

'And the Hanging Man was your usual rendezvous, was it?'

'No, not always. But it was always a car park somewhere.

189

The time before last it was a multi-storey car park in Dorchester. He always fixed the venues. Used to ring me at the office to tell me where to go. The second Monday in the month.'

'How about the time?'

'Ten forty-five.'

'Always?'

'Regular as clockwork. Monday was the first time I'd ever been a few minutes late. He was as foul-mouthed over that as he was that I hadn't brought all the cash.'

'Who left the car park first, you or him?'

'I did,' said Craven.

Roper lifted an eyebrow at that. According to Rubery and Bennett it was always Pope who had quit the scene first.

'And that was a regular thing too, was it?'

Craven shook his head. 'No,' he said. 'That was the first time he told me to go first. Usually I had to give him five minutes' start.'

'So on Monday you could have lain in wait for him afterwards.'

'I could have, but I didn't know which way he'd be going, did I?'

'How long d'you reckon you were in the car park with him?'

Craven shrugged. 'Minutes. Five, perhaps.'

'So you could have been back here in the house soon after eleven?'

'Must have been,' said Craven. 'My wife was in bed when I got home, but she may have heard me come in.'

'If she was in bed, you could have gone out again without her hearing you.'

'But I didn't,' said Craven. 'As soon as I came in I switched on the television to watch the late news. I watched that for a while, fell asleep on the settee, woke about one o'clock the next morning and climbed into bed.'

'Not much of an alibi, is it, sir?'

'Do I need one?'

'Very much so, sir,' said Roper. 'Since you were probably the last person to see Pope alive. And you more or less told us just now that you and him had had a bit of a barney.'

'I couldn't have done it,' said Craven.

'Why not?'

'Because I was too bloody drunk to kill anybody,' confessed Craven. 'I got well boozed up in Town before I got on the train. That's why I didn't have all the money for Pope. I could still hardly stand up when I put the car away. That's why I didn't go to bed as soon as I got in. It would only have started another bloody row.'

'Quarrel a lot, do you, sir, you and your wife?'

'Is that any of your bloody business?'

'Under the present circumstances, yes, sir.'

'Yes,' agreed Craven tiredly. 'We quarrel. We don't talk much but when we do it's usually to have a blazing row.'

'They ever get physical, sir, these rows?'

'No,' said Craven, with a brisk shake of his head. 'Never.'

'How about last Friday morning?'

'I've already told you. I wasn't here when that happened. You can check with the landlord of the Cherry Tree.'

'We did, sir,' said Roper. 'He remembers seeing you arrive, but not leaving.'

'There was a woman behind the bar . . .' Craven recalled hopefully.

'She didn't see you leave either, Mr Craven,' Roper said flatly. 'And yesterday evening, Sergeant Makins here took a statement from your wife. You'll be glad to know she's not pressing charges against you.'

'Charges about what?' asked Craven, blinking vaguely and generally looking bewildered. Which caused Roper his first grave doubts. Last Friday lunchtime, when Craven had faced Roper over his wife's unconscious body, Roper had been certain that Craven had been conducting a master-class in bluffing. Now he was not so sure. 'For

191

God's sake, you don't really think I did *that*, do you?'

'Your wife says you did.'

'She's lying,' retorted Craven. 'She's *bloody* lying!'

'It would be difficult for her to lie, Mr Craven,' said Roper. 'She knows to within a couple of minutes when you attacked her. She'd just put the phone down on Mrs Wicks. And those are the couple of minutes you can't account for, if you see my point, sir. What I'm saying is, Mrs Craven couldn't possibly have known that you didn't have an alibi for the few minutes either side of the incident, so she must have seen you, mustn't she?'

'Somebody could have told her I turned up here shortly afterwards,' Craven suggested angrily.

'Your wife had had no visitors before I spoke to her yesterday, sir,' said Makins. 'Made no phone calls, and her only contact with the outside world has been through the nurses. And the only message they were told to pass on was that your wife didn't want to see you. Other than telling you her state of health, of course.'

Craven's anger subsided as quickly as it had risen. Now he looked only puzzled and bewildered again.

'I swear,' he said, looking bleakly across at Roper. 'I swear, I have never – *ever* – hit my wife. And if she says I have, then she's lying.'

'Somebody did, sir,' Roper reminded him.

'Not me,' said Craven. 'I swear to God it wasn't me.'

And Roper, listening and watching for Craven's every nuance and change of expression, was almost tempted to believe him. But if Craven was telling the truth, then it would have to follow that his wife had lied to Makins when she had talked to him at the hospital last night. She might have lied out of spite, of course. Alternatively, wild idea though it was, she might have been lying in order to shield the real culprit.

Like her lover . . .?

'When I was here the other day, Mr Craven, you mentioned you suspected that your wife had a man friend.'

'I don't suspect,' said Craven. 'I know.'

'On the strength of the wristwatch you found, or d'you have anything else to go on?'

'The wristwatch was the second thing; I've never told my wife about that. A couple of weeks before that I found a pair of gloves. My wife said they were Mrs Chance's, but they were too big even for me. They were a man's gloves. That's when I first became suspicious.'

'But you don't have those gloves now?'

'No, I don't,' said Craven. 'My wife told me she'd give them back to Mrs Chance. That was the last I saw of them. They were padded, black driving-gloves with a yellow strap at the wrists. They were definitely man-sized.'

'How seriously are you taking all this?'

'Very,' said Craven. 'Last Friday morning in Dorchester, I called in to see a fellow called Jordan. He's a private detective. Got an office near the station. I gave him a down-payment of five hundred pounds.'

'To keep an eye on Mrs Craven, I take it?'

'Precisely,' said Craven. 'And when I came home, I found you people here and my wife unconscious on the floor.'

'It was a man who phoned for the ambulance.'

'Well, it bloody well wasn't me.'

Inside Roper's head a flickering image of Nicholas Chance, flitting through the shrubbery towards the Cravens' bungalow, came – and stayed.

'You've lied a lot so far, Mr Craven.'

Craven glared back coldly at him, but said nothing.

'You said, when you first met Pope, he kept his thumb over his name on his warrant-card.'

'He did,' said Craven.

'But you subsequently found out his name. How come?'

'I was told it,' said Craven. He made a casual throw-away gesture with his left hand. 'A neighbour along the way. Chap called Chance.'

Which astonishing piece of intelligence rocked even

Roper on his heels. 'That's Mr Chance along at Downlands Farm, is it?' he asked, just to be sure that they were talking of the one and same Nicholas Chance. He had suspected all along that Chance had known Pope – and was beginning to wonder now if there was anybody around here who hadn't.

'Yes,' said Craven, seemingly unaware of the hiatus he had caused. 'Nick Chance. I saw them together in a pub in Dorchester. A Saturday morning. Two or three weeks ago. Chance knew him, apparently.'

'You went up and spoke to them, did you?'

'Hardly,' said Craven. 'I turned sharply about and went into the other bar. I asked Chance about him the same evening, along at the Hanging Man.'

'And what did he tell you?'

'That he was a private detective. Chance had been losing a lot of stuff from the farm. Tools and pieces of machinery and such. Pope was going to look into it for him.'

All or some of which might be true, but it struck Roper as singularly suspicious that Nicholas Chance had not seen fit to divulge that simple explanation to him last week. And the fact that he had not put a whole new slant on things.

'Who d'you reckon it belongs to, George?' asked Roper.

Makins continued to speculate over the Avia wristwatch that Craven had reluctantly handed over to them. Still outside Furzecroft, the two of them sat in Roper's Sierra. It was coming up for four o'clock in the afternoon. Brake and his sergeant had driven back to County to raise the paperwork that would close the file on the death of Sidney Manley, Craven had gone with them to be formally charged and the rest of that particular business was down to the lawyers to make of it what they could.

'And who's Mrs Craven covering up for?' Makins observed, equally pertinently.

'How about Chance?'

Makins handed the watch back again. 'Reckon he's her piece on the side?'

'Somebody is,' said Roper. 'I don't think Craven was lying over that. And we can always check out what he told the private investigator he'd hired, can't we?'

'But that's not what we're supposed to be investigating, is it?'

'True,' agreed Roper. And even if Mrs Craven did press charges against her husband it would still be none of their business. Unless some kind of connection could be established between what had happened to her and the death of Gerry Pope. Through the windscreen, in the distance, a shabbily dressed man on a bicycle was pedalling along from the direction of the village. He dismounted the bicycle near Mrs Wicks' and wheeled it into the trees. It looked as if the Lees had already taken Roper's word for the deed and returned to their old camp site.

After a few more moments of reflection, Roper reached for his ignition key. 'Get back in your car and follow me, George,' he said. 'I think it's time we had another word with old Hobday.'

They paid a courtesy call on Mrs Wicks who pointed out the path to Hobday's hut. 'You can't miss it,' she said. 'Just follow the reek of pipe tobacco.'

But still they almost did miss it. Painted the same garish green as Mrs Wicks' front door, the rickety old garden shed with a tin roof was all but obscured behind an overgrown clump of rhododendrons.

Hobday was making the most of the spring sunshine. At his ease in an old deckchair that looked no more substantial than his hut, his feet resting on an orange-crate with a cushion on top, and with a ball of pink wool jiggling on his lap, he was dexterously knitting a sock. Despite the sunshine, he still wore his moth-eaten woolly cap. He glanced up over his needles as twigs crackled under Roper's and Makins' feet, but his old collie, sprawled on the ground beside him, only opened its eyes halfway then sleepily closed them again.

'See you're a man of many parts, Mr Hobday,' said Roper.

'Bed-socks,' said Hobday, laying the vivid pink tube on his lap. 'If I've got warm feet I'm warm all over. Gets a bit nippy around here o' nights. Something I can do for you, gents?'

'Need a chat with you, Mr Hobday,' said Roper. 'Sorry to disturb you on a Sunday afternoon, but it's important. It's about last Friday morning.'

'Oh, right,' said Hobday, his expression darkening to one of suitable gravity. 'Say no more. Give us a hand, will you son,' he said to Makins, clutching his ball of wool and his knitting in one hand and offering the other to Makins to be hauled up from his chair. The effort left him raspingly out of breath. He beckoned them after him into his hut, offered them his bunk to sit on and sat himself on a fisherman's folding stool until he had got his wind back. As befitted an old sailor, everything was shipshape. There wasn't a great deal of room – Roper's and Hobday's feet were almost touching as they sat facing each other – but Hobday's possessions were few, and those that weren't stuffed under the bunk were arranged on homemade wooden shelves above it. An old Valor oil-heater with a whistling-kettle on it stood in a corner and appeared to be his only concession to luxury. Belatedly, the collie followed them in and laid its chin on Hobday's knees.

'Get a bit puffed, when I bob up and down,' explained Hobday apologetically. 'The old boilers ain't what they was. Not done bad though. Eighty-two I'll be in a couple o' weeks.' But furred-up boilers or not, they didn't stop him taking a foul-looking pipe out of his shirt pocket and stuffing it into the gap in his beard where his mouth was, sucking on it contemplatively a few times, then lowering it to his knees. 'Friday, you said.'

'You were cleaning Mrs Wicks' windows.'

'I was.'

'And you saw Mr Chance.'

'I did,' said Hobday. 'Creepin'.'

'Certain?'

'Maybe fallin' to pieces but I still got eyes. Besides, I remember 'im bein' born. Watched 'im grow up, and take over the farm when old Jack Chance died. I'm *dead* certain. An' he was up to no good, an' all.'

'Remember what he was wearing, Mr Hobday?' asked Makins.

'Overalls,' said Hobday. 'One o' them boiler suits. A green one. And wellies. And a flat cap. Working clothes, like. He must have come this way over the fence you asked about the other day.'

'Was he carrying anything?'

Hobday shook his head. 'Not as I saw.'

'Mind showing us the route he took?'

Hobday reached out to the edge of the tiny table beside him and pushed himself to his feet. They followed him outside, where first he led them back along the path to within sight of Mrs Wicks' bungalow. 'I was swabbing the window to the left of her front door,' he said, pointing. 'And sort of turned to wring out the leather over me bucket, and that's when I first saw 'im. He was about where we are now. He was goin' that way.' He pointed in the direction they had just come from, turned, and again they followed him back along the overgrown path. Just as the roof of his hut came into view he stopped again and Makins almost bumped into him.

'He stopped just here and took a good look about, real crafty I thought he looked – that's when I thought he was goin' to my place. Then he cut through here.' Hobday beckoned once more and they followed him again, away from the path now, into the shrubbery and between the trees, then behind Hobday's hut and then, twenty or thirty yards further on, back on to the path again.

'I stopped just here,' said Hobday. 'Kept meself well

tucked in, like, and kept an eye on 'im. When I'd made sure he wasn't goin' to my place, I turns back and gets on with Elsie's windows again.'

'What do we come to if we keep walking?'

'Not a lot,' said Hobday. 'Except the back of Mr Craven's place. I'll show yer.'

Waddling ahead of them he led the way again through the trees. Roper could hear the murmur of water now, and from over on his right caught the occasional hum of fast traffic on the road to the village.

A few hundred yards more over rising ground and they reached the new post and wire fence at the western boundary of Craven's few acres, where the trees petered out and gave way to cultivated shrubs with a lush green lawn behind them.

All the doors and windows at the back of Furzecroft were tightly shut and there were no signs of life.

Roper plucked at the tightly-strung topmost wire of the fence and made it resound like a double-bass string. 'How long's this been here, Mr Hobday?'

'It's new. About six or seven weeks, I s'pose.'

'Craven install it himself?'

'He's not that sort. Some firm in Dorchester did it for 'im. Their van was parked outside here for the best part of a fortnight.'

'A fit bloke could vault that,' observed Makins.

And a thin man who was not so fit could easily have slipped between the strands, kept behind the bordering shrubbery and made his way to the back of the bungalow almost unobserved. And Sergeant Mallory, when he had arrived at Furzecroft last Friday lunchtime, had found the kitchen door unlocked.

'Remember the name on the van, Mr Hobday?' asked Makins, clearly having caught Roper's drift when he had twanged the wire. The fencing contractor might have left some wire behind . . .

'No, I don't, son,' said Hobday. 'Sorry. But the van did

have a Dorchester phone number on the side.'

... and Craven might have used that remnant of wire to kill Gerry Pope. Craven still wasn't completely out of the woods on that score despite Roper's niggling doubts to the contrary.

'One last question, Mr Hobday,' he said, on their way back to the hut. 'Where would I find Mr Chance's foreman, if he's got one?'

'Harry Cutler,' said Hobday. 'Tall, bearded bloke. Seven o'clock Sundays he'll be in the Hanging Man. Reg'lar as clockwork.'

SIXTEEN

NICHOLAS CHANCE WAS NOT PLEASED to see them. Roper even thought he saw momentary alarm flit across his face.

'And just what the blazes are you two doing creeping about on my property?' he demanded to know, still standing by the yellow tractor, the tyres of which he had been washing down when Roper and Makins had walked into the yard behind the house. The gouting hose was still in his hand.

'Need to talk to you, Mr Chance,' said Roper. 'Sorry to catch you by surprise, but we couldn't get an answer to the doorbell.'

'No, you wouldn't have,' grumbled Chance. He laid the end of the hose over a drain and moved away to turn off the tap on the standpipe beside his corrugated iron garage. 'My wife's gone along to the hospital to see Dagmar Craven. What do you want to talk to me about exactly?'

'Just making a few more routine enquiries, Mr Chance. Go inside, can we?'

Chance would clearly have preferred to stay outside in the yard. But he shrugged and mumbled, 'Yes, I suppose so, if we have to.'

He heeled off his green gumboots against the stone step of his kitchen doorway and padded ahead of them to his sitting-room at the front of the house. He did not suggest they sat down. And if Roper was interpreting his body language aright Chance was very ill at ease as he stood with his back to his stone fireplace and waited for someone to speak.

Coldly and deliberately Roper let the silence drag, until the moment came when Chance at last managed to look him straight in the eye.

'I want to talk about Gerald Pope first, Mr Chance,' he said then. 'Because you didn't tell me the truth the other day, did you, sir?'

'About what?' asked Chance.

'Knowing him, sir. You told me you didn't.'

'It's none of your damned business whether I knew him or not,' retorted Chance pettishly. 'I didn't see why I should have to discuss it with you. It was a private matter between him and me. And certainly nothing to do with his death. He spent a couple of weeks working for me, that's all.'

'That's fair enough, sir,' Roper agreed. 'So why didn't you tell me so at the time? Exactly what sort of transaction did you make with him?'

'Stuff was going missing out of the sheds. Pope was looking into it for me.'

'Did he catch whoever it was?'

'No,' said Chance. 'Not for certain. But between us we got a fair idea – I gave the man in question notice last week.'

Roper recalled the hot debate between Chance's workmen he had overheard the other lunchtime in the Hanging Man.

'Accuse him, did you, sir?'

'I made him redundant,' said Chance. 'It was safer that way. Better than having the Union lawyers breathing down my neck.'

'What made you choose Pope? Why didn't you get the police in?'

'Police are too damn busy, aren't they?' said Chance. 'And I'd seen an advertisement Pope put in the local paper.'

'You could have told me that the other day. Why didn't you?' Roper asked again.

'I've told you,' said Chance. 'I didn't want the police involved. Besides which, I'd got it all sorted out by then.'

It sounded a likely enough story, but truth, Roper had learned over the years, was an elusive commodity and difficult to recognise even when it was staring him in the eye, as Chance still was.

'Mind telling me your movements last Monday night, Mr Chance?'

'I was out,' said Chance.

'Yes, sir, you told me that last time. But I'd like to know *exactly* where you were, purely for the record.'

'I was with a friend,' said Chance, looking evasive again.

'From when till when?'

'I left here soon after nine o'clock. Got back around eleven-thirty.'

'And this friend,' asked Roper, carefully selecting a gender, 'he'll vouch for that, will he?'

'Yes, I suppose so. If it's absolutely necessary.'

'But he could only confirm the time you left him. Not the time you arrived home.'

'Not exactly, no,' agreed Chance. 'But he only lives six or seven minutes' drive from here.'

'You can give us his name and address, can you, Mr Chance?' chipped in Makins.

'It's a woman,' Chance admitted at last. 'And she's married. I can get her to phone you, if it's that vital.'

'I'd be obliged,' said Roper. Makins gave the telephone number of County to Chance who scribbled it on the margin of a Sunday newspaper, tore it off and stuffed it into a pocket of his green boiler-suit. 'I'll have her ring you later this evening,' he said.

Which still wouldn't prove anything. Chance could have primed the woman to tell the police anything that suited him.

'When did you last see Pope to talk to, Mr Chance?' asked Roper.

202

'Last Friday week,' said Chance. 'Lunchtime. I met him in the Red Lion in Dorchester. He gave me the result of the work he'd been doing for me. He told me he couldn't do any more and told me he'd put his bill in the post that same afternoon.'

'Did the bill detail the work?'

'It just said: for investigative services.'

'According to a witness, while he was working for you Pope was spotted over on the heath with binoculars and a camera. He was watching Mr Craven's place.'

Chance's eyes stilled. And he hesitated just a fraction too long. 'Then he must have been working for someone else at the same time.'

'Pope produce any photographs for you? Black and white ones?'

'No, he didn't,' retorted Chance, far too quickly this time, so that more and more was Roper certain he was lying.

'What were you doing last Friday morning, sir?' Roper asked, quickly changing direction. 'A few minutes either side of twelve o'clock.'

'I was here.'

'No, you weren't, Mr Chance. You were making your way through Mrs Wicks' back garden.'

'Rubbish!'

'You were seen, Mr Chance. And you were followed. You were last seen heading towards Mr Craven's bungalow.'

Chance shook his head vehemently. 'Not true. I was here. Working. I was in the office.'

'You were wearing a green boiler-suit, green boots and a cap.'

'I always wear those when I'm working,' retorted Chance. 'Anybody could have told you that.'

'It was a man's voice on the phone.'

'Phone?' protested Chance. But he knew what Roper was talking about all right, it showed in the fixed stare, the

203

way he was trying to stand perfectly still and relaxed, and couldn't, while all the time he was desperately trying to guess what Roper knew, or thought he knew, and what next he was going to try and prise out of him and what he ought to be bracing himself for. 'What bloody phone?'

'Mr Craven's phone,' said Roper. 'It was a man's voice that made the call for the ambulance for Mrs Craven.'

'I don't know what the hell you're talking about.'

But with every protest Chance was backing himself deeper and deeper into a hole that Roper was digging for him. 'Have a row, did you, you and Mrs Craven? Go a bit too far did you, call for the ambulance and then do a bunk?'

'Christ,' Chance spat back. 'What the bloody hell are you accusing me of now?'

'I'm not accusing you of anything, Mr Chance. I'm just making a few suggestions. You were seen going along the back path towards the Cravens' bungalow around the time Mrs Craven sustained her injuries. A man's voice put in the call to the emergency services. He said he was Mr Craven –'

'Perhaps it was Mr bloody Craven,' sneered Chance, breaking in.

'He says he wasn't there.'

'Can he prove it?' snapped back Chance. He had summoned up more resources from somewhere and his hands were bunched to tight fists, white knuckled. 'You take it from me, if Dagmar Craven didn't have an accident along there on Friday morning you can bet your bottom dollar Martin's at the bottom of it. He's a foxy bastard, that Craven.'

'We have talked to Mrs Craven, sir,' said Makins.

'So you know all the bloody answers then, don't you?' blustered Chance, but all the same Makins' interjection caught him wrong-footed – and it showed and he looked hunted and alone again. 'She must know damned *well* I wasn't there.'

'If we could go back to the question of Gerald Pope again, sir,' said Roper.

Another half-hour had passed. They were in the gloom of the brick store-shed where Chance kept his stocks of wire among a litter of tools and machinery.

'What's this one?' asked Roper, laying a finger on the rim of a massive spool of galvanised wire that hung on a rusty steel shaft between a couple of old axle stands.

'Fencing wire,' said Chance. 'It was only delivered last Thursday. I can show you the invoice for it.'

Roper glanced back quickly at him. 'Why d'you say that?'

'I just thought you'd like to know,' said Chance. He looked even more uneasy out here than he had indoors.

'How about this one?'

'It isn't wire,' said Chance impatiently. 'It's twine.' He reached out and ripped away an edge of the waxed paper wrapping to show them. The gesture was an angry one, so that Roper wondered if Chance was at last reaching the end of his tether under the relentless barrage of questions.

'And what sort of wire's this?'

'Baling wire,' said Chance. There were two spools of it, one opened, the other still wrapped. The two spools lay one on top of the other on the dusty floor, either one of them too heavy to lift without a lot of effort. Baling wire was thin, galvanised, easy to manage. At eighty miles an hour it would take a man's head off as easily as slicing a carrot.

'Strong, is it?' asked Roper.

'Strong enough for baling,' said Chance.

'When was the top one started?'

'How the hell would I know,' retorted Chance. 'We use the bloody stuff all the time.'

And then something caught Roper's eye on the unstarted spool beneath. A length of green plastic ferrule sticking out of the torn edge of the oiled wrapping paper. He had seen such a thing before . . . quick as a flash . . . a

205

glimpse out on the road last Monday morning . . . Charlie Brake had tossed one into the roadway the very instant Roper had come up behind him. It had looked unlikely evidence then of course because at that time no one had even guessed quite how Pope had met his end . . .

He dropped to his hunkers, took a good grip of the ferrule and tugged it off. Rising again, he handed it to Makins. 'Give Mr Chance a receipt for that, will you, Sergeant.'

'What the hell d'you want that for?' asked Chance.

'Evidence, sir,' said Roper, and left it at that as something else for Chance to worry about. He was going to call it a day here soon, confident that he had stirred up a hornet's nest of one kind or another. It would do no harm to let Chance sweat it out for a few more hours. That he had told one lie was certain. Tasker Hobday's boilers might be letting him down but there was nothing wrong with the old fellow's eyesight. Whatever Chance said, he had not been here in his farmhouse at midday last Friday. And if that green ferrule wasn't one of millions there was even a chance that the killing of Gerry Pope could be traced back to this dark, dusty shed. What the motive could have been was anyone's guess, but Roper's every instinct told him that somewhere along the line Chance was involved in it, and perhaps Craven was as well, and perhaps they were even in it together despite Chance's description of Craven as a foxy bastard.

'You'll be sure your lady friend rings me at the office tonight, won't you, sir?' said Roper, when they had returned to the house and he was picking up his briefcase from where he had been standing earlier.

'And when she does ring you, I shall be relying on your discretion, of course.'

The two-timers always said that, Roper had noticed – asked for discretion when the chips showed signs of tumbling about their own indiscretions.

'Your private life's of no interest to me, sir,' he said,

buttoning his jacket, barely able to keep the scorn out of his voice. He wondered if Martin Craven had a spare woman too. They were very much alike, Messrs Craven and Chance.

As Chance moved past him to show them out there came the rasp of a key in the lock of the front door, a draught of air, then a slam as the door was closed again. Brisk footsteps along the passage then and Mrs Chance's testy voice on sighting her husband in the doorway:

'. . . I've had to drive the last couple of miles with a bloody flat tyre. Oh . . .' the exclamation was quickly followed by a vivid smile at the sight of company as she brushed past Chance and caught sight of Roper and Makins in the room behind him. '. . . Can I get you a cup of tea or something? I'm absolutely gasping, myself.'

'No, thanks, Mrs Chance,' said Roper. 'We were just leaving.' From the tail of his eye he noticed that Chance's relief at seeing them off his premises had switched back to distinct unease now that his wife had turned up. 'Hear you've been along to see Mrs Craven. Coming along all right, is she?'

'So-so. Still looks a bit poorly, you know, but according to what she tells me they're stuffing her to the gills with codeine and stuff. She reckons on coming out on Friday. I think you ought to go out and look at that tyre, Nick,' she said as an aside to Chance, tossing him the keys to the Range Rover. 'It's practically down on the wheel-hub now, and I want to use the thing in the morning to go into Dorchester again. I've left it out front.'

Chance stared back at her for a moment with virulent hatred, then padded up to the front door, stabbed his feet into a pair of shoes beside the hallstand and slammed the door behind him as he went to do as he was told.

'Dagmar tells me you've had a chat with her,' she said, now that her husband was safely out of earshot, taking a grip on Roper's jacket sleeve and drawing him confidentially deeper into the drawing-room. She was wearing jeans and a sweater again today, her hair clubbed tightly at the back of her neck.

'Sergeant Makins did last evening.'

'Yes, so she said. So you know it was Martin, then? He pushed her over, apparently.' She stood very close, her hand still on Roper's sleeve. Still with a few red blood corpuscles flowing in his veins, Roper thought, and not for the first time, what an incredibly attractive woman she was, and wondered what the hell Nicholas Chance was doing seeking more illicit comforts elsewhere. But, on the other hand, she was probably doing the same, and perhaps even on her own doorstep with Martin Craven.

'Only allegedly, Mrs Chance,' he was careful to say.

Her hand fell back to her side. 'She tells me she doesn't intend to charge him. I told her that was crazy. I mean, he could do it again, couldn't he? I mean, what happens if he *really* goes berserk? Can't you do *anything* about it?'

'Not if Mrs Craven doesn't want us to, Mrs Chance. And it seems she doesn't. Stay with her long?'

'No,' she said. 'Only for a couple of minutes.'

'But you'd spoken to Mrs Craven on the phone? Before you visited her, I mean.'

'Not directly, no,' she said. 'Not until this morning. We just passed messages. Dagmar phoned me soon after breakfast.'

Which only served to confound further any idea Roper had that anyone but Craven could have been responsible for the injuries to his wife. Because if no one had communicated with Mrs Craven between the time Sergeant Mallory had arrived on the scene and Makins' chat with her last evening in the hospital, then she could not possibly have known of the few minutes gap in her husband's alibi. Ergo: she had to be telling the truth, and Craven was lying. And Mrs Craven had known of Pope, or at least his name, when Roper had mentioned it that morning in the bungalow. Between here and Furzecroft Pope had met his grisly end and somewhere between here and Furzecroft lay the answers to all the whys and wherefores.

But by now Chance was coming in again through the front door, his quick eyes anxiously taking in the fact that Roper and Makins were still there. 'It's a bloody roofing-nail,' he said.

'I must have picked it up in the hospital car park,' she said. 'They've got the builders in. Scaffolding and everything.'

'We'll be off and leave you to it then, Mr Chance,' said Roper. 'Thanks for your help. And yours too, Mrs Chance,' he added pointedly, at which juncture Chance's eyes flicked to meet his wife's, sharp as a carving knife, before flicking back again. Roper could feel the tension between them, tight as a bow-string.

'I'll see you out,' grunted Chance. He turned and led the way back up the passage, which was where Roper caught sight of a pair of black, padded driving-gloves with yellow wriststraps. They were stuffed into a flat tweed cap that lay on the hallstand.

'Your gloves, Mr Chance?'

'Yes, they are.' Chance's eyes had clouded over with suspicion again.

'Lost 'em lately?'

'Not that I recall, no.'

'Fair enough, sir,' said Roper, making sure that Chance knew that by no means was it fair enough and leaving him to sweat on that as well, as Chance closed his front door on them and went back to his wife.

Hughie Lee's flashlight lit the path along the heath, sweeping backward from time to time so that Roper could see the obstacle that Lee had just stepped over. It was almost seven o'clock in the evening, and dark now.

'Mind that,' said Lee, flashing the torch behind him again and showing up the handle of a child's pram that someone had dumped and that was sticking out of the

209

bushes. Roper stepped over it, then over a Safeway plastic carrier bag filled with empty drink cans. A pair of tiny glittering lights, momentarily frozen, turned into a rabbit that unfroze and scuttled quickly away into more undergrowth.

'Sergeant Mallory been to see you yet?'

"E come along just before dark. Just looked, though. Didn't get out o' his car.'

They moved on along the overgrown path. The moon put in a brief appearance but was quickly gone again behind a bank of cloud.

'Just 'ere it was,' said Lee. He had led the way into a semicircular rampart of rhododendron bushes, the opening of which faced away from the road and would thus obscure someone hiding behind it from the carriageway – and from Craven's bungalow which was immediately opposite.

'You're sure?'

'Certain,' said Lee. He shone his torch over the grass, crouched and gathered up a dozen stained and flattened cork-tipped cigarette ends and several dead matches. 'The dog-ends are all the same, see?' he said, rising again and holding his torch close over the collection of cork-tips. 'A bloke'd 'ave to be lyin' here for a good few hours to smoke that many snouts wouldn't he?'

'You ought to be a copper, Hughie,' said Roper.

One corner of Lee's mouth twisted in the pale glow of his torch. 'Not me, mister,' he said. 'Never on your bloody life.'

Roper took a plastic evidence envelope from his pocket, opened it and held it out for Lee to tip in the cork-tips and the matches from the palm of his hand. He pinched a thumb and fingernail across the opening of the bag to seal it, stuffed it in his pocket and from another pocket took out a pair of miniature, folding binoculars and focused them on Craven's bungalow.

Someone was home. Craven. Coming into view to draw the sitting-room curtains.

210

'Pope were lyin' down,' said Lee, lighting the moss and grass. 'Stretched out there, 'e was.'

Roper buttoned his raincoat and lay down on his stomach on the damp ground. By dint of shuffling a few inches either way on his elbows he eventually found a spot between the leaves and branches where he could again get a clear view of Furzecroft, and within half an arm's length of where Lee had picked up the cigarette ends and dead matches just before. The view became clearer still when the coach-lamp beside Craven's front door was switched on. A few seconds after that Craven came out and walked briskly across to his garage.

Roper got to his feet again and brushed off the front of his raincoat.

'Can I take a look?' said Lee.

'Sure,' said Roper, passing over the binoculars. Lee put them to his eyes, fiddled with the focus-wheel and turned slowly on the spot to take in whatever he could see on the heath. 'Aye,' he said with grudging approval. 'They're good bins, these, for little 'uns.' He went to hand them back again.

'Keep 'em,' said Roper. 'I was on the point of getting a new pair anyway.'

'I wasn't hinting,' grumbled Lee.

'I didn't think you were.'

'I got to give you somethin' back.'

'You just did, Hughie,' said Roper. 'More than you'll ever know, old son.'

A hundred yards away, Craven had driven his car on to the road and was walking back to close his front gate. From the way his car was facing he appeared to be about to drive off in the direction of Dorchester, which was where Roper, with the germ of an idea sprouting in his mind at last, would be heading himself at the crack of dawn tomorrow.

At a few minutes to seven-thirty Roper sat over a beer in the Sunday evening quiet of the Hanging Man. At the far end of the public bar two of Chance's workmen that he

211

recognised from last week were playing Russian pool, and over by the fireplace Tasker Hobday and another village elder were playing a game of cribbage. There was still no sign of the bearded Harry Cutler.

The next arrival was the young lad to whom Chance had given his marching orders last week, the one the others had called Jacko. Mrs Hapgood pulled him up a bitter-shandy. He took a sip as he picked up his change, then went to join the other two at the pool table.

It was almost seven forty-five before Cutler put in an appearance, by which time Mrs Hapgood was drawing up Roper's second half-pint.

'And one for this gentleman,' said Roper, passing a five pound note across the counter.

With one foot on the brass rail and his elbows comfortably on the counter, the black-bearded Cutler gave a surly glance along his shoulder.

'Only drink with those I'm on speaking terms with,' he said. 'Thanks all the same.'

'Mr Cutler, is it?'

'Aye, that's me,' grunted Cutler. 'What about it?'

Roper took out his warrant-card and slid it along the counter. 'The name's Roper, Mr Cutler.'

'Oh, aye,' said Cutler, unmoved, even after he had glanced at the card and slid it back again. 'You can make it a pint of lager then.'

Mrs Hapgood drew up a pint of lager. Roper paid for that and his own and rose from his stool as he collected his change. Cutler followed him to the table in the corner by the door to the forecourt.

'Cheers,' said Cutler, taking a swig of his lager, then wiping the froth off his moustache with a knuckle. He eyed Roper suspiciously from under thick black eyebrows with flecks of grey in them. He was about forty-five, thickly set and with shrewd eyes that showed he wasn't a man to be messed about with. 'So what's this all about then?'

'Hear you're Mr Chance's foreman.'

'So?'

'Get along all right with him?'

Cutler shrugged and took another swig of his lager. 'It's work,' he said. 'And that's hard to come by these days.'

'How long have you been with him?'

'Eight years. Coming up nine.' Cutler's hand curled around his glass again.

'So you're pretty well in with the routine of the place.'

Cutler's glass was lifted and tilted, his eyes still watching Roper over the rim of it. Mr Cutler was clearly a man of no mean capacity when it came to his lager. 'You could say,' he agreed, lowering it and dabbing froth from his moustache again.

'Talk to him much?'

'Only when I have to.'

With that tacit agreement made, Roper took another sip of his bitter and Cutler another hefty swig of his lager.

'Heard of any equipment going missing from the place?'

Cutler glowered. 'Who told you that?'

'A little bird,' said Roper. 'Some machinery, tools, gear like that.'

'You've been listening to the wrong little bird,' growled Cutler. He buried his nose in his glass again, his dark eyes still unwavering.

'You're certain?'

'It's all kept under lock and key. And only me and him's got keys.'

'Why'd he sack young Jacko?'

'If you're saying –'

'I'm not,' said Roper. 'I'm only asking why Chance sacked him.'

'Cash flow, so he said. Money's tight. That don't stop him buying a new bloody Range Rover every year, mind.'

'So nothing's been nicked?'

'Definite,' said Cutler. 'Whoever told you that's a bloody liar.'

'Ever see a stranger prowling about the place? A big, bearded bloke, a bit like yourself?'

Cutler shook his head. 'If Chance says anything's gone missing, you ask him to show you the inventory. Find out if he's told the insurance company, and if he has, you come and see me and we'll sort it out between us. All right?'

'Fine,' said Roper. 'I may do that.'

Four young lads came in noisily from the forecourt. Three went down the bar to annex the Space Invaders machine while the other one went to the counter to get the drinks in.

'How d'you get on with his missus?'

'What's that got to do with it?'

'Get on all right together, do they?'

'You'll have to find out for yourself, won't you,' grunted Cutler, pausing briefly to drain his glass. 'None of my business, that.'

SEVENTEEN

ONLY HALF THE LIGHTS IN the CID room were on, its sole occupant George Makins, who appeared to be making a late mail-delivery around the empty desks. It was coming up for eight-thirty.

'Thought you'd gone home, George,' said Roper, still at the doorway.

Makins swivelled around like a safe-breaker caught in the act. The swatch of large white envelopes he still held went swiftly behind his back. 'Standing in for Peter Rodgers, guv,' he said. 'He's got a very heavy date tonight. I did check it out with Dave Price.'

'Handing out more memos from the ACC about tightening our belts?' enquired Roper.

'No,' said Makins, still looking conscience-stricken. 'Not exactly.' Then, finally deciding to bare his breast, he brought the envelopes from out of hiding behind his back, shuffled through them, selected one, and came reluctantly across to Roper to hand it to him. 'They're wedding invitations,' he explained.

'Whose wedding?' asked Roper.

'Mine,' said Makins.

Roper frowned in astonishment. Despite the canteen and washroom grapevine, nobody had ever seriously believed that young George would actually buckle down and do it. 'You're kidding,' he said.

'Never been more serious,' said Makins, whose reputation as the County's Lothario had become the stuff

215

of legend over the years. It was said of George Makins that he suffered from a plague of adoring women as other men suffered from dandruff. A nimble young man, he had thus far adroitly evaded the clutches of all of them.

Roper ran a finger and thumbnail around the edge of the envelope. The invitation was about eight inches by six and deckle-edged. 'Feels like a big invitation.'

'It's a big wedding.'

'Anybody we know?'

'She's a solicitor,' said Makins. 'Got a practice in Dorchester. Met her in court about six months ago.'

'And she can keep you in the style to which you'd like to become accustomed, can she?'

Makins' gloom that he was at last to be revealed as a charlatan was considerably lifted over a glass of Scotch from the private cellar in Roper's bottom drawer. He waxed lyrical. Her name was Fiona. She was thirty-two. And not only was she highly intelligent but very seriously and considerably gorgeous.

'Hope she's worthy of you, George,' said Roper solemnly, raising his tumbler to this paragon among women.

'Yeah ... well ...' mumbled the love-struck Makins, shrugging coyly. With his dark secret off his chest at last he was quickly back to his old self. 'How d'you get on with Hughie Lee?'

'Pope was definitely watching the Cravens' place. For a good few hours too, by the looks of it.'

'Who for?'

'Nicholas Chance, I think,' said Roper, to Makins' obvious surprise. 'I'm not certain, mind. It certainly wasn't for Craven, or in the mood he was in I think he would have told us so. I don't think Craven knocked his wife down either.'

'He must have done,' said Makins. 'A, she said so; and B, she was knocked down in the few minutes that Craven can't account for. And she couldn't have known that he

216

couldn't account for them, could she, because for her first twenty-four hours in hospital she was more or less incommunicado except to us, wasn't she? I checked with the nurses. All they did was to relay messages and none of those were sus. Unless she was guessing, and struck lucky.'

'I don't think she was guessing, George. I think she knew. I don't know how but I'm bloody sure she did.'

'Covering up for Chance and putting the skids under her old man at the same time?'

But about that Roper was less sure. If Mrs Craven had really wanted to put her husband squarely in the frame, her best bet would have been for her to charge him with assault. She had already told Makins that what had happened in her hall last Friday lunchtime had been no accident. So why had she not gone all the way and preferred a charge against him? And why would she be covering up for Nicholas Chance – if indeed she was – unless he was her lover, or she thought he was? And had that, any of it, anything at all to do with the killing of Gerry Pope –

He stretched an arm across the desk as his telephone chirruped. 'Roper,' he said.

'Call for you, sir. A woman. She's ringing from a call-box. She says she'll give her name to you but she won't give it to me. Put her through, shall I?'

Roper motioned for Makins to pick up the extension. 'Put her on,' he said.

There was a click, and a long pause.

'Superintendent Roper,' he said. He could hear breathing, not Makins' because Makins had his hand cupped over his mouthpiece. 'Are you calling about Mr Chance?'

'Yes, I am,' the woman said. Then, after another hesitation, 'If I give you my name, would there be any need to take it further?'

'Hopefully not,' he said. 'But it depends, of course.'

'My name is Quick,' she said. 'Caroline Quick. I run

Quick's Flower Shop in Dorchester. It's in the Yellow Pages. If you need to see me – to speak to me – if you'd contact me there and not at home . . .'

'Understood, Mrs Quick,' said Roper. 'What did Mr Chance tell you to say exactly?'

'He didn't *tell* me to say anything,' she retorted, with a sudden flash of anger in her voice. It was a pleasant voice, deep for a woman, used to giving orders, no trace of any particular regional accent. It also had a hollow sound, as if she were making the call from a tile-lined room, perhaps her shop. 'He told me the police suspected him of something pretty serious and that they wanted to know where he was for practically every minute of last Monday evening.'

'Not every minute, Mrs Quick. Just from nine o'clock onwards.'

'At about nine-thirty we were in the Yellow Dragon. That's a Chinese Restaurant near the Hardy Memorial in Dorchester.'

'Which you left when?'

'About ten-thirty.'

'And after that?'

There was another pause. 'We went along to the shop. We stayed there for about half an hour. Then I collected the van from the yard and we drove back in tandem as far as East Knighton. We talked for a few minutes – ten, perhaps. Then Nicholas went back to his car and we went our separate ways home.'

'Do you recall the time you got home, Mrs Quick?'

'About half-past eleven, I suppose.'

'And how far do you live from Mr Chance?'

'A few minutes,' she said. 'Maybe five. Does all that make you happy?'

'Yes, that's fine, Mrs Quick. Thank you. But there is one more question I hope you won't mind answering. Exactly how long have you and Mr Chance been going around together?'

'Is that really any of your business, Superintendent?' she asked spikily. 'Or are you just being bloody nosey?'

'It's my business, Mrs Quick.'

'I can't think why, for God's sake,' she retorted. 'But it's about five weeks, if you really must know.'

'Thank you,' he said.

'That's all?' she sounded surprised.

'That's all, Mrs Quick,' he said. 'Thank you.'

'Sounds like a tough cookie,' remarked Makins, as he and Roper laid their phones back on their cradles.

'Sounded as if she was telling the truth though,' said Roper, sitting back in his chair and lighting a contemplative cheroot. Not that anything was certain yet, but if Mrs Quick had been on the up and up, then the glimmering of the idea that he had had while he and Hughie Lee had been out on the heath earlier on was beginning to look more and more like a bright light.

'Who's the duty WDS tomorrow morning, George?'

'Penny Wilmott,' said Makins.

'Well, if you see her before I do, tell her she and I have got a hospital visit to make in the early a.m.'

'Mrs Craven?'

'You've got it.'

'But she's already made a statement.'

'I don't think she's been telling us the truth, George. And I've got a sneaking feeling I know why.'

It was soon after nine o'clock on Monday morning when Detective Sergeant Penny Wilmott and Roper took the lift to the second floor and the ward where Mrs Craven was bedded down in a private room off the hospital annexe.

The staff nurse was unimpressed by Roper's credentials. She fetched the ward sister who, equally unimpressed, fetched the registrar in whose charge Mrs Craven belonged. The registrar, a tall and gangling young man, with receding fair hair and a white coat that had been made for someone half his height so that he appeared to be all legs and knobbly wrists, was impressed but cautionary.

'You can have ten minutes,' he said. 'She's still a bit on the jumpy side and needs all the rest she can get. So not too many questions. All right?'

In the event it was nearer a quarter of an hour. The staff nurse went in first to tell Mrs Craven that she had visitors, and as she came out again Roper and Wilmott filed in. Practically every horizontal surface in the room was banked with flowers. Mrs Craven, one side of her head shaved and swathed in a padded bandage, was sitting up against her pillows. That she was now a walking patient was evidenced by the colourfully embroidered kimono she wore over her pyjamas and the pair of furry bedroom mules standing on the floor beside the bed. Apart from a little pink lipstick she wore no make-up. But what Roper observed most keenly were her glittering blue eyes, wide and unblinking and wary. Her hands were tight knuckled around a book she had been reading, although it was Roper's more immediate impression that she'd grabbed it up quickly for something to hold on to.

'I hear you're improving, Mrs Craven,' he said, with a smile.

'Yes, thank you,' she said, sounding as if she'd tried to swallow a stone and it had stuck in her throat.

He introduced Sergeant Wilmott, whose slight and feminine presence seemed to discomfort Mrs Craven even more than his own. 'Why have you come again?' she asked anxiously, her Nordic accent far more pronounced than it had been the last time he had spoken to her. 'I spoke to another man and woman on Saturday. I told them everything.'

'We'd like a few more details, Mrs Craven. Mind if we sit down?'

She shook her head, said nothing. If eyes really were the mirrors of the soul, Mrs Craven seemed to be suffering from a remarkably unquiet spirit. Wilmott sat down in one

220

of the visitors' armchairs, Roper on the wooden arm of the other. There was a grey metal wastepaper tub by his left foot, several crushed balls of cellophane and pink and white tissue paper in it. It looked like the sort of wrapping florists used. So there had been yet another delivery of flowers already this morning. He wondered idly if Martin Craven had sent any of them. Somehow he doubted it.

'I am not making charges against him, you know,' insisted Mrs Craven. She watched Wilmott lift her briefcase to her knees and take out her pocket-book.

'That's your husband, I take it?' said Roper.

'Of course, my husband,' she said, after a cautious pause, her eyes swivelling back to him again.

'Your husband tells us he wasn't there, Mrs Craven.'

'He is lying,' she retorted. 'He was.'

Mindful of the registrar's warning, he gave her a breathing space. 'I'm really not here to bully you, Mrs Craven,' he said quietly then. 'I just want to know what happened.'

'He came home,' she insisted again.

'And you'd just put the phone down on Mrs Wicks?'

She stayed silent this time.

'Do you remember if your husband came into the house by the back or the front?'

'The back. I looked and he was there. I did not hear him come in.'

'And what happened then?'

'I told the man on Saturday,' she protested. 'I do not remember. I remember hardly anything.'

'You told him that Mr Craven had forgotten to collect some dry-cleaning for you.'

'To *take*. Not to *collect*. To take. It was a coat.'

'You told Sergeant Makins it was to collect.'

'It was to take! I told the man distinctly. It was to take . . . All these questions. It is making me confused.'

But what she had told Makins *distinctly* was that the dry-cleaning had had to be collected. George Makins just didn't make mistakes like that. And whether the cleaning had had to be taken or collected had been irrelevant to the matter, until now.

'And you had a row about that?'

'He had been drinking.'

'And he hit you?'

'I think so.'

'But you aren't certain?'

She lifted the book and slammed it down hard on her legs. She looked close to tears. 'I do not remember. I keep telling everybody. I do *not* remember!'

'So your husband came home, you asked him if he'd remembered to collect your drycleaning –'

'No,' she broke in. '*Not* to collect. To *take*. I keep telling you, to take.'

'I'm sorry,' he said. She really did seem irrationally persistent about that apparently innocuous detail. 'I keep forgetting. You asked him if he'd remembered to take your coat to the cleaners, he said he hadn't and the two of you quarrelled.'

'Yes,' she said. 'It was exactly like that.'

'Who hit who first?'

'He pushed me.'

'And you fell and struck your head on the table in the hall.'

'I did. I tried to get up and I could not. Then I was unconscious.'

'And how did the vase get smashed?'

She was stopped instantly in her tracks, her forehead creasing. 'What vase?'

'The blue Gallé vase; on the table in the hall.'

He could see she was floundering, her mind racing while she desperately tried to think of an answer to that. Because she might not know the vase had been broken, or how important it might be that she knew how – and why. She had known that her husband had been close to the scene when the incident had happened, she knew that he had come home the worse for drink, but she hadn't known about the Gallé vase being broken. And there could only be one reason for that. Whoever had fed her with the rest of her story hadn't known about the vase either.

'It fell,' she blurted suddenly, as clumsy inspiration came at last. 'Yes, it fell. I remember. It must have rolled off when I hit the table. I remember the sound of glass breaking.'

'It hit the carpet,' prompted Roper encouragingly.

'I suppose so.'

'Or could Mr Craven have struck you with it?'

For a beat or two her eyes were suddenly shrewd and sharp, as if she dearly wished she had thought of that little bit of embroidery for herself. 'No,' she said at last. 'I do not think so.'

'Did you see Mr Chance that morning?'

'No,' she said, her eyes slitting suspiciously. 'Why should I have?'

'He didn't pay a call? Around the time you were on the phone to Mrs Wicks?'

She shook her head.

'Did you know your house was being watched?'

The startled eyes again, a fractional sagging of the jaw. If ever Dagmar Craven got to court even a fledgling barrister was going to be able to tear her apart with one hand tied behind his back.

'On Friday?' she asked.

'A few weeks ago. A man called Gerald Pope. He was the fellow who was killed near your place last Monday night. If you remember, I called on you with Sergeant Makins to make enquiries about him. Mrs Chance was with you.'

She pretended to have forgotten that too, pleaded confusion again; but if Roper was interpreting her signals correctly she seemed greatly relieved that her house had not been watched last Friday, and less concerned that it had been under scrutiny a few weeks previously.

'I have told you before, I do not know the man. I do not

know why he was watching our house.'

'He was being paid to, Mrs Craven.'

She was instantly alert again. 'By my husband?'

'Why do you say that? Your husband have a reason for having your house watched in the daytime?'

'Of course not.' She turned her face away like a petulant child. 'And please, I want you to go now. You have made me very tired.'

'There's just one more thing, Mrs Craven,' said Roper, 'then we'll be off. Will you show Mrs Craven the wristwatch, Sergeant.'

At the mention of a wristwatch, Mrs Craven jerked her face back towards them and he distinctly heard her breath catch.

Wilmott produced the Avia wristwatch from her briefcase and held it out, but Mrs Craven wouldn't touch it, scarcely even looked at it. 'I have never seen it before. Why should I have?'

'Could it be Mr Chance's watch?' asked Roper.

'I tell you,' she protested, 'I do not know. I do not know what sort of watch he wears. How *should* I?'

'It was just a thought, Mrs Craven.' He rose and buttoned his jacket – kicking over the grey wastepaper tub in the process, stooping and setting it straight and deftly palming up one of the crumpled balls of tissue paper that had rolled out of it.

He waited in the car for Wilmott. The weather-guessers had promised intermittent showers in the south and west today but so far they had held off. Over on the right the maternity wing was caged in scaffolding and being re-roofed, a half-dozen tilers as casually at work as if they were on the ground and not fifty feet in the air.

On the dashboard shelf in front of him lay the sheet of florist's wrapping-paper he had filched from Mrs Craven's waste-tub, straightened out now and neatly folded. Whoever had sent Mrs Craven flowers this morning had purchased them from Quick's Flower Shop in Dorchester, which was a coincidence indeed since the owner of that shop was Nicholas Chance's current woman friend. The circle seemed to be getting smaller and tighter around the Cravens and the Chances, and a visit to Mrs Quick might even make it tighter yet.

Wilmott came briskly from the reception annexe. He leaned across to open the driver's door for her. She dropped her briefcase over on to the back seat.

'Any joy?' he said, as she swung her legs in and pulled the door shut after her.

'Nothing we didn't know, sir,' she said. 'All her phone calls out are logged on the switchboard and go on the bill when she's discharged. She only made the one call out. Yesterday.'

'How about calls coming in?'

'Her husband phones every morning and evening to see how she is – but he doesn't speak to her. The only other caller's been Mrs Chance, but she hadn't spoken directly to her until Mrs Craven rang her yesterday. And the only visitors she's had are Mrs Chance and ourselves, but again Mrs Chance didn't make her first visit until *after* George Makins took a statement from Mrs Craven on Saturday evening. Oh, and Mr Craven called in last evening, but he only spoke to the sister to ask if his wife needed anything – and to bring some more night-clothes and that kimono she was wearing. Mrs Craven asked him to bring those – but again the message was passed through one of the nurses. So there's really no way she could have known where her husband was last Friday lunchtime unless she saw him for herself.'

But there had been a way, and it was highly likely that the key to that way was presently sitting on the shelf of the dashboard. A pink and white candy-striped sheet of tissue paper with *Quick's Flower Shop, Dorchester* printed right in the centre of it.

*

'She must have changed her mind then,' said George Makins. 'She definitely told me that Craven had gone to *collect* some dry-cleaning for her.'

'I don't see why that's important,' said Dave Price, as Makins passed his pocket-book across Roper's desk with the relevant page opened.

'It's *bloody* important,' said Roper crossly. Price was very slow on the uptake sometimes. 'Because if he'd gone to collect some cleaning for her, and forgotten to pick it up, then it'd still be in the cleaner's, wouldn't it?'

'It could have been a slip of the tongue,' said Price. 'First, she's foreign, and second she was dosed with painkillers. She could easily have used the wrong word.'

'She wasn't *that* dozy,' said Makins. 'I got the impression she was telling me the story in a nice logical progression.'

'Because she was primed with the story to tell,' argued Roper. 'But whoever fed it to her didn't know all the story. For a start, they didn't know that the Gallé vase had been smashed. And I don't think they told Mrs Craven what the row between her and her husband might have been about; I think they told her to point the finger at her husband but left her to invent the reason for herself, only she slipped up and said it was about collecting a coat from the cleaners.'

'Which she corrected this morning,' said Wilmott's quieter voice. 'Adamantly.'

Roper sat at his desk, Makins opposite, Wilmott at one end and Price on the window ledge overlooking the car park. It was eleven o'clock on the same Monday morning. DS Rodgers backed into the office with five steaming coffees in plastic cups on a tin tray, and handed them around.

'Adamantly, as Penny says,' agreed Roper. 'Because since George spoke to her on Saturday evening, somebody pointed out to her that she'd slipped up badly by saying that Craven hadn't collected that dry-cleaning. Because if he hadn't collected it, it would still be on the cleaner's premises and we might set about looking for it, and when we couldn't find it we'd know she'd told one lie and we'd be looking around for some more.'

'And she doesn't want us looking around at all,' ventured Price. 'Which is why she's trying to keep last Friday's business in the family.'

'I reckon,' said Roper.

'And the only person she's spoken to between when I did and you did,' said George Makins, over the rim of his coffee cup, 'was Vanessa Chance.'

'Exactly,' said Roper.

'But how did Dagmar Craven know her husband could have been about last Friday lunchtime and that he'd been drinking?' asked Price from the window ledge.

'Because somebody told her before George talked to her.'

'They couldn't have,' said Price.

'Yes, they could,' said Roper. 'They sent her a letter.'

'She hadn't received any mail,' said Makins. 'I asked. And it wouldn't have had time to go through the post, would it?'

'Probably not,' agreed Roper. 'But they sent her flowers, didn't they?'

Caroline Quick sighed as she handed back Roper's warrant-card. 'I guessed you'd be paying a call somehow. Once you people get your teeth into something, you just can't leave it alone, can you? I told you everything I knew on the phone last night.'

'This is nothing to do with our conversation last night, Mrs Quick,' said Roper. 'It's to do with your business.' He and DS Wilmott were in the damp and aromatic fragrance of Mrs Quick's flower shop in the middle of Dorchester. 'D'you keep records of customers who ask for flowers to be delivered?'

'Have to.' she said. 'I'd be lost otherwise.'

'You'd have delivered these sometime on Saturday last. To a Mrs Craven. She's presently in the local hospital.'

There was clearly no need for him to say any more. 'That

was Mrs Chance,' said Mrs Quick, who was a short, sturdy and down to earth blonde, somewhere in her early forties, and so unlike the glamorous Mrs Chance that it was quite plain Nicholas Chance had sought something very different from the bug that had bitten him the first time. 'She ordered another couple of bouquets to be sent along this morning.'

'Does Mrs Chance know you?'

She shook her head. 'I didn't know her either; at least, not until last Saturday morning. It came as a bit of a shock actually.'

'She called in? She didn't phone?'

'No, she called in here, to the shop. I'd never seen her before.'

Mrs Quick went into a cramped little office at the back of the shop and returned with an order book. A carbon-copied page showed that Mrs Chance had ordered fifty pounds' worth of mixed flowers to be sent to a Mrs Dagmar Craven by midday last Saturday. A similar order had been placed this very morning, although Mrs Chance had placed that one over the telephone within minutes of Mrs Quick opening the shop at eight a.m. They had been despatched at eight-thirty.

'Did Mrs Chance send anything with the flowers on Saturday?'

'Yes, she did. A sealed letter that she asked me to wrap up with one of the bouquets, and one of our gift-tags.'

'Remember what she wrote on the gift-tag?'

'Couldn't read it. It was written in Dutch or German or something of that sort.'

'Or Norwegian?' proposed Roper. 'Could it have been written in Norwegian?'

'Possibly,' said Mrs Quick. 'If I knew what Norwegian looked like.'

Leather aproned and with a pair of safety-goggles hanging from an elastic strap around her neck, Elsie Wicks had been in her workshop when Roper and Makins arrived on her doorstep at a few minutes to midday.

'I only went into the bungalow as far as the kitchen,' she said, in response to Roper's question. 'Sergeant Mallory told me to wait there while he went out to the hallway.'

'So you didn't actually go out there to see what had happened?'

'No, I didn't,' she said. 'All I saw were the soles of Dagmar's shoes.'

'There was a lot of broken glass out there.'

'I didn't notice.'

'Sergeant Mallory didn't mention it to you?'

'No. He didn't say anything much, except that Dagmar was unconscious and that he was calling up an ambulance for her.'

'Who did you talk to afterwards? D'you remember?'

'Well . . . old Tasker. He was still here when I came back from Dorchester. And later on in the afternoon Vanessa Chance dropped in and we had a cup of tea together. I told her what had happened, of course, but she already knew because you'd been along to see her.'

'But you filled in a few details?'

'Well, yes. I did, as a matter of fact. She and Dagmar are pretty close buddies, so I really didn't tell her anything she couldn't have guessed for herself. Did I do wrong?'

'No, not really, Mrs Wicks. Did you tell her that Mr Craven turned up while you and I were talking in the kitchen? And that he might have been drinking?'

'Yes, I'm afraid I did. But then everyone who knows Martin Craven knows about his liking for the bottle.'

'Did she ask you what time he came back?'

Mrs Wicks frowned. 'Yes, she did.'

'She asked a lot of questions, did she?'

'Well, yes, of course she did. She was interested, wasn't she?'

'But you didn't tell her about the broken glass in the hall?'

'I told you,' she said. 'I didn't know about that.'

'I'm still not sure where all this is leading, guv'nor,' said Makins, as they trudged back up the steep driveway to his car.

'Mrs Craven's lover,' said Roper. Because that is what it was really all about, why Nicholas Chance had hired Gerry Pope to watch Furzecroft, why Craven had belatedly hired a private investigator last Friday morning to watch his wife, why Mrs Craven had been struck down in her hall and why Hit and Run Pope had finished up dead on the road to Dorchester. It was all to do with love.

'You've sussed out who the bloke is, then?' said Makins, as they reached the road and he fished out his car keys.

'Bloke?' said Roper, scowling at him across the roof of the car. 'Who says it's got to be a man?'

EIGHTEEN

NICHOLAS CHANCE LED THEM INTO his office and dropped the thick rubber gloves he had been wearing on to his desk. It was a tidy desk, Roper observed, the mid-morning mail still unopened on it, three wire filing trays labelled in, out and pending, a desk calculator with a print-out facility, and a green telephone. A cork notice-board on the wall displayed all the latest dogma from the Ministry of Agriculture, Food and Fisheries. In his business life, at least, Mr Chance was an orderly man.

There was only the one chair. Chance offered it to Roper, who declined it. Perhaps recognising that he would be disadvantaged if he used it himself, Chance perched himself on the corner of his desk, one foot slowly swinging. He looked uneasy, but then he had good reason to.

'Well?' he snapped, looking Roper straight in the eye. 'What's it about this time?'

'Gerald Pope, sir,' said Price.

'I've told you all I know about him,' retorted Chance.

'No, sir,' said Roper.

'Bloody yes, sir,' said Chance angrily. But he wasn't angry, not really. He was worried and he was playing for time. 'Or are you calling me a liar?'

'We'd like to look at your inventory, sir,' said Roper. 'The one that covers your machinery. I presume you keep one?'

Chance was no fool. Quick to see the point, his eyes

231

narrowed. 'If I do, it's none of your bloody business, is it?'

'We would like to see it, sir,' said Roper patiently. 'We can get a warrant if you like, but it's a lot of trouble, and I'd have to leave Sergeant Makins here while I went away and organised it. A waste of time really, sir, just for the sight of a piece of paper.'

'Unless you've worked a fiddle on your insurance company, sir,' added Makins. 'That'd be fraud, you see, sir. A criminal offence.'

'Or alternatively you can level with us and tell us why you really hired Gerald Pope, sir,' said Roper.

Chance looked from one to the other of them, then down at his green wellingtons. When Roper and Makins had arrived at the farmhouse there had again been no response to Makins' ring at the doorbell. They had found Chance in the yard at the back, sloshing about in water up to his ankles and rodding out a blocked drain.

Chance continued to gaze down at his boots. 'You wouldn't even begin to bloody understand,' he mumbled at last.

Roper reached into his pocket for the Avia wristwatch in its plastic envelope. Chance's sombre eyes lifted high enough to take it in.

'Your wife's watch, is it, sir?'

Chance nodded, looked down again. 'Where did you find it?'

'Along at Furzecroft, sir,' said Roper. 'Mr Craven found it one evening behind the shower curtain.'

Chance said nothing, showed no surprise.

'Hire Pope to watch Mrs Chance, did you?'

Chance nodded again.

'Because you thought she was seeing another man?'

Chance slowly shook his head, still gazing down at his boots.

'You knew she'd taken up with Mrs Craven?'

'Guessed.'

'Pope offer proof?'

Chance nodded again, his shoulders hunched, his hands tightly gripping the edge of his desk. His foot had stopped swinging.

'Photographs?'

Chance nodded; then lifted his face and looked Roper tiredly in the eye. 'Yes, he took photographs.'

'Clear?'

'No. Not very. They were taken through a window.'

'Along at the Cravens' bungalow?'

Chance nodded again.

'Black and white photographs?'

Another nod.

'Did he give you the negatives too?'

'Of course.'

'Keep them, did you?'

'Of course.'

'Mind if we see them?'

Chance hitched a careless shoulder. 'Why should I mind?' he said. 'I don't have much to lose now, do I?' He dropped his feet to the floor and went behind his desk. He stooped, opened a drawer, reached into it and tossed an envelope across the desk as he straightened up again and closed the drawer with the side of his boot. Then he slumped into his swivel-chair and waited.

Roper took up the envelope. It was a quality one, thick paper, pale blue, just like the ones he had found with the matching headed stationery in Pope's desk last Monday morning. The four photographs were grey and blurred and grainy, their horizons tilted, as if Pope had not been able to look through his viewfinder but simply held the camera above his head and the window-ledge and blindly squirted the shutter. A lighter grey stripe down the right-hand edge of three of them was probably the out-of-focus edge of a net curtain. Only in one photograph was it possible to define with any certainty that the two tangled figures on the bed were Dagmar Craven and Vanessa Chance.

The four negatives were equally drab and grey and underexposed. The staff in the photographic section back at the Forensic laboratory might get a better picture out of them than Pope had, but only just. Roper slipped everything back into the envelope and passed it to Makins to put in his briefcase. 'We'll give you a receipt for those, Mr Chance.'

Chance sketched a shrug, past caring any more.

'This is a new development, is it, Mr Chance? Or has your wife gone in that direction before?'

'I think it's been going on a long time,' said Chance. 'It was just that I lacked the nous to cotton on to it.'

'Shown those photographs to your wife yet?'

Chance's mouth twisted in a mirthless smile. 'What do you bloody think?'

'So you haven't?'

Chance shook his head. 'No,' he said. 'I was saving them for the big confrontation when it came.'

'Did you tell Pope you weren't going to use them immediately?'

'Yes, I think I did,' said Craven. 'I told him I'd need a couple of weeks to think about it.'

'Why did you go along to the Cravens' bungalow last Friday lunchtime?'

Chance shrugged, almost as if he had expected that to be the next question and was ready for it. 'She'd gone along there. Vanessa. Dagmar had rung here about ten minutes before. Some kind of argument. I don't know what it was about. I was in here, and she was using the telephone in the sitting-room. About five minutes afterwards Vanessa went out. I guessed she'd gone rushing along to see Dagmar, so I decided to follow her . . . I'd got some vague idea of catching them at it.'

'It?' enquired Roper.

'Whatever dykes do together,' said Chance with a sneer.

'Intend to do something violent did you, sir?' asked Makins.

Chance glanced up again angrily. 'Yes, I bloody did.'

'And did you?'

Chance shook his head. 'When I got close to the house, I heard them shouting and screaming at each other. They were in the kitchen. Vanessa had hold of Dagmar. Dagmar was in tears and Vanessa was trying to kiss her and Dagmar was trying to fight her off. Then I heard the phone ringing and they broke apart. Dagmar went to answer the phone and Vanessa followed her up the hallway. I saw Dagmar pick up the phone, but only for a couple of seconds.'

Which had probably been the call Elsie Wicks had made about returning the repaired engagement ring.

'I saw her put the phone down – but then pick it up again. That time Vanessa tried to stop her. I couldn't see what was happening exactly, just a couple of shadows struggling behind the front door. Then Dagmar went down – and stayed down. Vanessa crouched down beside her, stayed there for a few seconds, stood up, then came straight towards me.'

'She see you?'

Chance shook his head. 'I was watching through the kitchen window. I ducked out sharpish and tucked myself in behind the side of the house. She came running like hell out of the kitchen door, crossed the garden and went through the wire fence towards this place. She was still running. As soon as she'd gone I went into the bungalow. Dagmar was face down on the carpet. She was unconscious and she was bleeding – somewhere here.' Chance lifted a hand and touched his own head just above his right ear. 'I had a good mind to just leave her bloody well lying there. I loathed her, you see. Hated the bloody sight of her. I even thought for a moment of killing her there and then –'

'We have to caution you, Mr Chance,' warned Roper, before Chance committed himself too deeply.

' –but I didn't,' Chance went on heedlessly. 'But Christ, I really wanted to. I picked up that vase and I was going to smash her head in with it. But I didn't have the guts, not when it really came to it.'

'So you smashed the vase instead.'

'Yes, I smashed it,' said Chance bitterly. 'It was either her or the bloody vase.'

'Then?'

'I rang for the ambulance and got the hell out of there. I said I was Craven, gave them the address, and went.'

'Your wife know yet you saw all this?'

Chance shook his head.

'Can your wife speak and write Norwegian, Mr Chance?' asked Roper.

Chance nodded wryly. 'That's something else she learned from bloody Dagmar.'

'Did you ever voice a complaint to your wife about those two gipsies camped along the way?'

'No,' said Chance. 'Why should I? They don't bother me and I don't bother them.'

'Where's your wife now, sir?' asked Makins.

Chance smiled another of his death's head smiles.

'Can't you bloody guess,' he said.

The silence of the interview room was broken by the snap of Roper's lighter and the click of metal as Mrs Chance lifted her hands to take the lit cigarette down from her mouth.

'If you promise to behave yourself, those things can come off,' he said.

She stared malevolently at him. Blood still seeped from a laddered hole in DS Wilmott's tights just below her knee and Dave Price was sporting two deep fingernail slashes down his left cheek. Mrs Chance had not come quietly. In another interview room, further along the passage, Nicholas Chance was making his formal statement to Rodgers and Makins and a tape recorder.

'We know all about it, you know, Mrs Chance,' said Roper.

Her mouth twisted in disdain, and he wondered now why he had ever considered her a beautiful woman. 'So why don't *you* tell *me*,' she spat venomously, 'if you're that bloody clever.' The cigarette rose to her mouth and she snatched a lungful of smoke.

Roper said nothing. He went across to the other table where the meagre pile of evidence lay in plastic bags and brought it back to the table where Mrs Chance sat over her ashtray. He laid it all down in front of her and then seated himself opposite her.

'This is a ferrule off the end of a drum of the baling wire your husband uses,' he said, selecting that and pushing it towards her. 'A similar one was found near where Pope was murdered. And these are photographs that Pope took through Mrs Craven's bedroom window. And this is your wristwatch. The one you left behind the Cravens' shower curtain.'

She showed only a momentary flicker of interest, then glanced away again.

'I think Pope was blackmailing you and Mrs Craven, Mrs Chance. I think you agreed to meet him at a specific time on the road last Monday night, fixed up the rendezvous somewhere between your place and Mrs Craven's; and strung up a length of baling wire a couple of hundred yards before he was due to reach it so you could be sure he'd still be travelling flat out. Right, so far?'

She took another drag on her cigarette, still keeping her eyes averted and her face like stone. In the struggle at the hospital her lipstick had been smeared away from the right-hand side of her mouth and dragged down towards her chin. It looked like a streak of blood. The glass of her new wristwatch was cracked too. According to Price it had taken both him and Wilmott to subdue her and wrestle the handcuffs on her.

'And then Mrs Craven lost her nerve, didn't she? She rang you on Friday morning and told you so, and you went along hotfoot to see her and try to talk her out of it.

237

While you were there, the phone rang – it was Mrs Wicks – and when Mrs Craven put the phone down on her she picked it up again to telephone the police.' Most of which was pure invention based on what Nicholas Chance had seen through the Cravens' kitchen window. That it was fairly close to the mark was obvious from the sudden caustic stare that Vanessa Chance shot at him. 'You tried to stop her. The two of you struggled, she tripped and cracked her head on the table in the hallway. You thought you'd killed her – that's only a guess, by the way, because I haven't heard your side of the story yet – and decided you'd better make a run for it.

'Then I came along and told you that she was still very much alive –' He still recalled the dismay on her face, and the way she had clapped her hands to her cheeks. She had fooled him completely. ' –so you went along to see Mrs Wicks so that you could find out what had gone on at Furzecroft after you'd left and cobble some sort of story together that we couldn't break. And somehow you had to get that same story across to Mrs Craven without us knowing about it. So you sent her a letter – and a message-tag in Norwegian, probably telling her not to open the letter until she was alone – together with the flowers you ordered from Quick's Flower Shop. You told her just how she could fob off the blame for what had happened in the hallway on to Martin Craven.'

Like a poised snake she continued to stare at him, then struck as she angrily ground her cigarette to extinction in the ashtray. 'The bitch!' she hissed between gritted teeth. 'The stupid little bitch!' She sat back in her hard chair, her eyes blazing with contempt, her nostrils flaring with every noisy breath she took. 'She lied to me! She told me she hadn't talked.'

Roper didn't enlighten her. He had struck the tinder. All he had to do now was to wait for the fire to blaze.

As suddenly, she was icy calm again. She swivelled on her chair and offered her wrists to Wilmott. Roper nodded and Wilmott unlocked the handcuffs. Mrs Chance rubbed her wrists. 'It was all her bloody idea in the first place,' she muttered angrily. She said no more until she had stuffed another cigarette into her mouth and Roper had struck his lighter for her. Smoke briefly veiled her face. She waved it away.

'That pig of a man phoned Dagmar on the Friday afternoon.' Which was probably one of the calls Pope had made from Mrs Barr's house. 'Told her he'd got some interesting photographs of her and me together. He wanted money, he said. Two thousand. It wasn't blackmail, he said. It was a straight deal. We gave him the cash and he handed over the pictures and the negatives. If we played it right, we'd never hear from him again, that's what he told her.'

'Did she believe him?'

'She did, I didn't. I knew he'd be back. That sort always are. You pay once and you pay for ever. Anyway, we couldn't raise that kind of cash without Nick or Martin finding out about it.'

'So you decided to kill him.'

'We didn't know what the hell to do. But we certainly toyed with the idea.'

'So when did you decide?'

'The following Monday morning. He rang Dagmar again to find out whether we intended to pay or not. I was there when he rang that time. To buy time we said we'd pay him and would meet him somewhere with the cash.'

But Pope had proposed a rendezvous that very same evening which left them hardly any time at all. But then Pope had had little time to spare if he had wanted to play both ends off against the middle. Chance had told Pope that he needed a couple of weeks to think about what he'd do with the photographs Pope had sold him. If Chance had decided to change his mind before Pope had struck that deal with his wife and Dagmar Craven then there would have been no deal. Time had been of the very essence. Pope would be coming through Appleford shortly after eleven o'clock. He would meet them then. 'Dagmar went into a flap and tried to put him off, but he wouldn't have it. So I took over the phone and said I'd pay and Dagmar would be waiting for him on the road near the bungalow. Only I wanted to be sure that the money would be paid over to the right man. And he said he'd be on a motor-cycle and coming from the direction of the village. And he told me that if Dagmar flashed a torch he'd dip his headlight so she'd know he was the man. That's when I decided we'd have to kill him.'

'*You* decided to kill him?'

'One of us had to. Dagmar was running around in bloody circles.'

'Whose idea was the wire across the road?'

'Dagmar's,' she said. They had thought of several wild ideas before they had known that Pope would be on a motor-cycle. A carving knife, an iron bar, a plastic bag dropped over his head and Sellotaped tightly around his neck from behind. Martin Craven belonged to a gun club in the City and owned a .22 target pistol. Nicholas Chance had an up-and-over 12-gauge shotgun, but neither woman was sure how to load them, besides which both weapons would kick up a lot of noise at eleven o'clock at night. Then Dagmar Craven desperately threw in the idea of the wire stretched across the road. As a child, her noisy and extrovert grandfather had interminably bored the family with his blood-curdling bragging about his work for the Norwegian Resistance during the war. And one particularly horrific recipe Dagmar Craven had remembered because it had given her nightmares, was how to unseat a German military dispatch-rider, and gain a very useful motor-cycle into the bargain, by means of a wire stretched across a road in the dark.

They settled for that. Whatever happened, their tormentor would at least be disabled enough for them to finish him off without recourse to sheer physical strength.

Desperation propelled them to carry it through. By telling them he would be travelling on a motor-cycle Pope had virtually determined the manner of his death for himself. Mrs Chance knew where she could lay her hands on a suitable length of wire, and in the afternoon she and Dagmar Craven had slowly walked the road in order to find the best site to string it up. They chose the cattle-crossing sign and the silver birch tree on the edge of the heath. Mrs Chance had then paced out the distance between the two, and in the early evening, in her husband's store-shed, she had broached a drum of baling wire and snipped off the measured length plus half a dozen paces more in case she had made a mistake. For extra measure, she also selected the longest and sharpest carving knife from her kitchen.

Luck was with them. Nicholas Chance had gone out for the evening and Martin Craven had been working late – or drinking late – and at ten to eleven the two women had met by the cattle-crossing sign to set up the wire. As Roper had guessed, the wire had been secured to the silver birch first, then trailed loosely across the road to where Mrs Chance was going to wait in the shrubbery with a pair of pliers for Pope to appear from the direction of the village.

'He was late. Then bloody Martin came driving by on his way home. And that nearly screwed up everything because Dagmar was scared enough already. Then I heard this motor-bike, but stupid Dagmar almost forgot to flash him and I only just got the bloody wire rigged up in time before he could pick me up in his headlight, didn't I? I expected a crash, but there wasn't one. The bike just went on up the road and drove itself into the bushes. He just sort of somersaulted in the air and flopped down beside the verge. Something else rolled along the road. I thought it was something heavy that had fallen off his bike.'

'But it was his head,' said Roper.

'Yes,' she said. She spoke casually, with a shrug. 'We didn't mean to do that. I had to guess the height of the

241

wire. I got it wrong.'

'Then you robbed him.'

'No,' she said. She was very calm now, very cool, very composed. 'I cut the wire down first. Then I went through his pockets for the photographs he said he was bringing. They were tucked inside his jacket. Dagmar was supposed to join me, and give me a hand, but she didn't. When she realised his head had come off she wouldn't come near, just watched. Stood there gibbering, the stupid little bitch. I asked her where the bike had gone. She said she didn't know. I took all the stuff out of his pockets. I thought it would make him difficult to identify. That's when I found out his name. There were some business cards in his wallet. They said he was a private investigator.'

'Why did you take his head away?'

'Same reason,' she said, stubbing out her second cigarette and reaching towards the packet for another. 'So nobody'd recognise him.' She paused while Roper struck his lighter for her again. Smoke gouted out contemptuously between her teeth. 'Bloody Dagmar was nearly bloody hysterical by then. I reminded her that it was her bloody idea in the first place and that she was in it now as deep as I was, but if she was going to crack up then she'd better sod off home and I'd see to the rest myself. I wrapped the head up in Dagmar's scarf, and she went her way and I went mine.'

'Which way did you go, Mrs Chance?' asked Price.

'Down behind that hut of Tasker Hobday's. Then over our fence at the back of Elsie Wicks' garden.'

'And that's where you tossed the head into the stream,' said Roper.

'I thought it would sink,' she said. 'But it bloody didn't, did it. It just bloody sat there.'

'How about Mrs Craven's scarf? And Pope's wallet?'

'I stuffed them in the boiler furnace,' she retorted. 'What the hell else.'

'There were over five hundred pounds in that wallet,

242

Mrs Chance.'

She frowned in surprise. 'How the hell d'you know that?'

'Because I know the man who'd paid it to him about ten minutes before. What did you do with it?'

'Burned them,' she said. 'They were all brand-new fifties. I thought they might be trouble.'

'Smart,' he said, with grudging admiration.

'Just because I'm a bloody woman doesn't mean I'm a bloody half-wit too, you know,' she snapped back. 'All you bloody men make the same mistake, don't you?'

To her chagrin, however, in her first few feverish moments back in her kitchen, Mrs Chance discovered that Pope had indeed been carrying a set of compromising photographs of herself and Mrs Craven – which were doubtless duplicate photographs of the ones Pope had printed for her husband – but there were no negatives. And over the telephone, Pope had promised to bring the negatives. But of course he had already sold the negatives to Nicholas Chance by way of their legitimate business; although Mrs Chance would have been unlikely to have found that out until her husband had instituted divorce proceedings against her.

'They were somewhere else on the body, were they?' she asked Roper, nodding down at the envelope of photographs.

'No,' said Roper. 'Your husband gave those to us. He thought you were having an affair.'

The side of her mouth twisted in disgust. 'Don't tell me,' she said. 'He hired Pope to spy on us.'

'Right,' said Roper.

'You know,' she said, with lacerating irony, 'I never thought Nicholas was that smart. How about the watch? How did you get hold of that?'

'Mr Craven found it behind his shower curtain one evening.'

'That bloody stupid Dagmar again,' she sneered. 'As

243

soon as I'd got home I rang her and told her I must have left it somewhere in her bathroom. The silly cow told me she couldn't find it. Didn't look bloody hard enough, did she?'

'When I got home, Nicholas was still out.' Vanessa Chance was on her fourth cigarette and Wilmott had just brought in a cup of coffee for her. 'And Dagmar found Martin zonked out with booze on the sofa. So everything was fine until Dagmar started to get the jitters again last Friday morning.'

'Did you intend to kill her when you went along there on Friday?'

'That's a damned fool question, too,' she retorted. 'Of course I bloody didn't.'

'But you thought you had?'

'I panicked,' she said. 'She'd gone as white as a sheet and I couldn't find a pulse. I really thought she was dead.'

'And afterwards, the two of you were . . . reconciled?'

'We were never any other way,' she said. 'At least I thought we were never any other way until I walked out of her room this morning straight into the arms of your gorilla and gorillarette. I guessed then she must have got cold feet again and spilled the beans. And back there at the hospital she was still swearing black was white and that she hadn't told you anything.'

'Did you ever borrow your husband's driving-gloves and leave them behind at Mrs Craven's?'

'Yes,' she said. 'Once. I found them on the dashboard of the car. I wore them over my own. It was a bloody cold morning.'

'And did your husband tell you to complain to Sergeant Mallory about the Lees?'

'No,' she said. 'He couldn't have cared less about them, so long as they kept off his land. I was the one that did the complaining. I heard that Hughie Lee had been prowling about the heath that night. I was worried in case he might

244

have seen something.'

She paused then, dotting ash from her cigarette over the ashtray.

'You've got to tell me,' she said. 'What exactly *did* Dagmar tell you?'

'She only told us what you'd told her to tell us in that letter, Mrs Chance,' said Roper. 'The only snags were, she didn't know any more than you did about the broken vase we found in the Cravens' hallway, and your telling her she'd better change her story about that coat being collected from the cleaners'.'

'Yes,' she said, 'it wasn't very bright of her to invent that bit about the coat. But we didn't break that vase you kept asking her about.'

'We know you didn't, Mrs Chance,' said Roper. 'Someone else did that. There was a witness to what happened last Friday, you see. And if he hadn't been there, Mrs Craven could well be dead by now.'

She stared hard at him. 'Bloody Nicholas,' she said. 'I'll bet it was bloody Nicholas.'

But on this occasion Roper did not enlighten her.

NINETEEN

'NOT THAT I DOUBTED YOU were on the right track all along, Douglas,' said the ACC(Crime) from the depths of his luxurious and leather upholstered swivel-chair – which one particular wit at County swore was a cunningly disguised ejector-seat to launch the Speeding Spectre straight out into the car park to save him hanging about for the lifts.

'Funny thing you should say that, sir,' said Roper drily, well aware that the ACC was putting out the olive branch for drawing him off Craven. 'I thought you did.'

'No, of course not,' protested the ACC, with an airy flap of his hand. 'Never for a *moment*.' The hand that had flapped descended then to slowly caress the back edge of his highly-polished desk-top, which meant either that the ACC was meditating or that he had something else on his mind and was having a little trouble formulating the words. It was ten o'clock on the Tuesday morning. Mrs Chance would be formally arraigned before the magistrates at eleven, and Mrs Craven, again with a resident policewoman outside her door, would be following her on Saturday morning when she was discharged from hospital. Half an hour ago Roper had made his promised telephone call to Mr Jobling and removed any lingering guilt that Jobling may have felt that he might, remotely, have been partly responsible for his wife's suicide, as those left behind often did. Jobling had broken down, although he had tried hard to disguise it. Gerry Pope had created a lot of unhappiness for a lot of people.

'I heard something on the grapevine, Douglas,' ventured the ACC at last, his slowly sweeping fingertips still stroking from side to side over his expensive woodwork. 'Some gipsy girl told you what you were looking for would be near water. The rumour true, is it?'

'Yes, sir,' said Roper.

'And it was near water,' said the ACC.

'Yes, sir,' said Roper. 'But then most of Appleford village isn't very far from the stuff.'

'No,' agreed the ACC. 'Quite.' He obviously had more to say on the subject of Annie Lee's possible powers, but his eyes popped at the roaring and window-rattling interruption of what sounded like a racing car steaming into the pits at Brand's Hatch. In an instant he was on his feet and at his window, his forehead pressed against the glass to see what the commotion was down below in the car park. 'Good God!' he exploded indignantly, 'he's pinched the Chief Constable's bloody slot. Correction, it's a bloody *woman.*'

Roper joined him at the window. The car was a Lotus Elan, dashingly red, its engine still throbbing powerfully as its driver leaned across to make a loving and painstaking meal of her male passenger.

'And isn't that young George Makins in there with her?'

'Definitely,' said Roper. When he had presented the wedding invitation to Sheila last night she had been as flabbergasted as he had been. He had swiftly followed it with an invitation of his own. 'I've got a couple of rest-days owing. I thought we'd go up to Town. Spend a night up there and take in a show.'

'It must be contagious,' she'd said.

'What must?'

'All this romance in the air.'

'And what's wrong with that?'

'Nothing,' she'd said. 'Absolutely nothing.'

A happily beaming Makins finally climbed out of the

Elan, waved a hand to his lady driver and headed for the building. She loosed the brake, revved the engine, shot forward a few yards, then stopped again, threw open her door and went dashing after him with his briefcase in her hand. If anything, George Makins had greatly undersold her.

'I say,' exclaimed the ACC, his tone this time softened into one of frank admiration. 'She's a bit . . .'

'Very seriously and considerably gorgeous, sir?' proposed Roper.

'Yes,' said the ACC, delicately clearing his throat. 'Quite. Know who she is, do we?' he asked hopefully.

'Makins' fiancée, sir. Her name's Fiona. She's a solicitor. Got her own practice in Dorchester.'

'Has she, by gum. I wonder what his secret is?' enquired the ACC wistfully, as the dark, lean and elegant Fiona returned to her car.

'I wish I knew, sir,' said Roper. 'Except that I've left it a bit late in the day to find out.'

'Haven't we all, Douglas,' agreed the ACC, sagely and sombrely as the Elan sped off like a rocket. 'Haven't we all . . . As I was saying,' he said, snapping back quickly from his moment of mourning for his lost youth and glancing quizzically at Roper. 'That gipsy girl. Think she really did second-sight something or other?'

'Thinking of putting her on the pay-roll, are you, sir? To cut a few more shillings off the wage bill?'

Across the ACC's cadaverous face came the coy grimace that he used for a smile. 'It was only a thought, Douglas,' he said. 'Only a thought.'